Anonymous

Fairy Circles

Tales and legends of giants, dwarfs, fairies, water-sprites and hobgoblins

Anonymous

Fairy Circles
Tales and legends of giants, dwarfs, fairies, water-sprites and hobgoblins
ISBN/EAN: 9783337011918

Printed in Europe, USA, Canada, Australia, Japan

Cover: Foto ©Andreas Hilbeck / pixelio.de

More available books at **www.hansebooks.com**

Fairy Circles

TALES AND LEGENDS

OF

Giants, Dwarfs, Fairies, Water-Sprites, and Hobgoblins

FROM THE GERMAN OF VILLAMARIA

WITH NUMEROUS ILLUSTRATIONS

London:
MARCUS WARD & CO., 67 & 68, CHANDOS STREET
AND ROYAL ULSTER WORKS, BELFAST
1877

CONTENTS.

Illustrations.

FAIRY CIRCLES.

FREDERICK TAKES LEAVE OF GELA.

Barbarossa's Youthful Dream.

MORE than a thousand years have rolled away since a castle looked down cheerfully from a height amid the Franconian plains into the well-watered Kinzig Valley, with its pleasant villages and towns.

It belonged to the powerful Swabian duke Frederick of Hohenstaufen, whose young and valiant son loved this the best of all his father's proud castles, and often left his uncle's splendid palace to hunt in its forests, or to look down from its lofty oriel window on the blooming plain below.

His father and uncle indeed missed him sadly. His clear blue eye, and the cheerful expression of his noble countenance, seemed to the two grave and war-weary men so gladdening to look upon, that they were always unwilling to let him leave them.

But the young Frederick used to beg them so earnestly to grant him the freedom of the forest for just this once, that father and uncle smilingly granted him permission, though "this once" was often repeated.

So it happened the autumn of that year when Bernard of Clairvaux passed through Germany, calling prince and people in words of burning eloquence to aid in the deliverance of the Holy Sepulchre.

"Just this once!" said young Frederick again; and King Conrad and Duke Frederick granted him permission.

As he bent in courteous farewell to take his uncle's hand, the king whispered, "Be ready, my Frederick, to return as soon as my messenger calls thee. Great things are before us, and I can ill spare thy strong right arm!" And young Frederick smiled his own cheery smile, and answered, "I come when my king and lord calls!"

Then he galloped away as if he were bound that day to ride round the world. His Barbary steed bore him as on wings through the dark forests of the Spessart, and as the latest sunbeams sank in the waters of the Kinzig, he mounted the steep path towards the castle, and rode over the lowered drawbridge into the court.

Was it really the stags and boars in the vast forests, or the treasure of rare old manuscripts of the castle archives, which drew the young prince again and again to the small and lonely fortress?

So his father and uncle thought, but they knew not of his deep unconquerable love for the beautiful Gela, the daughter of a humble retainer. He had seen her while resting from the chase in the forest of the Kinzig Valley, and so great had his love for her become that he was willing to renounce all dreams of future power and greatness to live in blissful retirement with the beloved one whom he could not raise to his own rank.

But the lovers had to guard their secret carefully; they dared trust no confidant, lest their paradise should be laid waste before its gates had been fully opened to admit them. So they breathed their love to none but each other.

The prince passed Gela with cold indifference if he met her in the castle court or at her work about the house, and Gela made lowly reverence, as if she were the meanest of his maids, to him who counted it his greatest honour to do her service.

But at evening, when Frederick had roamed the forest since early morning, his bow on his shoulder and his faithful hounds by his side, the fair Gela might be seen walking along the high-road with a basket on her arm, or with a stock of newly-spun yarn, as if she were going to seek purchasers in the nearest town. But in the forest she would leave the broad path, and make her way through briars and underwood to a height on which her young prince awaited her beneath the shelter of a giant oak.

There they would talk happily and innocently till the last sunbeam was quenched in the Kinzig stream, and the convent bell resounded through the arches of the forest; then they would fold their hands in prayer before saying farewell, in hope of a meeting on the morrow.

So had it been for many a year. Their love remained unbetrayed, their hope unquenched, their faith unshaken. In the splendid halls of the palace, amid the proud and lovely ladies who surrounded the young prince with flattering marks of favour, the longing after the lonely forest in the Kinzig Valley and the fair and gentle loved one never died from his heart.

They had met thus one evening with the old, yet ever new tenderness. Frederick drew Gela's fair head to his breast, and spoke to her of the near and blissful future, which would be theirs in a few weeks, when he would be of age, and would be able to lead her openly as his wife to his castle in the fair land of Bavaria, to the inheritance of his dead mother. And the oak tree overhead rustled gently, scattering golden leaves on Gela's beautiful hair, for it was far on in autumn.

When the vesper bell of the forest cloister began to sound, it was already dark; the moonlight gleamed on the path, and Gela walked with her lover as far as the high-road, supported by his arm. But there the moon shone so brightly that they had to part, lest some prying eye should see them. "Meet me to-morrow, dearest!" said the young prince, once more kissing her blooming cheek; then Gela tripped lightly down the high-road towards the valley, while Frederick gazed after her till she vanished from his sight, when he called his dogs, and turned towards the castle.

But there the usual stillness and loneliness had given place to bustle and confusion. The young prince's aged tutor, who was the father-confessor and confidential friend alike of his father and of his uncle, had arrived a few hours before, accompanied by a troop of horsemen. Inquiries after the young prince passed impatiently from mouth to mouth, for the message was one which called for haste. At last he came riding over the drawbridge, his handsome face glowing as in a transformation, for his vision of the forest still hovered before his mind.

The old chaplain of the brothers of Hohenstaufen had been long and anxiously awaiting his pupil; now he hastened to meet him as quickly as his infirmities permitted, and greeted his dear one, who had left him but a few days before, as if he had not seen him for years.

Then they went together to the room with the oriel window, for there the young prince liked best to sit, as it afforded a view of Gela's lattice. They sat long in confidential conversation, and the light that fell on the pavement for hours after all others in the castle were asleep told Gela, who stood at the window opposite, that important and serious matters were being discussed by her dear one and his aged tutor.

Next morning the people flocked out of the castle chapel, where the old priest who had arrived the evening before had spoken to them in eloquent words, and claimed the arm and heart of young and old for the approaching crusade to the Holy Land. And not in vain. Men and youths were ready to venture wealth and life, and the aged were with difficulty persuaded to remain at home to till the ground and protect the women and the little ones.

All returned home to arrange their business hastily, and make needful preparations. One alone remained in the sacred place. It was Gela, who, when all had left the chapel, rose from her seat and threw herself prostrate before the altar, there to pour forth all the anguish of broken hopes, of parting, and of lonely sorrow that oppressed her heart.

She lay thus, her hands clasped, and her face uplifted in an agony of grief. There were light footsteps behind her, but Gela, lost in sorrow and prayer, heeded them not. A hand was laid on her shoulder; she looked up and saw the face of him on whose account she suffered.

"Gela," said the young prince tenderly and low, as if in reverence to the holy place—"Gela, we must part! We must wait a while for the fulfilment of yesterday's beautiful dream! I can scarcely bear it, and yet I cannot refuse, either as prince and knight, or as son and subject."

"No," said Gela calmly; "thou must obey, my Frederick, even though our hearts will bleed."

"And thou wilt be true to me, Gela, and wait patiently till I come back, and not give thy heart to another?" asked the prince, and his voice was full of pain.

"Frederick," said Gela, laying her hand on his shoulder, "bid me give my life; if it were necessary to thy happiness, I would give it gladly. Thine will I be through all the sorrow of separation; and if I die, my soul will leave heaven at thy call."

Frederick drew her to his heart. "I go content, my Gela; danger and death cannot harm me, for I am sheltered by thy love! Farewell till we meet again in joy!"

He hastened away to hide the tears that started to his eyes, and Gela sank again on the altar steps and bent her head in silent prayer.

She did not perceive the footsteps that once more broke the stillness of the place, and she only looked up when a second time a hand was laid on her shoulder. It was not into Frederick's youthful face that she looked this time, but into the grave countenance of the aged priest who had come to call her darling and the people of the surrounding country to the Holy War.

She shuddered as she thought that he had perhaps been a listener to their conversation, and had thus discovered the carefully guarded secret.

"Be not afraid, my daughter," said the old man gently; "I have been an unwilling witness of your meeting, but your words have fallen into the ear and heart of a man whose calling makes him the guardian of many a secret."

Gela breathed more freely.

"Thou art of pure heart, my daughter," continued the old man mildly; "who could chide thee for giving thy love to a youth to whom God has given a power to charm that wins the affection of almost every heart? But, my daughter, if thou love him thou must renounce him."

Gela looked up in terror at the priest.

"Yes, renounce him!" he repeated gravely, nodding his white head as he spoke.

"I cannot, reverend father!" faltered the maiden with trembling lips.

"Canst thou not?" asked the old man still more earnestly; "canst thou not give up thine own happiness for his sake, and yet thou art ready to give thy life if his happiness should demand it?"

"Oh, reverend father," Gela faltered, raising her hands to him entreatingly, "look not so stern! You know not what it is to renounce him, and with him all that I call happiness. But if his welfare demands it, my heart shall break without a murmur."

A gentle radiance beamed from the old priest's eyes.

"Thou hast well spoken, my daughter," he said gently. "Frederick loves thee now with the force of his un-estranged affection, and is ready to sacrifice rank and worldly prospects for thy sake; but he is a man and a prince, and, above all, of the house of Hohenstaufen, in whose soul lies a longing after great and praiseworthy deeds, though these aspirations are lulled to slumber by his love for thee. But when he comes to years of manhood, he will be unhappy that thou hast kept him from the tasks incumbent on one of his noble race. And then, my daughter, not he alone, but all Germany will blame thee, for every far-seeing eye recognises already in this heroic youth the future leader who is destined to bring this divided realm to unity and greatness. Canst thou think of the future of thy lover, and of us all, and yet act but for thine own happiness ?"

Gela raised herself as out of a dream.

"No, my father," she said in a firm voice, though the light of her eyes seemed quenched as she gazed at the priest; "no, I renounce him. But if he should ever think with bitterness of Gela, I ask of you that you will tell him of this hour, and why I have renounced him; because I loved his happiness more than myself. May this sacrifice not be in vain !"

The priest laid his hand, trembling with emotion, on her beautiful head. " Peace be with thee, my daughter !"

On a dewy May morning, two years after that farewell scene in the castle chapel, young Frederick rode over the drawbridge of the fortress on the height beside the Kinzig Valley.

The sun of Syria had dyed his white skin with a deeper hue, the toils of war and grief at dispelled illusions had drawn a slight furrow in the smooth brow, but on his flowing beard and hair lay the same golden splendour, and his blue eyes beamed brightly as of yore.

The castle servants flocked to greet their beloved

young master, who had meantime, through his father's death, become Duke of Swabia and their feudal lord. His princely mouth spoke many a gracious word, and his winning smile hovered among them like a sunbeam. His eye passed quickly from line to line, till it rested inquiringly on the features of an old bent man. It was Gela's father. Then he sprang from his horse, and ascended the stair to his favourite room.

The butler placed a goblet of the richest wine on the table, a drink of honour which he kept carefully in the driest corner of the cellar for the greatest occasions; and Dame Barbara, the housekeeper, brought in proudly the delicious pastry which she had prepared for this festive day; but the young duke gave no heed to these attentions. He stood in the oriel window, and looked down at a little lattice in the buildings that surrounded the castle court. There, in a green window-box, gilly-flower and rosemary used to bloom, and behind them he often had watched a face bent over the spinning-wheel —a face that he had not found surpassed by any even among the Flowers of the East.

But now all was changed. No blossom sent forth fragrance; the green box hung empty and half-broken; the clear lattice panes were blinded, and no dear face looked through to him in love.

A pang of dread presentiment pierced his heart.

"Who dwells in that room with the blinded window?" he asked as calmly as he could of Dame Barbara, who was rattling her keys to call her young lord's attention to herself and her masterpiece of culinary skill.

The old woman drew near, and looked at the desolate window to which the duke's finger pointed.

"Alas! my lord duke," said the loquacious old woman, "Gela used to live there, the good child; but she became a nun two years ago last autumn, and entered the convent of St. Clarissa, in the heart of the forest."

Frederick stood for a moment motionless, then he beckoned silently to the door, for his first sound must have been a cry of pain.

Barbara went, but her master sank into the window-seat, his gaze fixed on the deserted lattice.

There was a gentle knocking at the door, but the duke heard it not for the painful beating of his heart. Then the door opened, and on the threshold stood the old man on whom the prince's inquiring glance had rested on his arrival. He approached the window with a low reverence, and waited patiently till his young master raised his head. When at last he looked up, the old man started to see the beloved face that used to beam like the sunlight now covered as with the shadow of death.

"My lord duke," said the old man, when Frederick signed to him to speak, "I had an only child. I know not if your grace has ever noticed her. When the men went from the country round to the Holy War, she entered the forest cloister, because she thought she could there pray undisturbed for the safety and victory of our soldiers. Before she went she made me promise to give this letter into your hands as soon as you returned."

Then he drew from his doublet a strip of parchment carefully sewed in purple silk, and handed it to the duke.

And again Frederick spoke not, but silently took the missive, for his heart was full to overflowing.

The old man withdrew in silence. When Frederick found himself alone, he cut the silken covering with his hunting-knife, and drew out a piece of parchment; and when it was unfolded, he saw the childish handwriting which he himself had taught Gela in their happy hours in the forest, and with which she now bade him the last farewell, for she could not break her promise to the aged monk.

While Frederick, two years before, hastened to his uncle's palace, the holy man had gone on to other parts of the country to call on the people to join the Holy War, and from this errand death had called him.

The sun was already far past the meridian, but yet no sound had broken the stillness of the room where Frederick sat. The butler's drink of honour was untasted; Dame Barbara's masterpiece remained untouched.

At last the young duke rose, left the room, and descended the winding stair into the court; but when his steed was brought, the attendant esquire thought that this could scarcely be the same young and joyous prince who, a few hours before, had ridden across the bridge. He sprang into the saddle, cast a last glance on the desolate window, and then turned without a word of farewell to take the road which, but a short time before, he had galloped over with hopeful heart. It was the same road which Gela had so often followed with him to the little hill in the forest, and when he came to the narrow path, he led his obedient horse to one side, fastened the bridle round the trunk of a tree, and then walked slowly along the mossy path.

Now he stood beneath the oak. Its leafy roof and the moss at its foot were green and fresh as ever. Once he was like it in his love and hope, but all was changed! He sat down at the foot of the tree, and its rustling brought back to his soul the dream of his now vanished youth.

Suddenly bells sounded from the forest depths. But he could not, as in days gone by, fold his hands in pious awe, and pour forth every grief in a believing prayer. No; at the sound of these bells which now called Gela, his Gela, to devotion, it seemed to him as if he must rush to the cloister gate, knock with his sword hilt, and cry, "Come back, Gela, come back; for thy sacrifice will be in vain!"

He hastened down the hill to his horse, and sprang into the saddle.

"Away, my faithful steed!" he cried aloud. "Show me the way, for love and grief have bewildered my clear brain. Bear me where knightly duty and princely honour claim my presence—for I know not where."

And the good beast, as if it understood his master's words, rushed with him away farther and still farther south through the dim twilight, and beneath the bright beams of the full moon. Without weariness, though without rest, it bore him on, and when the morrow's sun stood in noonday splendour they had reached the goal, and the young duke stood before the gate of his own Staufenburg.

Gela's sacrifice was not offered in vain. The words the old monk uttered that morning in the castle chapel were fulfilled. After his uncle's death, young Frederick of Swabia was raised to the throne of Germany, and all that the realm and people of Germany had hoped from him was more than fulfilled.

His strong hand gave unity, strength, and majesty to the divided land, such as no ruler after him was ever able to bestow; and when the imperial crown of Rome was also placed upon his head, the proud people of Italy bowed before Frederick Barbarossa, did him homage, and acknowledged his power.

The laurels of many a victory rested on the Emperor's brow ; his house was happy, his race flourished, his name lay like a word of blessing on every lip ; and when Gela, still in the bloom of youth, closed her eyes in death, she knew that she had not in vain renounced Frederick and happiness.

Beneath the shelter of his favourite castle the Emperor founded a town, and named it after the unforgotten loved one of his youth, "Gelashausen ;" and when on his travels he came to the forest of the Kinzig Valley, he led his horse silently aside, fastened the bridle to a tree stem, and ascended the hill to the majestic oak. There leaning his head, amid whose gold full many a thread of silver gleamed, against the trunk, he closed his eyes, and dreamed once more the old delightful dream.

And the people called that tree ever after "the Emperor's oak."

The sun of Asia Minor once more sent its glowing rays on the head of the heroic Emperor, though they gleamed back now with a silvery radiance.

The cry of distress had risen once again from the Land of Promise, and drawn the aged monarch from his German home; he placed himself at the head of his army, and led it with prudence, courage, and military skill safely through the heat of the Eastern sun, in spite

BARBAROSSA IN THE HOLY LAND.

of the treachery and malice of the foe, in spite of the pangs of hunger and consuming thirst.

On a warm summer evening the army reached the steep bank of a foaming mountain torrent. There on the farthest side lay the road that they must take.

Barbarossa's son Frederick, that " Flower of Chivalry," sprang with a chosen band from the high rocky bank into the stream and reached the other side in safety.

The Emperor now prepared to follow. Without heeding the advice of his attendants, the aged hero, who had never known what fear meant, put spurs to his steed and plunged with him into the waters of the Seleph. For a few seconds the golden armour gleamed amid the waves, once or twice the reverend, hoary head rose above the stream, then the deadly waters carried horse and rider into their raging depths, and the beloved hero vanished from the eyes of his sorrowing army. His most valiant knights indeed and chosen friends plunged after him into the flood to save their honoured prince or die with him, but the wild mountain torrent bore them all to death. With bitter lamentations the army wandered up and down the stream, if perchance they might at least win the precious corpse from the waters. But night came and threw its dark veil over the sorrow and mourning of the day.

All around were wrapped in slumber, even deeper than was their wont. The moon stood high in heaven, and beneath its beams the waters of the Seleph flowed more gently like molten silver. Once more they roused their angry strength, and from their midst a white head rose, golden armour gleamed above the waves, and Barbarossa and his faithful steed slowly emerged from the waters. With noiseless hoof they wandered up and down the stream, and out from the depths mounted the troops of faithful ones who had followed their Emperor to danger and death. The drops gleamed like diamonds as they fell from head and armour with a gentle splash into the shining stream.

Silently the band of warriors rode along the waves; not a sound, not a footstep broke the stillness; thus they turned to the shore, and the horses clambered up the rocky bank.

There Barbarossa and his silent warriors halted on the height. For a moment the Emperor's glance rested on the slumbering army, he held out his hand as if blessing them in a last farewell, then he shook the reins, and horse and rider, freed from the laws of earthly gravity, swept onwards to the beloved Fatherland.

They passed over the Bosphorus. Far below them gleamed the towers of Constantinople with the golden cross on their summits, but Barbarossa heeded them not. His head was bent forward, so that his white locks fluttered in the night wind, and his eyes were directed solely to the land towards which the horses moved with the swiftness of the storm-wind on their cloudy path.

Soon German forests rustled beneath them, and round the Emperor's lips played something like the reflection of the old sunny smile.

To the south lay the Italian plains which had claimed

the best years of his life and his youthful energy, but the Emperor turned his head from these. Perhaps he saw already the destiny of his proud race, which must some day be fulfilled in those fragrant fields.

Now their native air surrounds them. The fir trees of the Black Forest scent the air, the waves of the Neckar gleam below them, and, bathed in the full moon's silvery splendour, there lies at their feet the Staufenburg, the cradle of the lofty imperial race.

Barbarossa raised his hand to bless its battlements and pinnacles, but still he held on his way northwards.

The Spessart forests rustled beneath him in the darkness of the night, not a moonbeam pierced their thickly-leaved summits. But there gleamed the waters of the Kinzig, the walls of Gelashausen in its gently flowing stream, and over on the mountain's brow shone the aged Emperor's favourite castle, with the high oriel window, and Gela's deserted lattice.

Barbarossa bent over his horse's neck, and cast a look of recognition on the scene of his early happiness.

Soon they hovered above the high-road, and then over the familiar forest with its spreading "Emperor's oak." The old man's head was still bent forward, as if his eye would pierce the whispering tree-tops. A sound of clear bells greeted his ear. Below in the convent they called to midnight prayer, and these tones, which had once well-nigh broken his heart, acted now as a spell to bring back the old loved images. His breast heaved as of yore in mingled joy and grief, and "Gela, my Gela!" was the cry that started from his lips and reached the convent in whose vaults the loved one slumbered.

But still the steeds held on their unhalting course over Thuringia's golden plain to the Kyffhäuser Mountain, within which Frederick Barbarossa must hold council to-night with his faithful ones about the people of Germany and their future.

The castle, which in bygone days had so often opened its hospitable gates to him and his court, within whose halls many a gladsome feast had been held, of whose magnificence and splendour old chronicles tell us—this castle still kept watch over the land with unbroken pinnacles, but Barbarossa knocked not at its gate.

Gently the horses sank to the earth, and halted at a hidden door in the mountain side.

The Emperor struck the stone with his sword, so that a loud echo answered from the hollow interior. Then the rocky door opened, and Barbarossa and his faithful warriors entered the spacious hall of the Kyffhäuser Mountain. The rock had not long closed behind them when a gentle tapping was heard, the magic gate swung open, and the lovely Gela entered, arrayed in bridal attire as she had been laid in the tomb.

The hand of death had touched her heart, but had not quenched her love. When Frederick's cry reached her ear, she had opened her eyes as out of a deep sleep, and had left the vault to seek her beloved with the swiftness of a spirit's tread. Now she stands before him in unchanged grace and beauty.

Barbarossa's youthful dream was fulfilled. Gela, his

first love, was now at his side to tend him and bless him for ever as she could never have done on earth. It was she, the faithful one, who ruled henceforth in the magic kingdom of the Kyffhäuser, and cared for the beloved hero and his trusty band. It was she who knew when Barbarossa's heart yearned over the memories of his glorious past. Then she would lead the knights—his faithful comrades in the Holy War—into his room. They would range themselves round the marble table at which Barbarossa sat, with his long white beard flowing round him like imperial ermine, and over the golden goblets, filled from the exhaustless stores of the mountain cellars, they talked with the hero about the glorious days that they had spent together, about " the golden age" of the Holy German Empire. And the minstrels, who had been wont to go with him to the Holy Land, and had entered with him the enchanted mountain of the " Golden Meadow," would strike their harps, and the song of the future, which still slumbered in their souls, rose to their lips and echoed loudly through the enchanted arches of the Kyffhäuser Mountain.

When Barbarossa's heart longed for news of the fatherland, Gela would pass at midnight out through the door in the rock, down through the " Golden Meadow," and listen at many a door, and look through many a window. Then all that she heard there of sad lamentation or joyous hope she would faithfully pour into the Emperor's ear on her return. And what Gela failed to find out was seen by other eyes and heard by other ears. Just as once Odin's ravens flew down from the dwelling

BARBAROSSA AND GELA IN THE KYFFHÄUSER.

of the gods to the home of men to tell the heavenly Ruler of all that happened on the earth, so did the ravens that built their nests in the clefts of Kyffhäuser hover through the plains to hear of joy and sorrow, and bear the tidings back in silence to their rocky home.

But at the still hour of midnight, when the mountain opened, and the little dwarfs who dwelt secretly among Barbarossa's vaulted halls slipped out into the moonlight, then the wise birds opened their mouths, and the little friends—like Solomon, learned in the languages of birds —heard all that the ravens told. The dwarfs in their turn brought the news to the old Emperor, before whom they appeared from time to time to fill his treasury with newly-coined gold.

With liberal hand Barbarossa gave of these hoards to pious and honest mortals, whom Gela led into the magic kingdom of the Kyffhäuser, that the beloved prince might be gladdened by the sight of the new generation, which, different though it was from that of his day, still held in loving remembrance the noble Barbarossa, and cherished a firm hope of his return to earth.

The fortress on the mountain mouldered to decay. Herds grazed where once the tread of armed men was heard, but once every century the walls stood at midnight in their ancient splendour; the drawbridge rattled, the watchman's horn sounded shrill and clear, and over the castle court, through the gates with their carved coat of arms, on to the brightly illumined halls of revelry, passed a brilliant procession. It was Barbarossa leading by the hand the lovely Gela, and followed by his knights and vassals, all eager to breathe the air of the upper world.

But while the knights were spending the few short hours with music and feasting amid the pleasures of the past, the Emperor and Gela mounted to the highest battlement of the castle, and looked down longingly on the plains of their beloved Germany.

All around lay wrapped in slumber. Night and peace had conquered all the cares that gnaw in daylight at the heart of man, but they had also stilled its hopes.

"They are all asleep and dreaming," said the old Emperor, "but the morrow will come, and my people will awake and find the strife that now divides their hearts laid at rest for ever. Brave men will draw the sword and wield it victoriously. Then the minstrels will seize their harps, and the fame of our great and united Germany shall sound from the North Sea to the fair gardens of Italy. Then will our watch be over, and we shall go to our eternal rest."

So spake the aged monarch, as he leant across the battlement to stretch his hands in blessing over his former kingdom. But when the first streak of dawn showed faintly in the east, Barbarossa and his Gela descended, the revelry ceased, the knights grasped their swords, and the glittering throng passed over court and bridge back to the heart of the mountain, while behind them the magic castle melted into mist.

The great morning has dawned; the nation has awaked; their strife is stilled. The imperial jewels, " Unity and

Strength," lie no longer buried in the waves of the Seleph, the German people henceforth have them in their midst.

Barbarossa may now cease his watch and enter on his rest, for from the North Sea to the plains of Italy is sounded the fame of the great united Fatherland.

Thus has the aged Emperor's prophecy been fulfilled, though it was but the nation's youthful dream.

VRENELI IN KING LAURIN'S ROSE-
GARDEN.

KING LAURIN.

N the Tyrol, that true home of the good little dwarf-folk, is a lovely valley where in olden days a substantial farm-house stood, whose owner had come from the other side of the mountain enticed by the beauty and fertility of this favoured spot.

In those days it was still possible to find good servants capable of forming a faithful attachment to their master and his household. But the farmer thought they were still better in his old home, and for this reason he generally brought his servants from the other side of the high mountain ridge.

Spring had returned ; the mountain pastures were green once more, and it was time for the herds to leave the valley ; but the old herdswoman who for years had had the charge of the mountain farm, and in whose capability and conscientiousness the farmer had the fullest confidence, now took ill and died.

This was a matter of some anxiety to the farmer and his household, for everything was ready for the removal of the cattle.

"Go over, Tony, to our native valley," said the old farmer to his only son and heir. "An aged cousin of mine lives there ; they say her daughter is a fine girl ; it might be a good thing if you could persuade her to come to us as herdswoman."

Early next morning the young man set out on his errand.

The shades of night still lurked among the rocks like giants in disguise, but the peaks of the glacier were already aglow with the light of morning. The youth, accustomed to the beauties of his native mountains, gave scarcely a glance to the splendour of the Alps, but hastened onwards with head and heart full of anxiety about his cattle. Soon he reached the narrow mountain ridge between the two lofty glaciers, from which the way led downwards to his native valley.

At this spot stood a tall cross, with dark arms outstretched over both the glaciers, as if it would tell of the dangers which had threatened the traveller who, out of gratitude for his deliverance, had caused a cross to be erected on this lonely height.

Tony knelt to pray, as was the custom in those times and in that country. His head was bent low, so that he did not see the grave face which looked down on him from one of the glaciers.

Surely it must have been carried thither on eagles' wings, for there, to that glassy height which seemed almost nearer the sky than the earth, no human foot could ever climb. Yet that figure stood there calm, strong, and erect. Long silvery hair flowed over the shoulders; round the head flashed something like sun-beams, or like a mysterious diadem of carbuncles; and the dark eyes pierced the distance, and rested on the kneeling one with an earnestness that went deep down into his heart.

The young man rose and descended the winding path to the valley. The apparition on the lofty glacier stood long looking after his receding figure, and then, with the sunbeams playing among his silvery locks, walked with sure footsteps that never slipped down over the gleaming field of ice.

Late in the afternoon Tony sat once more at the foot of the cross, with a lovely maiden by his side. She had placed her little bundle on the ground at her feet, her hands lay folded on her lap, and with an expression of mingled grief and newly-awakened hope she looked into the face of her companion.

Her mother had died a few days before, and poverty was even in those good old days a bitter thing, as the poor orphan learned to her cost. For the warden of the village told her bluntly that the cottage in which she had lived with her mother, being public property, was claimed now by another widow, and that Vreneli must make her own way in the world.

Many a farmer's wife would have been glad to hire the good Vreneli as servant, but the rough words of the warden had so frightened her that she determined not to stay in this inhospitable valley; and just as she had tied up her little bundle, Tony came to offer her a home in his rich father's house.

Joyfully she agreed, for the farmer was a relation, though a distant one, and she had a dread of going among strangers. So Tony and she set out together on the mountain path, and now they were resting under the old cross and chatting pleasantly.

Vreneli's beauty and innocence had taken Tony's heart by storm, and now he told her that he loved her, and that she, none but she, should be his wife. Vreneli clasped her hands and listened with her whole soul to these words so new to her. Ah! how sweet they sounded after the harsh tones that had made her so unhappy a few hours ago! Her heart went out in gratitude and love to the manly youth who had so generously offered his heart and his home to the poor desolate orphan.

" But I am poor, Tony, and I have learned to-day how evil a thing poverty is," said she at last.

"What does that matter, Vreneli?" answered Tony, cheerfully; "I have enough for both. And I do not like the rich bride that my father has chosen for me, she is ugly and empty-headed. When they see you at home, Vreneli, they must love you, you are so good and beautiful! And when you have tended the herds on the mountain with faithful diligence for the summer months, and when you bring back the well cared-for cattle at the end of the season, you shall be my wife—I will soon bring my parents round to my mind."

"Ah, how delightful that will be!" said Vreneli, smiling. "How I will love you, and what good care I will take of your old parents! Are you sure you are not making fun of me, Tony?"

The young man put his arm around her graceful form. "How can you talk so, Vreneli? Do I not love you better than any one in the whole world? and if it makes your mind easier, I will swear love and faithfulness to you under this cross—I will swear that none but you shall be my wife."

He put his right hand in hers and took the oath. Perfect stillness reigned around them; the spirits of the mountain listened in silence; noiselessly the beams of the evening sun hovered above the cross, and then sank, as if in blessing, on Vreneli's braided hair; while far overhead at the summit of the glacier stood the dark figure that had watched Tony on his journey that morning. The poor orphan and her lover did not see the grave countenance that looked down on them from the lofty peak, but Tony's words of solemn promise floated upwards on the evening breeze to the lonely old man's ear.

Again he cast a searching glance on the kneeling youth, but when his eyes rested on the sweet maiden that listened to those earnest words, the stern expression of his countenance melted, and the wrinkled features bore traces of some sad memories that seemed to be awakened by the sight of her beauty and grace. He leant gently forward, so that his shining locks flowed down like a silver stream, and his eyes followed the two young people with an expression almost of longing, as they walked cheerfully on. But soon the twilight laid its dim veil over hill and valley, and the receding figures faded altogether from his view.

The rich farmer owned the pasture of a whole mountain, and Vreneli was to have the sole charge of the herds that grazed on it, while on another mountain the herds of the other villagers wandered, watched over by several herdsmen.

" Now, Vreneli," said the old farmer next morning, when the cows had been let out of the stalls, and were already climbing the well-known mountain path to the music of their jingling bells—" now, Vreneli, do your duty faithfully, and take good care of my herds, and if the produce of the mountain farm be richer than that yielded in the days of my former herdswomen, I will not be stingy about a reward."

Vreneli blushed, and cast a stolen glance at Tony, who stood behind his father ; she could not but think of the reward which he had promised her. She assured the farmer that she would do her duty, shook hands with the whole household, and then turned to follow the herds.

Tony went with her; he wanted to show her everything in the senner's cottage, and to point out the richest pastures on which the herds were to graze, taking a different place each day, till at last they returned to the first, which by that time would be covered with a fresh growth of grass.

It was a lovely spring morning. The distant glacier was radiant with sunlight, the bells tinkled softly on the necks of the cattle, and wild flowers bloomed at the edge of the torrent which rushed foaming over the moss-grown rocks. But what was all this external beauty in comparison with the blooming world in their own hearts?

They exchanged looks, and words, and happy smiles. Not till the herds had been milked and led to rest on the night pasture did Tony say good-bye. Vreneli stood at the door of the cottage, her hands clasped, and her eyes brimming with happy tears, and watched him till a turn of the road hid him from her view.

Inside, in the cosy cottage, it seemed to her, all the time that she was filling the milk vessels and putting everything in order, as if she still heard his caressing words, and as if his brown eyes looked out on her from every corner. Love and hope quickened her hands, so that her work seemed mere child's play. Then when everything was done, and the fire had died out on the hearth, she stepped out again to the door.

Like a faithful senner she looked first at the night

pasture where the herds were resting peacefully. Now and then one of the beautiful animals would lift its head, and the bell at its throat would tinkle softly ; the night-wind moved gently among the lofty trees, making the long moss of their stems wave to and fro like dark soft veils. Then Vreneli's eyes sought the valley, and to the moonbeams which hastened, in their glittering robes, down the rocky path to the village she entrusted tender messages of love. And when she turned back into the cottage she knelt at her mossy couch beside the hearth, and mingled with her evening prayer words of joyful thanksgiving. Her last thought before she fell asleep was this, that she was the happiest herdswoman and her Tony the handsomest and truest fellow in the whole land of the Tyrol.

Sunny days succeeded to nights filled with golden dreams. When the first sunbeams flashed from the summit of the glacier, the goat-bells sounded below in the valley, and the goat-herd led his flock to seek the juicy plants that grew on heights inaccessible to less sure-footed herds.

Then Vreneli ran joyfully to meet him, for he always brought some message from Tony, or some other token of his love. With joy-quickened energy she went then about her daily toil. The cows left their nightly resting-place, and came to Vreneli to be milked, and then she led them to some new pasture.

And while the cattle grazed there, she leant against a rock and carefully watched each step of the animals entrusted to her care, lest any one of them should go too near a precipice, or, enticed by the plants that grew most richly beside the torrent, be hurried away in its mad whirl.   And when evening sank on the mountain, and clothed the ice-columns in a splendour of red and purple, the goat-herd led his flock back to the valley, and received every evening from Vreneli's hand a bunch of mountain violets for her beloved Tony.

Then she drove the cows again to the milking-place, and repeated the task of the morning.   But this did not end her day's work.   She was busy for hours in the cottage, and moon and stars had long looked down on the slumbering mountain before Vreneli had finished arranging her milk vessels in the dairy, or placed the newly-made cheese to dry, or rolled out her golden butter-pats.

Then after a simple prayer she lay down on her lowly couch, and when the distant thunder of avalanches broke the silence of the night, and the mountain torrent roared close behind her tiny cottage, Vreneli slept as sweetly as a child, and round her head dreams of love and home hovered on golden wing.

So the weeks flew by, and the day arrived when the butter and cheese which the mountain farm had hitherto produced was to be taken home to the farm-house. The farmer and Tony were to come to bring it, as the goat-herd had told Vreneli yesterday, and her usually dexterous fingers trembled with glad excitement just when it was most needful to show the farmer that he had entrusted his property to capable hands.

At last—how often she had looked impatiently along the path—at last the old farmer came toiling up, and behind him, not Tony, as she expected, but two servants with tall baskets on their backs.

Vreneli was bitterly disappointed, but she controlled herself and walked out calmly to meet her master. In spite of the sunny morning dark clouds lay upon his brow, and it did not clear even when Vreneli took him into the faultless dairy and showed him the rows of large rich cheese and the golden butter. Silently they were laid in the basket, and the servants returned homewards with heavy burdens.

Then Vreneli led the farmer to the meadow where the herds were grazing, and his keen eye told him that the beasts were well fed and cared for. It was a faithful hand to which he had entrusted his property—*that* he must acknowledge, however unwillingly. " You have done well, Vreneli; see that you go on as you have begun!" he said bluntly. How harsh the words sounded compared with those with which he had sent her to the mountain! Then when he turned to go home, and she politely begged him to taste the fritter that she had prepared for him according to the custom of the country, he refused it, looking all the time so gloomy that Vreneli did not dare to ask for Tony, though her heart throbbed in anxiety and longing. So he left her, and Vreneli stood watching him with a heart full of sadness and disappointment.

It was evening, and the firelight fell as brightly as ever on Vreneli's lovely face, but it did not show the joyous expression of other evenings. Her movements were languid, and now and then a tear stole down her cheek.

Why did not Tony come, as he had said he would? Why was the old farmer so gloomy? Why did the goat-herd refuse to take the daily bunch of violets, in return for which she might have hoped for some message from Tony? These were questions on which her life's happiness depended, and yet there was no one there to answer them.

She sighed deeply. There had been a gentle knocking at the door, which Vreneli, lost in her sad thoughts, had not noticed; but at her loud sigh the door opened, and a figure of mysterious aspect stood on the threshold. Long silvery hair flowed down over the shoulders, and from the serious yet kindly eyes spoke a majesty which diadem and purple robes would not have been enough to give. Vreneli let fall the milk bowl in her astonishment, and she bowed low as to a mighty prince; then she wiped the low bench before the fire, the only seat which the simple cottage offered, and asked her strange guest to be seated.

The old man nodded pleasantly, and sat down at the fire, leant his head on both hands, so that his silvery locks flowed almost to the ground, and directed his earnest gaze so searchingly on Vreneli that it seemed to her as if he could see into her very soul.

" Why art thou so sad to-day, Vreneli?" he said at last very gently.

Vreneli started. How did this stranger, who seemed

KING LAURIN IN VRENELI'S COTTAGE.

to come from some distant land—how could he know her
name? She looked at him, half in reverence and half
in fear. "Come, Vreneli, wilt thou not tell me?" said
the old man, and his eye rested almost with love upon
her face.

"I am an orphan," she faltered out at last, "and
sometimes a painful feeling of loneliness comes over
me."

"And is that all, Vreneli?" asked the old man;

"canst thou not confide in one who means well towards thee, and who has both the power and the desire to help thee? Dost thou think thyself unknown to me? Did I not see thee on the mountain side beneath the cross? Did I not hear the young man's oath, and see how love and hope had driven sorrow from thy heart? From that hour I have been thy friend. Dost thou think that thy care and watchfulness could have kept the dangers of the mountains far from thy roof and from thy herds? When thou wast asleep on thy couch of moss, and fair dreams led thy soul to golden meadows, I kept watch up there upon the rock, and warned the elements to leave thee and thy charge unhurt; I directed the course of the avalanches, and the flight of the snow-storm, so that they turned aside, and only softest breezes and the gentle starlight ever touched thy brow. Dost thou still mistrust me, Vreneli?"

Vreneli had clasped her hands and drawn nearer to her venerable friend.

"I thank you for your protection," said she, bowing once more in lowly reverence; "whoever you may be, to me you have been a benefactor, and such a one has a right to my confidence. But tell me how you read my heart and learned my love for Tony? For you know already what its burden is. I am troubled about what has happened to-day; I cannot understand it. Above all, I am disappointed at not having seen Tony, after I had looked forward so joyfully to meeting him"

The old man cast a searching glance on her lovely face, as she stood there with the firelight falling brightly on her, and her blue eyes turned towards him in sorrow and touching confidence.

"And wouldst thou like to see him now?" he asked gravely.

Vreneli's eyes shone with delight.

"But, Vreneli, the fulfilment of our wishes often brings something quite different from our hopes; we go to seek faithfulness, and we find treachery."

"Ah!" said she, with the smile of unshaken trust, "that will not be the case with me. Tony is good and truer than gold, and did he not swear to me beneath the cross?"

"Thou dear child!" answered the old man, while painful memories troubled his grave features; "if every broken oath could make a step, we would soon be able to reach the moon."

"Stranger," said Vreneli, confidently, "you may have met with faithlessness enough in your long life to make you lose your confidence in human nature, but you do not know my Tony!"

"Come then, Vreneli, since thou wishest it," said the old man, rising, "though I would fain have spared thee this pain." And they stepped out together into the night.

Led by the old man's hand, Vreneli climbed up to the point of rock from which he had kept nightly watch over her and her herds. They went forward to the edge of the precipice. Far below, veiled by the darkness, lay Tony's home. High walls of rock and wide pasture-lands separated them from the farm-house, so that no human eye could pierce the distance.

But the old man pulled down a branch of the lofty pine above them, and told Vreneli to look through a tiny knot-hole. She did so; the laws of space yielded, and her anxious glance flew to the distant farm-house. She looked through the lighted windows into the well-furnished rooms. All the costly vessels and ornaments, which were usually carefully laid past in chests and cup-boards, were to-day displayed on the festive board, round which the most distinguished residents of the village were chatting and laughing merrily. Next his parents sat Tony, and at his side a richly dressed maiden. His eyes shone, and his mouth smiled and whispered, just as on that evening when he had sworn love and faithfulness to Vreneli beneath the cross on the mountain. His father's threatening words and the wealth of the bride so long chosen for him had quickly shaken Tony's purpose, and while the gentle Vreneli was thinking anxiously about his non-appearance, the fickle youth broke his solemn oath, and betrothed himself to the unloved but wealthy bride.

Vreneli looked at the scene in tearless silence, then, when she could no longer doubt her lover's faithlessness, she let go the branch and turned her eyes away, so that once more night and distance covered the scene that had ruined her hopes. Vreneli silently descended the rock, but she did not seek the shelter of her cottage. She hurried past it, and wandered on aimlessly over the wilds of the mountain. It seemed almost as if she wished to reach the icy glacier heights.

"Vreneli," said the voice at her side; "Vreneli,

whither wilt thou go?" She turned her head as in a dream. Stony sorrow had fallen on her gentle features, and her once bright eyes were cold and fixed. "Whither?" she said quietly, "whither? I would like to go to the grave, but, since that may not be, I will go at least away, away as far as my feet will bear me."

"Wilt thou come with me, Vreneli?" said the old man. "My home shall be thine, and the love and faithfulness which thou hast lost here thou shalt find there a thousand-fold."

Vreneli looked into his mild eyes.

"And who art thou, kind old man?" she asked with faltering voice.

"I am King Laurin, the ruler of the powerful nation of the dwarfs, who for centuries were bound to men in faithful love. The impress of divinity which we spirits recognised in you, and before which we humbly bow, attracted us to your race. But in every generation we traced it less easily, and at last, despised and deceived in return for our kindness and help, we retired to the recesses of our mountains. There in the heart of the rock whose brow is crowned by the shining glacier, there stands my palace, adorned by my people with all the splendour of the precious stones which, hidden to mortal eyes, shine deep down in the heart of the earth.

"There I live, but I have led for centuries a lonely life, for my only daughter, the last flower of a blooming garland, died long, long ago. Her rose-garden, to tend which was her greatest delight, still blooms in unfading beauty, but as often as my eyes fall on its wondrous flowers, I think with grief of my long-lost child. Thou, Vreneli, art a pure-hearted maiden like her, and since I first saw thee and looked into thine eyes, it has seemed to me as if I had found my child. I have watched over thee with a father's care, and I am ready now to love thee as my daughter."

"Poor lonely king!" said Vreneli, in a tone of gentle pity, while the tears ran down her cheeks, "I will go with you to your mountain palace; I will love and honour you as your child once did, and I will tend the rose-garden that she loved; for I have no home and no heart to love me. But grant me one thing before I leave the sunlight."

"Thou hast but to ask and it is granted!"

"Ah, King Laurin!" said Vreneli, and her tears flowed faster, "I am still young, and this is the first disappointment that my heart has felt, and though it is almost broken, yet I have still a faint hope left. I cannot quite let go my faith in Tony."

King Laurin looked even more gravely than before on the weeping maiden.

"No, do not be angry!" she begged, raising her hands entreatingly to him; "call it not foolish weakness; remember that it needed hundreds of years before your noble heart would close against our deceitful race. I know that Tony has been persuaded by his friends to take this step; but he still loves me, and it would grieve him if I were to go without farewell. When he brings his bride up the mountain to-morrow, on their way to the wedding in the next valley, let me go out to meet him as he is passing my cottage—let me say farewell and part from him in peace."

"Do as thou wilt, my child," answered King Laurin with gentle sadness, "though thou wilt find but a new sorrow. And now, Vreneli, it is late. Go to thy cottage, and lie down on thy couch, there to forget thy griefs for a few short hours at least."

"Ah no!" said Vreneli, entreatingly; "let me stay here with you beneath the stars, for I dread the loneliness of the cottage. Wherever I may be I cannot sleep, and the shadows of past happiness would there trouble my soul. No; let me stay here and share your watch."

They climbed the rock, and sat down side by side beneath the lofty pines. Vreneli folded her hands and looked up to the stars, while her prayer for peace and comfort arose to Him who sits enthroned above the sky.

Not a word was spoken. King Laurin gazed in silence on the moonlit glacier, while his mind wandered back to the memories of a thousand years, and on Vreneli's brow lay the deep shadow of her young grief.

Gradually her eyelids closed, and her head sank gently to the old king's shoulder. He placed his arm tenderly round the slumbering girl, and stretched out his right hand towards the lofty glacier.

Then the storm-song in its icy clefts grew suddenly still, but the moonbeams still played around its jagged peaks; like glistening serpents they moved across the glassy sea, and then flowed slowly in a broad shining stream down on the crystal road. The mountain torrent meanwhile checked its thunder, and moved more gently on its rocky way.

The night that hung above the mountain seemed but a pleasant twilight, and through the mild, soft air a bell tinkled gently now and then from the night pasture where the cattle lay at rest. All was peace. Nothing stirred save the summer breeze and the golden starlight, which ventured near to kiss the tear-stained cheek of the maiden who lay in sweet forgetfulness of sorrow on the old king's arm.

And now it was once more morning, and Vreneli's cheek grew pale as she thought of the sorrowful parting with him whom she had once called her Tony. But she was determined to do her duty to the very last, so she led her herds to the pasture, by the side of which the road ran, that she might be at hand to tend them while waiting by the wayside for Tony and his bride.

The sun rose higher and higher, and the minutes of painful waiting seemed hours to the poor girl. Suddenly voices and loud laughter sounded in her ear, and soon two figures appeared from round the rock. For the first time since the morning when she brought the herds up the mountain Tony stood face to face with the poor orphan whose life's happiness he had ruined, and he started as he looked into the face so beautiful, but deadly pale. For one moment he remembered his oath. Then the rich bride at his side cried mockingly—"I suppose this is the servant girl of whom your father spoke, who had the presumption to dream of becoming a rich farmer's wife? Fancy the little beggar entertaining such an idea!"

The scornful words cut deep into Vreneli's crushed heart.

"I should never have thought of it myself," she said, sadly; "it was Tony who wished it, because he loved me so that my poverty seemed no obstacle."

"Oh! indeed, Tony," said the bride, haughtily, "that is rather different from what you told me yesterday evening. Did you not tell me that you had never troubled your head about her, and that you had always wished to marry me? Tell this girl that she lies, or if you cannot do that, then you are free to choose this beggar still. I have plenty of suitors left!"

Tony grew red with shame and vexation, but he did not vent his anger on the haughty bride, but on poor innocent Vreneli. "You lie, girl," he cried; "I never made you any promise; I never loved you!"

"Tony," answered Vreneli gently, "do not bring needless guilt on your head. Have you forgotten your oath beneath the lonely cross on the mountain? But I am not angry with you for forsaking me. Perhaps your parents persuaded you to do it; but I could not refrain from coming to say farewell, and to wish you happiness and prosperity."

"Keep your farewell and your wishes to yourself!" cried Tony, white with anger and shame; "you were a fool, if you took my words in earnest. I and a beggar like you!".

With a loud mocking laugh he turned away, gave

his arm to his bride, and passed on without a word of farewell.

Vreneli looked after him in speechless amazement. The wise king was right, then ; she had met but a new blow, and this one more crushing than the first. She turned, and saw behind her King Laurin, who had been an unseen witness of Tony's shameful treachery. His eyes glowed, but he uttered not a word. Vreneli stooped again to raise his hands to her trembling lips. "I am ready to follow you !" she said in a low voice.

Then the rock opened before them ; Vreneli gave a farewell look at the midday sun, then, led by King Laurin's hand, she entered the magic kingdom of the dwarfs.

That very moment an avalanche was set free from the snow-clad slopes of the glacier, rolled down with angry thunder, and at the cross where once Tony had sworn faithful love to Vreneli it overtook him and his heartless bride, and buried them so deep that their bodies were never found. Thus King Laurin avenged his adopted daughter.

Vreneli had found a home, and, instead of the one worthless heart that she had lost, a thousand hearts beat true to her in unchanging love.

King Laurin loved her as he had once loved his own lost child, and she returned his affection with all the warmth of her young heart, while the little dwarfs obeyed her every wish with that cheerful eagerness with which they had once served their lost princess.

She tended the rose-garden beside the king's crystal palace with such loving care that it bloomed once more as in the days in which the magic-mighty hand of the princess had moved among its fairy blossoms, and the sweet fragrance that the roses breathed into her very soul healed every wound of disappointed löve.

She did not miss the sunlight in this fairy kingdom, for the mild radiance of unseen stars lit it day and night; she never longed for earth, for here was unchanging spring; warm breezes kissed her brow, and the wild chamois, shy dwellers of the mountain solitudes, came up in friendly confidence, and let her stroke them with her snow-white hand.

Many a time on starry nights she went by King Laurin's side out to the glacier peaks, to look around upon the slumbering land. Her eye, made keen by the light of the fairy world, pierced the distance and the darkness of night, and she gazed, even unaided by any "magic ring," far beyond the boundaries which limit human vision. And what had once driven her from the region of sunlight she saw always and everywhere—sorrow, injustice, and untruth.

And when she looked into many a joyless cottage and many a sorrowful heart, she would turn to the old king by her side, kiss his hand with loving reverence, and say, smiling—" Come, King Laurin, let us go back to our home, to our peaceful kingdom, where tears and guilt and fickleness are all unknown."

The Dwarf of Venice takes his Departure for his Native Land.

The Dwarf of Venice.

VENING was falling with the mild beauty of spring on the mountains and pasture-lands of the Tyrol. The latest sunbeams which streamed down from the lofty glacier bore the tones of the vesper bell through the quiet village street, and floated over the brook and in at the open windows of a substantial farm-house which stood at the end of the little valley. A neatly carved balcony surrounded the house, the window-panes gleamed like mirrors, and the orderly arrangements of the farm-yard showed the owner to be a man of some wealth.

At the table in the oak-panelled sitting-room sat the rich farmer himself, but in spite of his possessions he seemed discontented and unhappy, for between his brows was a deep frown, and his eyes were dark and lowering. Opposite him sat his beautiful young wife, whose soft eyes looked anxiously into her husband's face. On her lap she held her only child, a lovely little girl, with eyes as blue as the flax blossom, and hair that shone like gold : she folded her little hands, as her mother did, as long as the vesper bell continued to call to prayer ; but her eyes looked longingly, now on the pancakes that lay piled on the bright pewter plate, now casting a friendly glance on the boy that sat at the furthest end of the table, with his hands folded in devout reverence.

It was Hans, the son of a poor relation, to whom the rich farmer, with unwonted generosity, had granted a place in his house and at his table, and who in return had to drive the goats every day up to the highest pastures on the mountain, to places inaccessible to other herds. He had just returned with his nimble charge, and had brought to little Anneli on her mother's knee a bunch of alproses, for he dearly loved the child.

The bell had ceased ringing, the hands were unclasped, and the mother began to help the delicate pancakes. There was a gentle knocking at the door, and in walked

a little man in a sombre and threadbare garment. His
back was bent, either with the weight of years or by the
wallet which hung from his shoulder; his hair was silver
grey; but the dark shining eyes told that in this decrepit
body lived a strong unconquered spirit.

"Good evening, sir," said the little man humbly;
" might I beg you for a bit of supper, for I am starving,
and for a night's rest on your haystack, for I am tired
to death."

"Indeed," said the farmer angrily; "do you take my
house for a beggar's tavern? if so, I am sorry your sight
is so bad. You may seek elsewhere, for you will not
find what you want here!"

The dwarf looked in astonishment on the master of
the house, who, regardless of the hospitable customs of
the country, could thus turn a poor man away from his
door; but the farmer took no notice of his surprise, nor
of his wife's looks of entreaty.

"No, wife," he said harshly, "this time you shall not
have your own way. I will not keep open house for all
the beggars in the land. Did I not give in to you about
that boy over there? You might be content with that."

Poor Hans blushed crimson at this allusion to his
poverty, but when the little man turned away with a sigh
and left the inhospitable threshold, sympathy with the
poor old man overcame his fear of his employer; he
seized the plate with the pancakes, and the great piece
of bread which the farmer's wife had just given him, and
ran out of the room.

"What's the boy after?" asked the farmer angrily.

"He is just doing what we ought to have done," answered the wife, with gentle reproach in her fair face; "he is sharing his meal with the poor man."

"Yes, yes," growled the man, "birds of a feather flock together."

Meantime the old man was creeping with weary steps across the yard, and had just reached the gate when Hans seized him by the arm.

"Here, good little man," said he in mingled pity and fear—"here is my supper; come, sit down there on the well and eat."

The old man's dark eyes rested with a pleased look on the boy. "And what hast thou for thyself, child, if thou givest away thine own share?"

"Oh! that does not matter," said Hans unconcernedly, while he led the dwarf to the stone wall which surrounded the well. "I am not very hungry, and the farmer's good wife would give me more if I asked her."

The old man sat down and began to eat, while Hans watched with delight how his aged friend enjoyed it. Soon the plate was empty, and the little man rose with thanks to set out on further wanderings, and to seek a night's shelter under a more hospitable roof.

Hans went with him to the gate, and whispered hastily, "Do not think ill of the farmer for having refused you; he is not always so churlish, but to-day something has occurred to vex him—he was not re-elected as burgomaster of the village, but his bitterest foe was successful; that has soured him, and so every one who comes in his way must suffer for it. But listen, little man ; to the right there, on the rock over which the path leads to the mountain, stands the hay-loft with *its* roof touching the stone. That's where I sleep, and if you climb a little way up the rock, and wait there till I go to bed, I will open the trap-door, and you can creep in to me among the hay."

"Thou art a good boy," said the old man ; "I will do as thou sayest, and wait for thee there upon the rock."

It was night when Hans was at last allowed to seek his couch. More nimbly than usual he sprang up the slender ladder to the hay-loft, and then he quickly unfastened the trap-door which opened on the roof.

The full moon stood large and bright above the mountain, and its pale beams played round the jagged brow of the glacier, and wove a veil of silver round the beech woods that adorned the mountain landscape.

The old man was sitting silently on a ledge of rock ; his hands lay folded on his lap, his head was bare, and the night wind moved lightly through his grey tresses. But the old man heeded it not. His eyes gazed fixedly on the night sky, as if they could, like the seers of olden time, decipher the records of the stars, and his features were ennobled by such a look of majesty that the boy gazed at him in astonishment, not daring to disturb him. At last he said softly, "Do not be angry, sir, at my troubling you, but the night is growing cold, and the dew is beginning to fall. Would you not be better in a warm bed ?"

The old man sighed, as if his thoughts returned unwillingly from their flight. Then he nodded pleasantly to the boy, went up to the trap-door, and let himself down upon the floor of the loft. He lay down silently on the fragrant hay, and was just about to close his weary eyes when he felt the boy's warm hand passing over him.

The little fellow had taken off his jacket, and was now carefully spreading it over the old man that the night wind might not hurt him. With a silent smile the dwarf accepted the service of love, and soon their deep breathing told that slumber had fallen on the eyes of both. Several hours had passed by, when something like a flash of lightning woke the boy. He rose quickly ; the trap-door was open, and the old man was rummaging busily in his wallet ; he had just taken out of it a very bright hand-mirror, and the light of the moon, reflected with a flash from the crystal, had awakened the boy.

The dwarf now threw his sack over his shoulder, took the mirror in his hand, and began to go through the trap-door to the rock.

Hans could bear it no longer. "Oh, sir," he begged, "take me with you into the mountains, for that you are bound thither the mirror in your hand tells me. My dear mother has often told me about the mountain mirror, by means of which one can see into the depths of the earth, and watch the metal gleaming and glittering in its veins. And although you have not said so, yet I know that you are one of the mysterious strangers who come from far-off lands to seek the gold of our mountains, which is hidden from our dim eyes. Oh, take me with you !"

The old man turned his face to the boy. "That is

idle curiosity, my son," he said gravely, and his eyes shone almost as brightly as the mirror had a few minutes before; "stay at home and tend thy herds, as a good boy should."

"Oh no, sir," begged Hans earnestly; "I have always longed to see the wonders of the mountains, and I will be quiet and silent as is befitting in presence of such marvels, and I will help you and serve you to the best of my power. Take me with you!"

The old man thought a minute, glanced searchingly into the boy's eyes, who had come nearer to him in his earnestness, and then he said—"Come, then, and remember thy promise."

They stepped out together, shut the trap-door behind them, and clambered up to the top of the rock, from which the broad footpath led up to the heights and abysses of the mountain. The moon poured its mystic radiance down from the deep blue sky of night, and the young foliage of the beech wood gleamed like silver as it fluttered in the breeze. Not a footstep was heard on the mossy ground, only their shadows glided in company with the lonely wanderers, who in silent haste pressed on deeper into the recesses of the mountains. The wood lay behind them, and the path led to a ravine, at the bottom of which a raging torrent rushed; they stood now at its edge.

None save Tyrol's boldest mountain climbers know this path, and even they, though provided with ice-shoes and alpenstocks, tread its steep ascent with trembling hearts. But the little man seemed to heed no danger;

fearlessly he set his foot upon the highest point, and securely, as if on level ground, he went down the side of the precipice, where one false step would have been certain death. The boy followed him with beating heart. The moonlight broke through the overhanging bushes and the lofty rocks overhead, and made its way down into the ravine.

The wanderers stood now at the edge of the raging torrent, and walked along it to the high rock over which the glacier stream fell into its rocky bed, and which seemed to them, as it stood veiled in night, like one of the giants of old who, the old legends tell us, were turned to stone. Even in the distance they had seen the moving cloud of vapour above its head, which hovered in the light of the full moon, like a giant eagle, above the rushing waters. The milk-white billows of the torrent that rushed down from this height rolled in the moonlight like silvery tresses down from the rock's giant head. The old man walked quietly through the noise and foam round the foot of the rock and into a narrow cleft, which was the opening into the heart of the mountain ; here he laid down his wallet.

Now, now the boy's heart beat even more loudly than it had done amid the dangers of the abyss, when the old man silently beckoned to him. He held the mountain mirror in his hand : Hans stepped timidly to his side, and looked into the magic glass. Mists impenetrable as the curtain which parts the present from the future rolled over its crystal surface, but they became lighter and lighter, and soon the interior of the mountain lay open before the eyes of the delighted child. Through the wide rocky gates his eye pierced into a land of wonders such as are never seen on earth. Through the blue air rose the pinnacles of a crystal palace; the golden roof and the windows of precious stone shone in the splendour of another sun; and in the lofty star-spangled hall sat King Laurin, the hoary king of the dwarfs, on his emerald throne. Round him stood his subjects, the wise and aged dwarfs, who had long since forsaken the wicked world to lead an active but peaceful life here in their magic kingdom, where the malice and inquisitiveness of mortals could not come to disturb them. They listened with heads bent in reverent attention to the words of their king, and then went in different directions to obey his commands; but Laurin descended from his throne, laid aside crown and sceptre, and went down the golden steps to the rose-garden, which his beloved daughter, the only one left to him of all his circle of blooming children, tended with skilful hand. The lovely maiden was walking among the garden paths, tying up the young roses and moistening their roots with water from the golden vessel in her hand, when she saw her royal father coming. She hastened to meet him, took his strong hand with respectful tenderness, and led him joyfully through the blooming beds. Meantime, the little dwarfs had set busily to work: some were leading their herds of chamois through a secret gate out to the mountains of the upper world, that they might there enjoy earthly air and light; others hastened to the clear silvery springs which watered this realm, to guide their waters of blessing up to the meadows

HANS SEES KING LAURIN'S KINGDOM IN THE MAGIC MIRROR.

F. C., p. 62.

and woods of the children of men, that they might yield a more abundant increase ; others, again, took pickaxes, mallets, and dark lanterns, all made of precious metal, and went into the heart of the surrounding mountains to bring their hidden wealth to light, and to increase still more the royal treasure, countless though their king's hoards already were.

Glittering veins of gold streaked the stone, and out of the dark rock bubbled springs, whose clear waters flashed and sparkled, as if they bore onward with them grains of the precious and much longed-for metal. In a dark grotto lay something white and motionless like a slumbering eagle; but at the flash of the lanterns it roused itself, and the white serpent queen lifted her gem-crowned head. The drops that trickled down the walls of the grotto gleamed like jewels in the light of her diadem ; but the serpent bent her head again, and coiled herself up for further sleep, for she knew well that the little dwarfs, unlike the robber sons of men, would never stretch forth their hands to seize the jewel on her brow. And there, at yonder spring, knelt a dark form busily engaged in gathering the gold sand from the bottom of the water, and putting it into the wallet beside him ; but the figure could not be recognised in the shadow which lay deep at that spot. But when some of the industrious little men drew near with their flickering lanterns, the man at the spring turned his head and nodded to them a friendly greeting, which they returned as if he was an old and dear acquaintance.

Then the boy recognised by his grey locks and his dark

eyes full of gravity and wisdom the old man who had been showing him the mountain mirror. He raised his eyes in astonishment from the magic glass, and now for the first time he perceived that he held the mirror in his own hand, and that the old man was no longer by his side.

"Ah! how thoughtless I am ; I promised to help him, and now the kind old man is tiring himself, unaided, with his heavy work," said Hans in self-reproach. Then he hid the magic mirror in his bosom and turned towards the hole which formed the entrance to the treasures of the mountains. But just as he was stooping to creep in, the old man himself came out, bearing on his shoulder the shabby wallet with its priceless contents. "Forgive me, sir," begged Hans in a tone of true sorrow, "for having kept my promise so ill, but my mind was spell-bound by the wonders I beheld."

"It matters not, my son," replied the old man mildly ; "I have always had to work alone and without help, and I will continue to do so. All I ask of thee is a night's rest on the hay and a bite of bread when thou canst spare it. But come now! Seest thou how the cloud above the waterfall is gleaming rosy red? It is the reflection of the dawn. I would not that thy herds should wait for thee, and thy harsh master find thee behindhand with thy work. So let us hasten!"

And back they hurried on the dangerous path by which they had come ; the beech leaves gleamed in the first light of the new day as they passed through the wood, and the thrushes were just beginning their morning song.

Soon they stood on the ledge of rock, and a few minutes brought them to the trap-door. The old man slipped in to snatch a little slumber before he began another day's wanderings, but the boy could not think of lying in his dark loft after all the splendour he had left behind, so he went to let out his goats and take them to the mountain. But to-day he could not bear to stay as usual in the tiny cottage where he performed the light duties of the mountain herdsman, while the goats clambered alone up the steep walls of rock in search of juicy plants, and came back uncalled at the sound of the evening bell. To-day he climbed with them up to the highest peaks, for he hoped to find some opening through which he might see into the magic kingdom which the mountain mirror had held before his view.

It was, indeed, a wondrous land which stretched far and wide before him in fresh and fragrant beauty. It was his native land shining in unimagined splendour. Crystal lakes gleamed in the distance, and the snow-crowned mountain peaks glowed in the morning sunlight like the roses in King Laurin's magic garden. But there was no palace here, no lovely maiden among her flowers, and no old and yet nimble dwarfs. But there, far away, scarcely visible even to the sharpest eye, a little black dot moved along the winding mountain path, and the flashes which now and then darted from it over to the rock where Hans was standing amid his goats told him that it was the old man with the magic mirror.

"Oh! how I wish it was evening," sighed the boy, looking longingly at the sun, which had scarcely run a

quarter of its appointed course.   At last it was evening,
and herd-boy and herds hastened homewards.   The boy
did not stay long in the house.   With a great piece of
bread and meat in his hand he climbed the steep ladder
to the hay-loft, and found to his joy the old man there
already, waiting to receive the food with humble thanks.
Hans lost no time in going to sleep, that the longed-for
hour of the night journey might come the more quickly;
and when again a sudden light flashed across his eyes,
he opened them in delight and rose.   But it was not the
brilliance of the magic mirror that had awakened him,
but the beam of the morning sun.   He looked round in
astonishment; he had slept so soundly that he had lost
his expected journey.   It was now clear daylight, and
the goats were loudly calling their young master to his
duty.   He gave a hasty glance at his companion, who
still lay in deep slumber.   Whether he had slept thus
since yesterday evening, or whether he was resting after
his nightly labours, Hans had no time to ask.   Quickly
he ran down the ladder into the farm-yard, where all was
life; then he took his shepherd's bag, which hung behind
the door, already filled with the daily portion of food,
and hurried with his impatient flock up towards the
mountain.

Again he looked wistfully from his high rocky seat
down on the blooming meadows, and recognised the
little man with the magic mirror in the remote distance,
and determined to keep his eyes open the whole night.
But when evening came, and he sought his couch,
scarcely had he lain down by the side of his aged friend,

when deep sleep fell on his eyelids, and left them only at the glance of the morning sun. Haste and timidity always prevented him from disturbing the old man in his sleep, and telling him once more the fervent wishes of his heart; and so every morning he bore his unfulfilled desires up with him to the mountain. Thus summer passed, and when one morning the first rough breath of autumn chilled the boy's brow, there was a rustling behind the rock on which he sat, and the old man, who had been his companion for so many months, stood before him. The wallet on his shoulder was full, and in his hand he held a staff as if he was ready to return to his distant home, for so indeed he was.

"I come, my son," said the little man with his old grave kindliness, "to thank thee for shelter and food, and to ask thee if thou hast any wish which I can gratify."

Hans shouted with joy; but the old man raised his finger gravely—he seemed to read into the boy's very soul.

"Neglect not sacred duties for the sake of idle curiosity," said he in a tone of warning, and the boy blushed and was silent. Then Hans thought of his good mother down in the valley, whose cottage he passed every morning and evening, and found the poor woman always at the window waiting to whisper a loving word, a motherly blessing to her only child. But this morning her eyes had been dim with trouble, and when he asked what was wrong she had answered with a sigh—

"Nothing, my good child, that thou canst alter; I am only thinking of the approach of winter, and how the cold wind will whistle through my battered cottage, and how I have no warm clothing to protect me from the cold."

All this flashed like lightning through the boy's mind; tremblingly he clasped his hands, and a prayer for help fell from his lips.

"That is right, my son," said the old man kindly, handing the boy a little coin. "Despise this not for its mean appearance, and never use it foolishly; and when I return next year, let me find thy hand as open and thy heart as pure as I have found them now. Farewell."

He nodded kindly to the boy, took the cloak from his shoulder, spread it on the rock, and placed himself on it, staff in hand, and with the burden on his shoulders. Immediately the mantle rose, and hovered before the boy's astonished eyes, bearing the little man up into the air. The old man waved farewell from his airy height; then he pointed southwards with his staff, and swift as an arrow flew the magic mantle towards his far-off home. The boy watched the wonderful journey with devoutly folded hands. Like the beat of eagle's wings was the motion of the dark garment through the white clouds, and the little man kept his balance perfectly, he guiding his flight with the staff in his left hand, while the magic mirror in his right gleamed in the beams of the morning sun like the diadem of carbuncles on the head of the serpent queen. The last flash died away at last, and the boy sat once more alone on his rocky seat, dreamily gazing on the gold coin in his hand. It had evidently passed through many a hand before, for it needed a sharp eye to trace the impression on its surface ; on one side the lion of San Marco stretched his royal limbs, and with raised head kept guard over Venice, the Queen of the Sea, whose foot the Adriatic kisses with its caressing waves, wedded to her anew each year by the Doge's ring.   The other side bore the name of one of the rulers of that proud Republic.   It was scarcely legible, and it had been long eclipsed by a younger glory.

The boy, indeed, had no key to the understanding of the image and inscription, but he felt confident the gift out of such a hand must bring blessing in spite of its mean appearance, and so he kept the coin carefully in his pocket.   To-day he started joyfully at the tone of the evening bell, said his prayer with more than usual fervour, and hastened with winged feet after his thriving flock.

"Just look, dear mother, what I have brought you," he cried joyfully through the window of the cottage, showing the old man's gift.   "Do not despise it," he begged earnestly, as he saw his mother's doubting smile ; "he told me not to despise it, the kind, powerful man who gave it to me.   Put it with your savings, and let us see what will happen."   As he spoke, his eyes shone so brightly with joy and confidence that his good mother could not bear to vex him by her doubts ; she promised to lay the gold piece in the drawer, and bade her boy good night with a loving smile.

Ten springs had passed over Tyrol's mountains and valleys, and there had been many changes in the time.

The young trees had grown tall and leafy; the children had become men and women. Hans was no longer a goat-herd, but a clever senner, as they call the mountain shepherds in the Tyrol, and now the farmer's herds had been entrusted to his sole care during the rest of their stay on the higher pastures, to which he had led them early in spring. The setting sun glowed on the lofty glacier before him, and its reflection flowed down to the night pasture, and hung like a golden veil over the pine trees, beneath whose wide branches the herds had lain down for their nightly rest. But Hans stood before his cottage, which he had entered to-day for the first time as senner, and gazed joyfully on his new charge.

The valleys were already slumbering in the evening shadows, but the peaks of the glacier were aglow with purple, and reminded the young man of an image that he had long borne in his soul with secret longing; he thought now, as he had not done for months, of the rose-garden before the crystal palace, and of the little man who had been his yearly companion in the farmer's hay-loft, and who, every autumn, had climbed the mountain side to say farewell to him, and then with his wallet full of gold had returned on his magic mantle to his distant home. He had never asked the old man for a glance into the mountain mirror since he had received that grave warning about idle curiosity, and these memories of King Laurin's realm had gradually faded. But his reverence for the strange old man had remained unchanged, and every day he had shared his supper with him out of gratitude for the parting gift which Hans had long ago taken home to his mother. He had not hoped or promised too much. With the little man's dim old coin blessing had come into the hut of poverty, and the money in the drawer had never grown less. There was always some left, even when they erected on the site of the tumble-down cottage a firmly built and comfortable house, and though after that they bought many a much needed piece of furniture and warm clothing for the winter. There was no need now to creep in secretly at even to receive the gifts of the kind-hearted farmer's wife without her miserly husband's knowledge. They were able first to keep one cow, and then two, and then—Hans looked joyfully round on the slumbering herds—four fine cows now rested there, his mother's property, which he had been allowed to lead up to the mountain pastures to graze with his master's cattle. The churlish farmer, indeed, had never granted him this favour, but his unkindly eyes had closed for the last sleep the autumn before, and the eyes which now shone in the farm-house were so mild and lovely that it was a pleasure to obey their glance. What were these eyes like! Hans tried to remember as he gazed at the glacier, whose purple had changed to a pale rosy hue. Yes, yes, now he knows. The eyes of Anneli, whom he had loved from childhood as his own dear little sister, were just like the eyes of that fair maiden who used to walk in the rose-garden by the dwarf king's side, and this brought him back to the beginning of his reverie.

And now he began to wonder if the little man, if he returned, would rest at night in the farmer's hay-loft, or, according to his old custom, climb up the mountain to seek him here. Then he heard, not far off, something like the sigh of a weary wanderer. The youth's sharp ear was directed attentively towards the path which led from the village to the senner's cottage, and which was now veiled in the double shadow of the trees and of the falling night. Yes, it was coming from that direction, and immediately Hans was ready to offer help. He took his lantern in his hand, seized his alpenstock, and ran down the path between the rocks and the dew-covered bushes. He had not far to seek, for there, on a stone by the wayside, sat a dwarf in a dark and shabby garment, and a well-remembered wallet hung from his bent shoulders. The young man cast a hasty glance at the figure, and then shouted aloud with delight. It was the old man of whom he had just been thinking, and it was with grateful emotion that he found that his old friend had not forgotten him, but that, in spite of the darkness and his increasing infirmities, he had toiled up the path to the mountains.

"Good evening, sir," said he joyfully, bending as reverently to kiss the dwarf's withered hand as if he had been a lord of the land. "You must be tired; take my arm, and let me carry your sack; that's the way. And now, courage for a hundred steps or so, and we are at the end of our journey." And with such care and reverence as are shown rather to great princes than to such a poor little dwarf, Hans led the old man over the last difficulties of the mountain path, and over the threshold of his hut. Then he hastened to take the covering off his couch of moss and spread it over the wooden bench before the hearth, that the old man might rest his tired limbs on a softer seat. Next he kindled a fire, and made a fritter which the senner who had preceded him had taught him how to make. He had no drink to offer but good, sweet, new milk; but Anneli's hand had provided richly for the wants of the new senner, and the little wooden cupboard in the corner was stocked with good things from the farm-house. The young man searched in it joyfully for something dainty for his guest, and felt proud and happy in his unwonted work. A white cloth was spread over the coarse oaken table, and on it was placed the delicate fritter, with a plate of eggs and bacon sending forth fragrance by its side. Proudly the young man brought his guest to the well-set table, and both enjoyed its good things in silent comfort. Then Hans led the old man, tenderly as a child his beloved father, to his own couch of moss, and when the little dwarf sank on it with a look of love and gratitude, the young man spread the covering over him as he used to spread his jacket years ago in the hay-loft. Then he sat down before the fire that the flickering flame might not disturb the old man, and when at last his deep breathing told that he was asleep, the youth rose and went out into the open air. The moss-couch in the senner's cottage was not broad, and Hans must not spoil the old man's comfort, so he went to the night pasture, where the herds lay sleeping, and sank to rest in the soft moss beneath the aged pines. They let their evergreen branches fall over him protectingly, and the long moss that hung from them served as covering to the youthful sleeper, while the glacier torrents in the distant ravines sang his lullaby.

The days passed by in keener enjoyment than even his boyish dreams had pictured. The hours were bright with happy sunshine, in spite of the double burden of work which he, contrary to the custom of his predecessors, had undertaken in the consciousness of his own powers and fidelity. And when the day had flown by with its quick succession of pleasure and toil, the evening hour would come when the beloved guest sat at the fire and at the oaken table, and sometimes the hitherto so silent lips would let fall words of grave wisdom.

Then came the hour of rest, calling the old man to the moss-bed under the senner's roof; but Hans slipped out when the fire was dead to the shelter of the old pine trees, and slept in their protection, lulled to slumber by the song of the glacier stream.

One warm spring evening, when the jagged ice-crown of the glacier gleamed with a bluish light beneath the full moon's beams, he did not turn towards his soft couch beneath the trees, but hastened to the grove of pines which rose above him on a steep wall of rock. With a sharp axe on his shoulder, gleaming brightly in the moonlight, he stepped along the well-known path across the green meadows to the dark ravine which separated him from the wood on the rocky height. Was the dream of his childhood now really fulfilled—was he going to look through the magic mirror into the heart of the mountains? Oh no. The spirit world had lost its power over his soul. His thoughts and desires belonged now more than ever to real life.

A few days ago Anneli had come up with her mother to the senner's cottage to see about the produce of the mountain farm, as the farmers are in the habit of doing when the herds have been some time on the high pastures; and while the mother inspected the dairy, tried the cheese, and tasted the balls of butter, Anneli stood outside with Hans and the grazing herds, and chatted with him pleasantly as in days gone by.

"And do you remember, good Hans, what day to-morrow is?" she asked with an arch look in her eyes, when Hans, after thinking in vain, shook his head.

"Do you not know?" she said, laughing. "Why, Hans, to-morrow is the first of May, and I am curious to know if I shall have a May-pole raised for me."

"You, Anneli!" cried Hans, looking in astonishment on her beautiful face—"you will have many a tree; they call you already 'the pearl of the valley,' and the rich farmers' sons will fight for the honour," he added in a low sorrowful tone.

This tone thrilled Anneli's heart; she leant towards him with innocent confidence, and said with emotion—"Let them, Hans; but you know that I shall take pleasure in no May-pole but *one*."

It was these words which were driving Hans now in the silence of night through the dangerous ravine and the foaming torrent, and up the steep precipice to the pine wood. Here he felled the chosen tree skilfully, tore the bark from the smooth stem, and bore the trunk carefully on his shoulder through shrubs and narrow mountain ways down into the valley. His path was dark and difficult, and jutting rocks often hemmed his footsteps; but his love for Anneli kept him from feeling weary, and the thought of her joy always gave him new strength. Thus, after hours of toil, he arrived at last in the village, and stood before Anneli's door. Then he took a packet carefully out of his shepherd's bag, and with the prettiest ribbons which his mother had been able to find in the nearest town he adorned the tree; and that Anneli's heart might make no mistake, he tied at the top a bunch of alproses, such as he used to bring every evening when he was the goat-herd and she a lovely little child. Then he planted the pole firmly in the ground right before Anneli's window, and with a glance at the bright ribbons fluttering gaily in the wind like the streamers from a ship, he turned joyfully towards the mountain and his slumbering herds.

It was evening, and the farewell sunbeams shed their gold on the mountain meadows and the senner's dark flowing hair, as he went with pail and stool to milk the herds just returning from the pasture. Well he loved the mountain, the herds, and the evenings full of sunset splendour and of peace. But to-day he had no eye for the glory around him; he thought of the valley and of Anneli, who was to join to-day for the first time in the village dance, and who would be led by some richer hand. Hitherto, he had thought himself passing rich; to-day, for the first time, he sighed over his poverty. He sat down beside his favourite, Brownie, and began to milk ; but in the middle of his work his hands dropped on his lap, and he began to wonder who besides himself had set up trees for Anneli, and whether she had known his among them all. Surely she must have. The bunch of alproses at the top would tell her, and he smiled to himself, and began again to milk.

Then a well-known voice called to him from the cottage, "Hallo, Hans! where are you hiding? I have been searching the whole place for you."

Hans shouted back an answer, and there appeared above the hedge the face of Seppi, the only one of the farm-servants who did not grudge Hans his place in Anneli's favour, and who had always remained his firm and faithful friend.

"Well, Seppi, what good news do you bring?" asked Hans, with a feeling of presentiment. "What brings you so late to the mountain?"

"It is Anneli, self-willed girl," answered Seppi, laughing. "She will not go to the dance without you. Quick, quick, put on your best clothes. The fiddlers are ready, and the maidens waiting to be fetched. I will stay here in your place to-night." Hans darted up like an arrow and flew into the cottage, while Seppi took his seat beside the cows, and went on with the unfinished work.

In a few minutes Hans appeared in holiday clothes, and in his hat a garland and a ribbon like those on Anneli's May-pole. " Now, Seppi, take good care of the cattle," said he, coming back to the hedge. " You have known the beasts for years—ever since you were here for a while as under-senner. Good-bye." And he hurried off.

But suddenly he remembered the little man, and that he had not told Seppi about the expected guest. Notwithstanding his eagerness about Anneli and the evening's merry-making, he ran back and commended the dwarf to the care of his astonished friend. But now nothing kept him back. Swift as the chamois before the hunter he flew down the steep path, and reached the gate of the farm just as the festal procession was moving along the village street to escort the "pearl of the valley" to the dance.

She was waiting for him at the gate, and watching impatiently for his coming. "I am so glad you are here at last," she said, stretching out both her hands towards him. "You shall be my partner; I have chosen you out of all the lads who have set up May-poles for me. Just look how yours looks down on the other contemptible little things. Seppi, the good fellow, went up to bring me the bunch of alproses and the ribbon, that I might wear them for your sake."

She pointed smilingly to her fair head, which was gay with a sky-blue ribbon, and to the bouquet at her breast. Hans looked at her in a rapture of delight, and grasped her dear hand more firmly, for the procession had now reached the farm-house, and the youths who had set up May-poles in Anneli's honour came out from the rest and stood before her, that she might choose one as her partner in the dance. But great were the astonishment and envy of them all when they saw that the former goat-herd had been preferred to them, and although they had to consent to this arrangement, yet poor Hans owned from this moment a number more of bitter foes. But he neither thought of this nor feared it ; he led the " pearl " which had fallen to his lot out through the gate, and his face shone with happy excitement as he joined the

ANNELI SEES THE MAY-POLE ERECTED BY HANS.

procession, and led his fair partner to the linden-trees where the dance was to be.

Hans had always counted himself a happy fellow, but as he now led the lovely Anneli in the merry dance beneath the green linden-trees, it seemed as if he had never known before what happiness meant, and his whole past life he counted now as nothing. But this life offers no lasting happiness, and the purer it is the shorter is its reign. Anneli looked up at him with unconscious tenderness, and whispered that she would not dance that night with any one but him. The maiden's softly spoken words reached the ear of Nazerl, the son of a rich neighbour; and anger and envy blazed forth in his soul.

"Anneli, you must dance once with me," he said, stepping up to her; but his petition sounded more like an imperious command.

"You know, Nazerl," answered the girl, "that Hans is my partner; you must ask his consent." Now Hans was just bringing a glass to offer Anneli some refreshment.

"Listen, goat-boy," said the rich farmer's son haughtily to the poor senner, "I will let you know that I mean to dance now with Anneli." And he seized her hand.

Hans was of a peaceable disposition, and his new happiness had not made him proud, but this taunt was too much for him.

"Let go her hand, Nazerl," he said quietly, though his voice trembled. "She may not dance with you."

"May she not, indeed, you beggar?" cried Nazerl; "then take this," and he struck Hans in the face with clenched fist.

Anneli screamed, and poor Hans lost all control over himself; without thinking, he hurled the glass in his tormentor's face, and with a loud groan Nazerl fell pale and bloody to the ground. Again a cry of terror escaped

Anneli's lips, but it was not for the sake of the fallen Nazerl, but for Hans, whose thoughtless deed must bring him into trouble.

The music ceased, and all hastened to the motionless form that lay stretched on the grass to offer help, while Hans stood by in speechless astonishment at his own mad act.

Then he felt his hand seized, and Anneli's gentle voice whispered in his ear, " Flee, oh flee, dear Hans, at once, for a minute's delay may make flight hopeless."

But when Hans still hesitated, she caught his arm and, unnoticed by the others, drew him away till they stood at some distance from the lindens, and were hidden from their companions by the trees.   Hans still looked stunned and paralysed.

" Hans," she said more earnestly than before, laying her little hand upon his arm—" Hans, listen to me and follow me.   Flee as quickly as you can, for all, all are against you, because I chose you in preference to them. Flee, and hide yourself somewhere till the noise of this is over and Nazerl is recovered."

" Ah, Anneli," answered Hans shuddering, " he is dead! Did you not see how pale and motionless he lay ?"

" Then there is all the more need for you to flee," said the maiden decidedly; " listen, they are coming ; go, go," she urged anxiously.

" Farewell, Anneli.   Do not be angry with me, and never forget poor Hans," and he looked down at her with sorrowful eyes.

" Never, never, Hans," she said in a firm voice, for the

experience of the last few minutes had ripened her self-knowledge and her will. "But you will come back some day, guiltless and happy; I know you will. But now go. They are coming to look for you."

He stooped, and, overcome with the sorrow of the moment, pressed a kiss on her sweet lips.

"Farewell, farewell, my Anneli," he whispered once more, and then he turned and fled like a hunted chamois. It was dark on the path along which he hastened, but darker in his soul. The short-lived happiness to which he had so joyfully opened his heart was gone, perhaps never to return; even the thought of Anneli's love, which she had so frankly revealed to him, could not scatter the dark shadows.

If Nazerl was dead, then he was a murderer, and must remain so all his life, no matter what might be his punishment and his repentance. He shuddered, and hastened trembling up the very path which his joyful footsteps had pressed a few hours before, when his heart was full of vague but sweetest hopes.

How all, all had changed in so short a time!

The moon, which before had beamed almost with the golden light of day, seemed now as pale as Nazerl's face; the night wind moaned through the trees like the sighs of a dying man, and the harp-like music of the glacier stream sounded like avenging thunder. Hans flew onwards, despair in his heart, great drops of anguish on the brow so lately crowned with calm content. There lay the night pasture. The moonbeams fell across it, and showed him the slumbering animals. He pressed his lips closer at the thought that he must say farewell to the herd that had grown so dear to him.

Soon he stood at the senner's cottage. He looked through the window. All was peaceful as usual. The bed was still unoccupied, and the old man was not at the table; but Seppi was merrily turning the fritters and whistling a cheerful tune.

"Seppi, Seppi!" cried poor Hans outside, as he knocked with trembling finger against the panes.

Seppi turned his head in surprise, and when he saw Hans standing out in the moonlight, he came to the window and drew back the bolt.

"What's the matter, Hans? Is anything wrong?" he said hastily.

"Alas! yes," sighed Hans, and he told his friend in hurried words the misfortune that had befallen him.

"The impudent fellow," cried Seppi angrily. "You may be sure your reminder will not do him any harm; and as for his being dead, you know, Hans, 'weeds wont die.' So don't be vexing yourself beyond measure. And are you going away? Where will you go?"

"I do not know, Seppi," answered Hans sadly—"as far as my feet will carry me; away from my beloved country, perhaps for ever;" and he wiped a tear from his cheek. "But you must do me one kindness, that I may go content. As soon as you can get down to the valley, go to my good old mother, and tell her not to grieve too much. Tell her that I will try to do right, though I must leave the mountains of the Tyrol; and beg Anneli never, never to forget me. And one thing more, Seppi.

Take good care of the little man, and let him want for nothing. Promise me this."

Seppi nodded, and his good, honest face had a cheery smile on it as he gave his hand to his friend, who hurried away on his restless wandering. He gave a hasty glance at the night pastures, which he now reached ; the long mossy veil of the old pine-trees, beneath which he had so often slept, fluttered in the wind like mourning banners. His favourite brown cow raised her head slowly, and the bell round her neck sounded like a sad farewell. Hot tears flowed from his eyes, but he had no time for long leave-taking, he must hurry on. Yonder rose the rugged brow of the glacier, with its furrows lighted by the weird moonbeams. He passed it by winding paths through the gloom of the fir-trees, now climbing steep ascents, now descending into a ravine with its foaming torrent— paths known to no eye and foot save those of the boldest mountaineer.

At last he stood on the lofty ridge from which the road led downwards into an unknown valley and unfamiliar fields. He threw a last glance back towards his own loved mountain, then he hastened without further delay on his sorrowful journey.

The golden sunlight of evening lay once more on mountain and valley, and floated on the waves of the lovely river Inn, which flowed as peacefully as if it had never tried to foam and rage like its brothers in the mountains. A youth was descending the mountain with tottering footsteps. It was the last of the hills that had lain between him and the great and populous town that stood in the valley below. His blue eyes looked dim and sunken, his long hair hung tangled round his head, and his once respectable clothing bore traces of hasty and toilsome journeying.

The son of the quiet mountains looked down in amazement at the bustle in the town below, and a deep sigh escaped his lips. But he collected himself, and descended the last declivity to the bank of the stream, across which a bridge led to the town. At one end of this bridge stood a watch-house, for it was a needful thing in those unsettled times to keep a sharp look-out on friend and foe. Two soldiers sat at the oaken table before the door. The young man went up to the building, and stood timidly a few steps from the men. At last the elder of the two raised his head.

"Look, Franzerl," said he, after a hasty glance at the young wanderer; "there comes a lad from your mountains, but he does not look so cheerful as you did when you came."

Franzerl looked up, but scarcely had he met the wanderer's eye than he sprang up and with a cry of joy caught his arm.

"Hans, dear Hans, where have you come from?" he cried. "Do not you remember me? Do you not know Franzerl, with whom you and Anneli used so often to play, and with whom you so often shared your bread and cheese, when my poor mother had nothing to give to her hungry little Franzerl?"

Hans—for it was he—looked with joyful surprise at

F

the cheerful young face, and recognised at once his old playfellow, who years ago had left his native valley to push his fortune in the great world, and whose friends had long believed him to be dead. He had become a soldier; but in spite of his stern employment his heart had remained as warm and true as ever. He drew his old friend to the table where the other man sat, and offered him some of the fiery drink in the glass before him.

"Drink, my good fellow," he said pressingly, "drink—you seem to be in need of refreshment—and then tell me what brings you hither."

The rough kindness touched the poor wanderer's heart, and acted like magic on his weary spirit. It was the first familiar face that he had seen for many days—the first pleasant reminder of days gone by, and he found it sweet to open his heart to this friend of his childhood, and tell him of the folly that had driven him from home, and how he had wandered since from mountain to mountain begging a bite of bread and a drink of milk from kind-hearted herdsmen; for he had not ventured to go down to the villages, where the news of what had happened might have arrived before him. "And now," he said, "I am going away—away to some far-off country, where they know nothing of Nazerl or of Hans, or even of the beautiful land of the Tyrol."

"You are very foolish," laughed Franzerl. "Are you quite sure that Nazerl is dead? He had always a thick skull, as I know full well. Don't be a fool, but stay here and become a brave soldier like us. Believe me, it is a merry life, and it is possible to be a good man even under this coat."

Hans hesitated a moment; he had never thought of this, but Franzerl overwhelmed him with persuasive eloquence.

"Look here, Hans; to-morrow or next day we are going to Italy, a country that, they say, is even more lovely than our own. Ours is a cheerful life, and when you come back in two or three years grass will have grown over the whole affair, and they will not dare to say a word to you after you have worn the Emperor's uniform."

"But Anneli?" sighed Hans.

"You cannot see Anneli for a time at any rate, and if she is really worthy of you, she will be true to you."

Yes, Franzerl was right, Hans saw that; so he agreed to his proposal, and went with his friend to the recruiting sergeant, who was glad to receive the fine fellow into his ranks.

It was autumn. The morning wind swept over the Adriatic, rippling its deep blue waves, and played with the dark hair of a youth who leant in deep reverie against the archway of the Piazza di San Marco, gazing dreamily at the flow of the Grand Canal, which, after cutting Venice with its great curve, mingles its waters with the waves of the Adriatic.

It was Hans. The mountains and valleys of his native land lay far away. It was long since he had left the last mountain-pass of the Tyrol far behind, but he could not leave his love for home there at the boundary—it filled him with secret longings in this beautiful, but foreign land. What good did all the splendour of this strange country do him—all the lofty palaces and art-trophies of the queenly city—all the sweet melody of this unknown tongue? Could one of those musical sounds be compared with Anneli's voice when she said, "I am so glad you have come, dear Hans"? Could one of these marble towers attempt to rival the jagged glacier peaks when they shone with the purple of the evening sky? And when the horn sounded at sunset through the mountains, echoed a hundred-fold from clefts and deep ravines, and dying softly amid the shades of the valley, who would compare with that the tones of the music which day and night hovered on the waters through the streets of Venice?

Hans raised his tearful eyes: the sky, at least, must be the same which spans the valleys of the Tyrol. Then he noticed a figure on a slender pillar—a figure which he must have seen long years before. A brazen lion with a proudly flowing mane raised its kingly head, as if keeping watch over the city below, and over the sea that kissed its feet. The young man dashed the rising tear from his eye, and looked thoughtfully up at the kingly beast. Yes, indeed, that was the same lion which was marked on the coin that the little man gave him long ago, and which in the secret drawer had kept watch and guard over his mother's treasure. A smile passed like a sunbeam over his troubled face as he thought of that sunny autumn morning when the old man said good-bye to him, and when he watched him from the rock as he sailed through the air on his magic mantle.

"Oh! I wish I had such a ship," he said with a sigh. Then, in the familiar accents of his native tongue, the words sounded in his ear, "Good morning, Hans."

Hans started—there was no one near. Had a dream mocked him? But no, there it was again—" Look up, Hans, up here." And Hans looked up.

Above him, out of the high bow-window of one of those proud palaces, leant a familiar head with snowy locks and dark earnest eyes that smiled kindly down on poor Hans.

He uttered a cry of joy, his first since he came to this foreign land, and quick as an arrow he darted into the archway, and entered the portal of the palace. His foot flew over marble steps and velvet carpets; but he had no eye for that. On he went, up to where, leaning over the golden banister of the landing-place, a noble and well-remembered face awaited him. Full of emotion, he stood before the old man, who gave him his hand in loving greeting. No longer a shabby coat, but a garment of black velvet covered his form, and his withered but wonder-working hand gleamed with costly diamonds. But the youth's affection broke the barriers of this marvellous change, and tenderly, as on that spring evening on the mountain when he had brought the old man into his cottage, he pressed his lips against the kind hand, and said from the fulness of his heart, "God bless you, sir. I bless Him for letting me find you here in this foreign land."

"Not a foreign land, Hans; I am in my own country," answered the noble Venetian, as he led the young man through the splendid halls, whose stately walls were adorned with the masterpieces of those immortal artists who called Italy their home.   Then they sat down

HANS RECEIVES A HEARTY WELCOME FROM AN OLD FRIEND.

together in the wide bow-window, and Hans looked joyfully into the old man's venerable countenance.

"So you did not forget the poor herdsman in your splendid home?" said he.

"Forget thee, Hans!" replied the noble Venetian— "forget thee, who didst think of me in the midst of love and pleasure, and even in thy flight, when thy heart was filled with deadly anguish! No, indeed. I long to reward those years of faithful love, and perhaps the opportunity has come at last."

"Oh, sir," cried Hans with shining eyes, "will you tell me how things go at home, where you have been more lately than I? Tell me if Nazerl recovered, if my mother has ceased to grieve about me, and if Anneli still remembers me."

"Nazerl is dead—but through no fault of thine," said the old man soothingly, for Hans had looked terror-stricken at his opening words. "He soon recovered from the trifling wound caused by thy hand; but his own foolhardiness drove him up to the highest points of rock after a chamois, and a rash step hurled him into the ravine. It was not till long afterwards that they found his mangled corpse. As for thy mother and Anneli, thou mayest see for thyself."

So saying he rose, stepped up to a richly carved cabinet, and took from a secret compartment a flashing jewel. The young man recognised it well; it was the wondrous mountain mirror; and now he held it once more in his hand, and looked searchingly on its shining surface. Light mists rolled over it; they grew gradually thinner and thinner, till at last there lay before him in the splendour of the morning sunlight his own beloved valley, and the substantial farm-house, Anneli's home. He gave no heed to the cheerful stir in barn and stable, nor to the busy preparation for the returning herds. No, his eye pressed through the clear window-panes to a well-remembered room. It was quiet and cosy, as in days gone by. At the window sat Anneli, fair and lovable as ever, but her countenance bore traces of gentle melancholy. The snow-white thread rested in her hands, and her lips moved in earnest talk with the two women at the other window—the farmer's widow and the old mother that Hans was longing to comfort. It seemed to Hans that the conversation concerned him, and as if now and then his name fell from Anneli's rosy lips. And every time she raised her eyes towards the opposite wall, Hans followed the direction of her gaze, and saw, carefully preserved by glass and frame, a well-remembered blue ribbon and bunch of withered mountain flowers. At this sign of faithful memory tears started to the young man's eyes, and when he had dried them, and looked again on the magic mirror, the dear vision had vanished, and the glass flashed once more in the light of the Italian sun.

"Listen, my son; I will tell thee the wish that my heart cherishes for thee," said the old man, as he laid the magic mirror carefully back in the cabinet. "I am alone and lonely, the last representative of a name of ancient renown. When I was young and strong, I was filled with a desire after secret knowledge. I sought the gold of the mountains far and near—thou knowest this well—heaping treasures on treasures, and all the while I never noticed that I was growing old, and was still alone in life. Stay now with me. I will enrich thy mind with the treasures of my knowledge, and thy heart shall remain pure. Thou shalt be my son, the heir of my wealth; and thy name shall be inscribed among the noblest names in the golden book of Venice."

The young man clasped his hands, and leant towards his aged friend. "Forgive me, noble sir," he begged humbly, "if I cannot gratify your wishes; but what can riches and honour do for a heart that is pining with longings after home? The scene which I have just witnessed—the vision of Anneli and my home—has shown me where alone my happiness must be sought. But if you wish to grant me a favour, then loose the fetters that bind me here, and let me go as quickly as possible back to my loved mountains."

The old man sat a moment in silent thought. "I would fain have kept thee with me," he said at last, "for thy heart is true and pure; but my wishes must yield to thy happiness."

So saying, he rose and once more opened the cupboard which hid his magic hoards. From its most secret recess he brought a dark object, and when he unrolled it, it proved to be the magic mantle, the air-ship of which Hans had thought so longingly a short time before. The old man spread it on the balcony, embraced the astonished youth with the tenderness of a father, and led him towards the mantle.

"Now stand on it," he said; "take this staff to guide thy flight; and think of me with love."

Hans obeyed as in a dream. The old Venetian waved

his hand, and the mantle rose and bore the young man up into the air.

Not till his eyes met the full light of the open air, and the fresh wind played with the folds of the mantle, did Hans awake to the reality of his situation. He looked sorrowfully back at his noble friend, who still stood in the bow-window looking after him, with a smile on his aged features, and waving a farewell with his withered hand. Hans stretched out his arms towards him, and cried in a voice of deep emotion, "Farewell, farewell, noble sir," and the mantle bore him onwards with the swiftness of the storm-wind.

For a moment the Queen of the Sea gleamed far below, in the splendour of her towers and palaces ; the sunlight flashed from the high windows of her churches, and the black gondolas glided noiselessly over the winding canals. But soon this scene grew faint in the distance, and nothing was left of it all but the sea stretching in a blue line along the horizon. Hans turned his face homewards, and directed his course towards the north. Swift as an arrow he flew onwards; the air rustled around him like the sound of eagles' wings ; in the dim distance lay the mountain peaks of his native land, but they began to shine out more and more clearly from the blue mists. Soon he was floating above that rocky pass which long months before he had trodden with deadly sorrow in his heart ; and now he breathes the air of his native land.

With beaming eyes he looked down over the side of the magic eagle whose dark pinions were bearing him onwards to his home. Far below him lay the mountains with the grazing herds; from his cloudy height they seemed no larger than the lady-birds with which he used to play when a boy, and the senners' cottages like the round pebbles in the village brook. He almost felt as if he could touch the glacier peaks with his hand, so near did they seem in the splendour of the midday sun. He looked down into their icy clefts, and saw the glacier torrent rolling far below in milk-white waves; but the magic boat sped further and further, still bearing Hans swiftly onwards to his home.

The young man now began to view the country more carefully, and soon he directed his course westwards. Then he uttered a cry of joy, for they were sailing towards a well-known mountain, and the mantle, as if it knew exactly its appointed task, sank gently downwards, till Hans found himself on a projecting rock. It was the same spot from which he had often, when a goat-herd, looked down longingly on the smiling meadows, searching for the entrance to the dwarf king's magic realm—the same spot where the old man bade him farewell that autumn morning long ago, before taking his airy journey to his distant home. Hans sprang joyously from his magic boat, laid the staff on it with whispered words of thanks, and immediately the mantle rose, and flew swift as an arrow up into the clouds. Hans stood watching it for a few moments, then he hurried down the old familiar path. A little below herds were grazing—his herds— and Seppi was leaning against a rock watching them, and singing the while in his own cheery way. Hans glanced joyfully at the distant scene, and hurried on. There was the night pasture, and now he arrived at the senner's cottage ; he did not wait, however, even to peep in at the window, so eager was he to reach the village. With flying footsteps he hurried down the rocky path which he had climbed a few months before with deadly anguish in his heart.

But to-day—to-day all was changed. With joy throbbing in every pulse-beat Hans felt the stony path softer than the grass of the pasture-lands, and the sound of the stream seemed sweeter than the melody of harps. At last he reached the valley, and just as he entered it the evening bell began to ring. At the sound he stopped, bared his head, and knelt by the wayside ; but when the last tone died away he rose and hastened up the village street, then with a bound he crossed the brook and reached the farm-yard gate. There was no one to be seen, for the servants were at supper in the house. Quickly, but noiselessly, Hans slipped through the yard, and stood with beating heart at the door of the sitting-room. There was no sound of life within. Hans put his ear to the key-hole and listened. Then he heard Anneli's sweet voice saying, "Come, Lord Jesus, be our guest, and bless Thy gifts. Amen." And when the Amen was said, Hans opened the door and stepped over the threshold.

"Have you any of God's gifts to spare for a poor wanderer ?" he said softly.

"Hans, dear Hans !" was Anneli's glad cry, for in spite of the twilight and his unfamiliar dress she recognised him at a glance, and soon she lay weeping with joy in the tall soldier's arms.

Next May-day a stately May-pole stood, as before, at Anneli's window, richly adorned with fluttering blue ribbons and with the bunch of alproses at the top, and Anneli once more walked on the arm of her Hans to the dance beneath the lindens. But this time the rich farmers' sons could not say a word of protest, for Anneli was now a fair and happy bride.

Meantime, the brave Franzerl had tired of the merry soldier's life, for it had grown dull to him since the return home of his dear friend Hans. So he had laid aside the Emperor's uniform, and come back to his native valley.

HACO THROWS THE TREASURE OF THE
NIBELUNGEN INTO THE RHINE.

RHINE GOLD:
A Tale of the Nibelungen.

EVENING'S dim shadows
had ceased to hover in
vague mystery around the
walls of Worms. They had,
hours before, gathered in
dark masses in every nook
of the royal city, hiding like traitors from the light of
the clear full moon that flooded with silvery splendour
the Rhine river and the Wonnegau on its banks, where,
transformed by the soft touch of the moonbeams, stood
the proud seat of Burgundy's mighty kings.

Slumber and silence reigned in the palace which, but the morning before, had resounded with the clash of weapons and a cheerful bustling life; for King Gunther, accompanied by his brothers and his bravest men-at-arms, had that day set out on a warlike expedition, leaving the town and the castle and his fair queen Brunhild to the care of the truest of the true, bold Haco, in whose courage and wisdom he placed the fullest confidence.

With a loose velvet mantle half hiding his gold-gleaming armour, Haco paced the streets of the lonely city, and listened attentively for some sound to break the stillness of the night. A distant noise like the rumbling of many wheels reached his ear, and an eager look came into his eyes. He glanced over at the palace, in the safest room of which lay Brunhild, his honoured queen. Out of love to her he had murderously slain the noble Siegfried, the immortal hero of the Nibelungen ; and the shame of the deed will last to the remotest ages, dimming with rust the splendid escutcheon of his fame.

When he had convinced himself of the undisturbed repose of the royal household, he turned and walked towards the minster, in whose shadow lay another palace. There dwelt the beautiful Kriemhild, King Gunther's sister, and widow of the noble Siegfried, whose death she mourned with inconsolable grief. The stillness of repose hovered also round these walls. The windows were dark, the doors barred, and amidst her maids lay the royal widow in her first deep sleep.

The moonbeams glided over the roof of the palace,

and glanced suspiciously at the dark figure of the man who stood gazing anxiously up at the windows. When he saw that there was no movement, he went towards the tower built of huge blocks which guarded the entrance to the castle, took a bunch of rusty keys from under his mantle, and opened the locks and bolts of the ironbound door which led into the vaults. The last bolt was loosed, the heavy gate opened, and the moonlight streamed in freely over the treasures which were here displayed in splendid piles. Crowns of gold richly adorned with diamonds, bracelets and chains gleaming with jewels, lay there in rich profusion. Wrought by the skilful hands of the dwarfs, they had been kept hid by the little folk in secret mountain recesses until Siegfried came, and Alberich, the dwarf-king, had been obliged, notwithstanding his magic power and cunning, to yield to the might of the hero's arm, and give him the precious hoards of jewels. And beside these, heaped up to the very roof, were bars upon bars of uncoined gold, only waiting the impress of the mint to change them into an exhaustless hoard. This was the treasure of the Nibelungen, the widow Kriemhild's rightful possession, which the heroes had brought her a few weeks before from the land of the Nibelungen. With full hands she had scattered gold among these heroes, and had also given rich gifts to the vassals of her brother, the king of Burgundy, for she had now come to live in his land that she might be near the corpse of her beloved husband. And what Kriemhild's beauty and misfortune had failed to do, her bounteous gifts accomplished. The hearts of the Burgundians were turned towards her, so that Haco, the watchful hero, began to be anxious about his own influence and her probable revenge. So he determined to rob her of the Nibelungen treasure, that she might be deprived of the means of working his ruin.

At a place not far from the royal city, where the Rhine flows in a still deeper channel, stood Haco a few hours later in a boat on the river, and watched the high-piled waggons, the first of which now passed over the shaking bridge, rolled on with threatening rumble, and stopped close to the low parapet. Haco stretched forth his stalwart arm and removed the back of the waggon, so that its precious burden slid into the depths below.

The stream gleamed brightly in the radiance of gold and precious stones, the jewels whirled round and round in the rapid waters, then sank down flashing from wave to wave, till they had reached the still, deep bed of the river. Waggon after waggon was silently emptied by Haco's powerful hand, and each time the costly load made the Rhine river flash with borrowed splendour. So hour after hour went by in silent and restless haste. When the last gold bar had disappeared beneath the water, the drivers swore an oath of eternal secrecy, received rich rewards of gold, and led their waggons away in endless line. Haco stood alone in the boat, and watched them till the last man had vanished in the shades of night; then he stooped to gaze down into the stream.

There far down lay the treasure of the Nibelungen, and the Rhine flowed on in silence over the golden secret that it hid. No tongue would ever tell the tale, no arm would ever reach the hoards. Why, then, did Haco still stand lost in thought?—why did he gaze down gloomily into the river depths? Was it that the shadows of the past, or visions of a bloody future, rose from the gleaming waves? Was he thinking of Kriemhild's beauty and the passionate love which his now hard heart had once felt for the beautiful princess, and which, when rejected, changed into anger and hatred that moved his arm to the murder of Siegfried and the robbery of the Nibelungen treasure? Or did he see with prophetic eye that time in which the now helpless one should take revenge on all who had injured her—a revenge which should exterminate the heroes of Burgundy to the last man.

Many hundred years had passed over the world since that night robbery; blood and tears had been shed, dried, and forgotten; new nations had arisen and the old ones fallen, so that there was scarcely a page of the world's chronicle to tell of their struggles, hopes, and tears. All things had changed. The new had taken the place of the old, only to yield in its turn to a newer order still. Nothing was the same but ever young, ever beautiful, ever innocent nature, and the human heart with its love and hate. The Rhine still flowed and the Wonnegau on its banks still bloomed as of old, but its name was changed; the Cathedral of Worms still pointed to the sky, but it was not the same building in the shadow of which Kriemhild's palace used to stand. The generation that now trod the same soil knew nothing of the Nibelungen—the tradition of those heroes lived only in some half-forgotten songs. The sunken treasure had long since been thought a myth, and with an incredulous smile the wise men of those days pointed to the stream which was said to hide such a "golden secret."

Nevertheless, it was no myth; the treasure still lay beneath the waters. Not a crown, not a bracelet was lost; not a diamond had fallen from the brilliant setting; for, as if held together by magic hand, the jewels had remained firmly united; but wave after wave had rolled on unceasingly, day and night, from year's end to year's end, and softly and gradually the treasure had been pressed on further into the bed of the river. The Wonnegau lay behind it; there the waves foamed, whirling over the hidden reefs beneath, and further on towards the sea they roared loudly against the walls of the Pfalzburg, then flowed caressingly past the blooming vines which wound their clustered garlands round the white cottages of the vine-dressers.

The treasure of the Nibelungen had been carried in safety, though without any guiding hand, past all these different scenes, and the waves had borne it further and further into the shadow of the bank, bit by bit, until, after many years, it lay at the foot of a rock that rose high and bold above the waves. The moonbeams wove a silver garland round its granite brow, and for centuries tradition echoed round its jagged peak; but a row of crags surrounded the foot of the rock, and the foaming rage of the waves kept away even the boldest. There into that deep rocky bed the waves bore the treasure, and now it rested safely hidden at the foot of the Loreley rock.

But treasures which have once gleamed in the sunlight, and been grasped by human hands, can never rest in darkness; they strive to reach again the light of day and the warm living hand of man. Slowly they rise from year to year, till at last they glow in the light of the sun, and await a pure hand to set them free, to do good with their riches, and so to expiate the guilt which was attached to them. It was thus that the treasure of the Nibelungen pressed upwards. It rose slowly, slowly, for sighs and blood and tears hung more heavily on it than on other sunken hoards. But at last, about a thousand years after that night when Haco threw the treasure into the stream, it had made its way up through the water.

It was just such a delightful spring night as that memorable one long ago; work had long since ended in the blooming vineyards, rest and peace lay all around. The night-wind came softly from the mountains and bore the fragrance of the vines across the Rhine; the moon stood high in heaven, its light glided trembling down on the ledges of the Loreley and kissed the feet of the rock, which until now had lain in deep shadow. There in magic radiance floated the jewels of the Nibelungen treasure, so that the Rhine shone brightly as its waves played round the golden hoard. The nightwind blew more strongly, bearing on its wings something like a spirit, which sank in a veil of mist round the point of the rock, and then stood in that majestic beauty which had in days long past touched Haco's proud heart and won the love of the hero Siegfried. It was Kriemhild, once Siegfried's sorrowing widow, and afterwards King Etzel's queen in the distant land of the Huns. As Queen of Hungary, she invited the Burgundian heroes to her kingdom, that she might demand the stolen treasure from Haco, or take revenge on him for Siegfried's murder and the robbery of her gold. But the vengeance which should only have overtaken one fell upon all, even on her own little son. Kriemhild's proud heart was softened by the blow, and with a pang of keen repentance she thought of those other mothers whom her mad revenge had rendered childless. One way only was left her of giving happiness instead of sorrow. With a desire that rose to heaven like a prayer, she thought of her lost treasure. If she could but get it now, what troubled hearts would be soothed by her who had heretofore brought misery to happy ones! But the swift sword sent her to the grave with her longings unsatisfied. The same slaughter that had freed her from her enemies had robbed her of her child and of her life.

Her spirit hovered often round the scenes of her youthful happiness, seeking the hidden treasure in the river-bed. That night, when it rose to the surface, and its golden radiance was seen bright and clear, Kriemhild came, thinking to set it free. Her eyes gazed longingly on the floating gold, and her arms, light and transparent as the moonbeams, were outstretched over the rock as if she would fain grasp the moving treasure. Then she glided with spirit tread down over the jagged moonlit rock by paths which no human foot could follow, and soon she stood on the narrow ledge over which the Rhine river flowed in gleaming ripples. Her white foot was covered by the water, but she heeded it not; her eye gazed fixedly on the treasure for which she had longed unceasingly in life, and which now hovered close to her feet in the dancing waves. Her lips moved softly, her hands were clasped as if in earnest desire, and she stooped to reach the golden crown which now knocked with a metallic sound against the rock and almost touched her foot; but when she stretched out her transparent hand, and thought she had touched the point of the diamond cross, the crown shrank from her fingers, sank into the stream, and was borne away out of her reach by the mighty waters. Kriemhild sank on her knees; the waves wet her long flowing locks, and the hem of her purple robe—but she felt them not. Only one thought, one feeling, lived in her heart—the longing to recover the treasure. She bent forward once more; her white hands clutched again and again at the jewels which shone around her in tempting nearness, and yet always shrank from her touch. Other treasures floated towards her, the bars of gold came close to her feet, then started back when the white hands grasped at them, and gradually all disappeared in the middle of the stream.

Kriemhild's cold lips trembled, her transparent hands ceased their useless toil, and were clasped again in prayer. Then there was a louder rushing in the river, and a majestic shadow floated down the stream. Kriemhild's eye watched its onward movement; nearer and nearer it came, till it passed through the foaming gold stream,

CHARLEMAGNE MEETS WITH KRIEMHILD.

F. C., p. 108.

and approached the rock where the Queen now stood erect and majestic.

It was Charlemagne, once Germany's beloved and mighty ruler, who every year leaves his tomb at Aachen, glides along the Rhine to bless the vineyards on its banks, and then lies down again in the golden coffin until the fragrance of a new spring awakes him to another beneficent progress. Now he stood before her on the river, clad in his purple mantle and his golden crown, with the sword which formerly decided the fate of nations in his cold right hand. His foot rested on the shield of Roland, his beloved nephew, which they had laid beside him in the tomb, and which now bore him like a trusty boat. The water rippled over the golden edge, and washed the grave-dust from the flashing emerald which the hero of Ronceval once won from the giant and fastened as an ornament on his shield.

"Who art thou?" asked the dead Emperor, when his gaze had rested long on Kriemhild's face. "Thou art no mortal woman; I know that by the glance of thine eye, which speaks to me of bygone ages. It was thus that Fastrada's eyes shone; her golden hair was soft and silken as thine. I have not forgotten it, though I have slept for more than half-a-thousand years in the dark vault—yet thou art not Fastrada, the Emperor's beloved wife."

"No, great Emperor," said the Queen; "I was once Kriemhild, the wife of Siegfried, the hero of the Nibelungen, who ruled over the land which was also subject to thy sway. The present generation know almost nothing of his glory, but in thy times, O Emperor, his renown was still bright."

"I know him well, that model of all knightly virtues," said the Emperor thoughtfully, "and his fate and thine are familiar to me. It was but the old and yet ever new song that sounds through all time—the song of the victory of evil over good—which made my life also one of pain and trouble. But what brings thee hither, O Queen ?"

"If thou knowest my fate, noble Emperor," answered Kriemhild, "thou knowest also what I seek for here. Thou knowest the misery I caused in life. When repentance came it was at the last moment, and my time was gone for earthly works of love. But now, perhaps, my spirit may be permitted to grasp this treasure, cause of so much sin, and use it well and wisely, till as many tears are dried as have been shed, and as much sorrow healed as was once caused by me.

"See yonder, noble Emperor! there gleams the Nibelungen hoard, the bequest left me by my husband, but of which Haco robbed me. It has risen, and awaits only the delivering hand ; but no one comes. So I would fain grasp the treasures and seize the moving bars of gold. Then in the stillness of the night I would take them into the abodes of poverty and misfortune, so that when the inmates awake Kriemhild's treasure might dry the tears of need and despair. But it is not permitted me."

The Emperor turned his face and ·gazed searchingly down at the jewels, which floated in bright clear radiance on the waters of the Rhine.

"Thou askest a thing impossible, O Queen," he said at length; "knowest thou not the limits which debar spirits from the deeds of mortals? It is only a guiltless, living, human hand which may change the sentence that hangs over them. But the Nibelungen treasure has long since been forgotten. Yet look! Thou no longer seest the jewels in the full size of olden days. Wave after wave has gnawed at them; the waters have worked unceasingly through long centuries at this tedious task. See how the ornaments on the bracelets and crowns have shrunk, and how slender the links of the chains have become. The Rhine has taken the gold of thy treasure, and with it fertilised the blooming meadows on its banks. Nightly the gold set free rises in light mists above the stream and sinks in blessing on mountain and valley, and when autumn comes thy gold gleams in every cluster, ripens in every ear of corn. Freer, stronger, more joyous are the people of these meadows—and that is the blessing of the Nibelungen treasure, which rests unseen in earth and air and water—thus will the guilt and tears be done away with which once lay heavy on this hoard. Then have patience, O Queen, for a few short years—then thou wilt search in vain for thy treasure. Meantime other ministries are thine."

The Emperor bowed his head in courteous farewell, and sailed on his magic boat up the moonlit stream.

Kriemhild gazed after him. The emerald in the point of the shield flashed brightly in the moonlight, and the wide purple mantle fluttered above the gleaming waves. The Emperor blessed the vineyards as he passed; and when the last glimmer of his crown grew pale and the veil of night concealed him, the Queen once more looked at the gold hoard at her feet. The dead Emperor had spoken truly; her eyes now perceived it too; so she could wait in patience till the last crown, the last gold bar, had melted in the sparkling river.

The treasure's time of freedom was passed; no delivering hand had come. The jewels slowly shrank together round the foot of the Loreley and fell into their watery bed. Their splendour was extinguished; still and dark the river flowed. Then Kriemhild turned and ascended the rock. She gave one long farewell look at the meadows of her former home, and then vanished like a mist in the distance.

Again centuries have passed. Kriemhild no longer hovers round the Loreley, for the Nibelungen treasure has melted in the waves; only its diamonds rest uninjured in the river bed, and any one gazing into its depths on starry nights may see them flash and sparkle far below. But the gold runs freely through the Rhine, so that its waters flow in bright, clear waves; and on summer nights the precious substance rises to the clouds, and then falls in fertilising dew on the meadows and vineyards all around. Gold shines in the ripening berries and gleams in the waving corn; with the clear ring of gold sound the songs of the Rhenish people; pure as gold is their honesty—that surest safeguard against every foe.

That is the German Nibelungenhort—that is the Rhine gold.

THE COUNTESS MATILDA RESTORES THE
DWARF-QUEEN TO HEALTH.

The Friendship of the Dwarfs.

PART I.

THE DYING DWARF-QUEEN.

STATELY and strongly-built fortress stood many hundred years ago on a high rock of the Thuringian Mountains. The lord of this castle was descended from one of the noblest families in the land, and had chosen this place from all his numerous estates as a home for himself, his wife, and his little son, because its cheerful situation and mild climate were best suited to the Countess Matilda's delicate health.

They had come home to it, after a long journey, on the evening which preceded the night on which my story begins, and the Countess, wearied with all the ceremonies of the reception, had just fallen into a gentle and refreshing sleep. Crimson curtains hung in heavy silken folds round the lady's couch; through them the lamps shed a softened light on the sleeper, lending to her cheeks a rosy glow which was, alas! but seldom seen there.

It was midnight. Every one in the castle was asleep, resting from the exertions of the past day, when the lofty door was noiselessly opened, and a little tiny man with a long grey beard approached the couch of the slumbering Countess, and let the light of a lantern fall on her delicate features. He was scarcely three feet high, and his figure was of ungraceful build. But in the rather large head gleamed a pair of bright and intelligent eyes, and in the aged features shone an expression of benevolence and truth. The little man's clothes were of a plain dark colour; his little smock-frock was bound by a girdle with a silver buckle; under his arm he carried an invisible cap, a little black head-dress with a long point, and ornamented with silver bells. Very gently he drew near the couch, raised his lantern, and softly touched the arm of the Countess, which was carelessly thrown over the silken coverlet. The Countess awoke, looked in amazement on the queer little figure, and asked at length, " Who are you, little man ?"

The dwarf bowed low and answered politely, " I am

one of the race of dwarfs, gracious lady, who live in great numbers in the rock below your castle. Our Queen lies at the point of death; her only hope of recovery is in the touch of a human hand. The King, therefore, sent me, when he heard of your arrival, to beg you to show this kindness to our beloved Queen."

"Alas!" answered the Countess sadly, "I am so ill myself, can I be of any use to another?"

"It will be all right, gracious lady, and will cost you no fatigue," answered the little man, "if you will only trust yourself to my care."

The Countess turned to waken her husband, and to ask his advice, but the dwarf begged earnestly, "Let him sleep, noble Countess. Long before he wakes you will be back again. No evil will befall you. We have always honoured your race—have lived in peace and friendship with them through long centuries, and have secretly done them many a good turn."

The Countess was of a kind and obliging disposition; so, notwithstanding her delicate health and present weariness, she agreed to follow the dwarf. She was also afraid of making the powerful little people angry by a refusal, and thus bringing evil on her family. She threw her cloak quickly about her, and prepared to go with the dwarf. With noiseless tread he led her through hall after hall, room after room, till they came to a little round bow-windowed chamber in the tower on the western side of the castle, whence they descended by a narrow winding stair into the castle garden.

It was a lovely summer night. The little guide

darkened his lantern, for moon and stars threw a clear light on their path, and thus they went on in silence along the foot of the castle rock, beneath overhanging trees, which showered down their fragrant blossoms on the lady's dark hair. At last they came to a rock which projected somewhat into the road, and the foot of which was thickly covered with ferns. The dwarf parted them asunder, and the Countess saw a narrow passage which led away into the heart of the mountain. They entered. The dwarf opened his lantern again, and its light showed the walls of a vaulted cave, which, at first low and narrow, became wider and higher as they went on, till at last they walked through a beautifully arched corridor. Soon they arrived at a door, and when it opened they entered a room with crystal walls, which shone as with the radiance of a thousand lights. Among the points of the crystal darted countless little lizards, whose bodies seemed made of transparent emerald; on their heads were little golden crowns set with rubies; and when the pretty little creatures with their shining diadems slipped so nimbly and lightly through the crystal points, the walls gleamed and flashed so strangely that the Countess was filled with astonishment. But the roof of this room seemed an ever-changing picture of living wonders. Great white and blue snakes with diamond eyes, and slender bodies transparent as the air of heaven, wound in endless circles the one through the other; and as they moved in gleaming coils, sweet music and refreshing fragrance filled the crystal hall. Here in this subterranean kingdom sin and enmity seemed unknown. Creatures which on earth fight and oppress one another lived here in friendly intimacy. So fair and lovable seemed these little animals to the Countess, and they looked down on her with such soft intelligent eyes, that she wished one of them would come near enough for her to stroke and caress it. Absorbed by these wonders, she had not noticed that her little guide was already at the further end of the room, and was holding the second door open and beckoning to her to enter. At last she saw him and followed.

The walls of the second hall gleamed with brightly polished silver ore, out of which bloomed flowers of such beauty as are never found in earthly gardens. They were carved out of precious stones so skilfully as to deceive the eye and to tempt one to bend over their cups to breathe their fragrance. Bright silver ore formed the pavement, and the light that streamed from a huge diamond in the centre of the ceiling trembled in thousand-fold reflection on the silver walls and the jewel-flowers.

In this hall were many of the dwarfs assembled. All were simply clad, like the dwarf that had acted as guide to the Countess ; all had grave, wise countenances and beaming eyes, dimmed now with anxiety and grief. As the Countess entered they bowed low, holding in their hands the little caps with the silver bells, which, by making them invisible, enable them to play many tricks on the human race. Now they arrived at the third room, which was the Queen's bed-chamber. At the ceiling of this room hovered a golden eagle with its wings outspread, and holding in its beak four diamond chains, on which the Queen's bed swung gently to and fro. The bed was a single gigantic ruby, skilfully cut, and on it rested on pillows of white satin the dying Queen of this enchanted realm.

The stillness of death reigned in the place. Goldemar, the mighty dwarf-king, stood by the ruby couch, sunk in silent grief. His hair and beard, gleaming like silver, flowed down over his mantle of royal purple; he had taken the shining crown from his head and laid it at the feet of the dying Queen. His nobles stood in a wide circle round the King, and seemed to share his grief.

The Countess went up to the couch. There, on pillows of white satin, rested the loveliest being that her eyes had ever beheld ; she was smaller than her subjects, while her husband, on the contrary, exceeded them in stature ; but her form was exquisitely symmetrical, and her tender limbs seemed formed of wax. Round her closed eyes and blanched lips the smile of youthfulness and kindliness still hovered, while her wondrous hair flowed round her whole form like liquid gold. The Countess bent silently over the dying Queen, listening for a breath, but in vain. Not a sound disturbed the solemn stillness. Only the golden eagle flapped his mighty wings, making a current of cool air through the lofty apartment, so that the rosy flames flickered in the crystal vessels, and threw a quivering reflection on the gilding of the walls and on the diamond crown at the dying Queen's feet.

"It is too late!" thought the Countess; but she did as her little guide directed, laying one hand on the brow, the other on the breast of the dying Queen, and then awaited the result in anxious silence.

Slowly and sorrowfully the moments passed by. The Countess was about to remove her hands, when she saw Goldemar's eye fixed on her in earnest entreaty, and she had not the courage to rob the sorrowing King of his last hope; so she let her warm hand remain a little longer on the rigid form. Suddenly, whether it was a reality or only her own fancy, a slight tremor seemed to move the delicate frame, then a second and a third time, and gently, very gently, the heart began to throb once more.

The Countess bent again over the Queen, and listened to her breathing. Gentle and sweet like the fragrance of flowers the breath passed in and out over the beautiful, half-parted lips, and life once more tinged the sweet face with a faint bloom. It was not the gleam of the candles or the ruby lights that caused the rosy hue that now overspread her face; it was life, true life. At last she opened her eyes, raised herself, and looked round in astonishment.

"Am I still with thee?" she said to her husband, whose glance rested on her in delight, as she held out her soft white hand. "How did it happen? Tell me."

Goldemar pointed to the Countess.

"Oh, my deliverer!" she exclaimed, turning in surprise to the noble lady; "how shall I thank you?"

The news of their beloved Queen's recovery soon

H

spread to the rest of the dwarfs, and they came flocking in, their grave faces lit with a serene content. They crowded round the royal pair with affectionate congratulations, and poured forth their thanks to the Countess. Then a band of servants drew near, carrying vessels of precious metal, wherein lay fruits and flowers carved in precious stones of incalculable value, and so cunningly and wonderfully wrought that the treasuries of earthly princes have not their like to show.

"Pray, accept these," begged the King, on whose brow the crown once more shone.

"Pray, accept them," said the Queen, her beautiful eyes fixed in entreaty on the face of the Countess.

The Countess shook her head gently. "Let me have the pleasure of having served you without reward," said she. "I have wealth enough; and now take me home again."

"Thou despisest our gifts," said the beautiful Queen in a tone of disappointment, "and our laws do not permit us to leave any benefit unreturned. Thou hast surely some wish; name it, then, that we may fulfil it."

The Countess shook her head, then all at once she thought of her child. The celebrated physician, to consult whom she had undertaken the long journey from which she had returned the evening before, had not concealed the truth. The span of life that remained to her was very short, and soon her beloved child Kuno would be left motherless. Perhaps he might some day need the help of the friendly dwarfs.

"One petition, indeed, I have," she said with a faltering voice. "My child will soon perhaps be motherless, and if he should ever need protection, will you befriend him?"

"From this moment," replied King Goldemar, "he is under our care, and we will hasten to his assistance as soon as he needs it."

Then the dwarf who had acted as guide to the Countess before conducted her back through the castle garden; and soon she rested, tired, but with a peaceful and happy heart, once more on her couch.

ECKBERT'S WILD RIDE ON KUNO'S
HORSE.

PART II.

THE FRIENDS IN THE ROCK.

SUNNY terrace of the castle hill became the last resting-place of the Countess Matilda. It had been her favourite spot both in her days of health and of sickness. Here she had spent part of every day with her Kuno, and with him looked down on the fruitful plains of Thuringia; and here she had taken a sad farewell of the blooming life around. She did not wish to rest in the dark and gloomy vault, but here on the lonely height, with flowers around her and sunshine above her head.

It was an autumn afternoon. There were no longer any flowers in field or garden, but around the grave of the Countess was a freshness and fragrance as of spring, and the sun in which she had so delighted let no day pass without looking kindly down on the lonely grave, if only for a few minutes.

The wind was shaking the lofty trees of the castle garden, and playfully driving the yellow leaves along the paths, when a little figure with a pale sad face came up the broad gravel walk, climbed the rock, and threw himself on the grave. It was Kuno, Countess Matilda's only child.

How one year had changed everything!—his dear mother dead, his father gone to distant scenes of war along with many noble knights, and he left alone with heartless and ill-natured strangers! A distant relation, the Lady Von Allenstein, had been asked by the Earl to preside over his household, and to act the part of a mother to the little Kuno. She was a woman as heartless as she was clever, and so successfully did she ingratiate herself into the favour of the unsuspicious Earl, that before he left he gave her full control over his vassals and his estate. Her son Eckbert, a lad of about fifteen years of age, had the reputation of being well brought up, because in the presence of strangers he could assume fine courtly manners ; but he had a mischievous and malicious disposition, and was both feared and hated by the castle servants.

That Kuno, this child, this dreamer, who in Eckbert's opinion possessed no knightly qualities whatsoever, should be some day lord and possessor of so many noble castles and estates with their numerous dependants, while to his lot had fallen nothing but one small and half-ruined castle, to which not even a single village was attached— this vexed him, and in his heart burned envious hatred towards the orphan child.   Hitherto Kuno had borne all Eckbert's malice with the gentleness which he had inherited from his mother ; but when the news came that the Earl had been dangerously wounded, and when the messenger spoke of his master's death as probable, Eckbert counted himself freed from restraint, and tormented the little Earl with greater spitefulness than ever.

To-day he had cut him to the heart. Kuno's little horse, which had borne him when he was scarcely more than a baby, and which had never felt either whip or spur, had been mounted to-day by the cruel Eckbert. For the first time Kuno ventured a decided protest, and Eckbert, seeing by this unusual courage how dear the animal was to its young master, struck the spurs with all his might into the horse's sides, so that it reared suddenly and then dashed with bleeding flanks out by the castle gate.   When Kuno, after Eckbert's return, ran to the stable to see how his favourite had borne the dreadful ride, the horse did not turn his head as usual to greet him with a joyous neigh ; he lay panting on the straw, covered with foam and blood, his feet stretched out, his head drooping, and his breast heaving with a loud rattling sound. Kuno threw himself down beside him, put his arms round his neck, and called him by the tenderest names. Then the creature opened his eyes, fixed his last look on his young master, and with a feeble attempt at a neigh, that sounded like a death-sigh, he died.

Kuno's tears were dried; he remained speechless before his dead favourite, and gazed with tearless eyes upon the body. Thus Margaret, the castellan's wife, Kuno's old nurse, found him. She had seen Eckbert mount the horse, and heard Kuno's words. When she saw the dead animal and the child's grief, her anger at Eckbert's malice knew no bounds. She went at once to Lady Von Allenstein, and said what she thought of Eckbert's shameful deed with vehemence such as the proud lady had never before witnessed in an inferior.

"Do you know," said the lady, with flashing eyes, "what you deserve?—a place in the dungeon among frogs and toads. But I will be merciful. In one hour you and your family leave this castle; that will serve as a warning to your fellow-servants, and will make Master Kuno more submissive to me and my son, as he will no longer have you to encourage him in his obstinacy."

So they left. In one short hour the last true friends of the poor orphan left the castle, although he clung to Margaret and besought her with passionate weeping not to leave him quite alone. He watched them as long as he could, and then crept back through the garden to his mother's grave.

Here dreams of bygone days passed before his mind. He thought of the happy hours which he had spent here on the solitary height with his beloved mother ; when he had looked down with her over the blooming country, and listened to her tales of the wonders of foreign lands, of our lost Paradise, and of the heavenly home which she soon hoped to reach.   Then when, at the thought of the coming parting, his little heart shrank, his mother would take him in her arms and try to comfort him by telling him about the friendly feelings that the good dwarfs cherish towards poor defenceless children, and about the splendour and beauty of the enchanted realm below the ground.

And now ?   He knelt down beside the grave, laid his head on the grass, and sobbed, till at last, tired out with grief and weeping, he fell asleep.   The sun set, but he did not know it ; the stars rose, and the child slept on, with his head pillowed on his mother's grave.   A gentle touch on his shoulder woke him.   He started up in surprise.   Before him stood a tiny little man of insignificant appearance, and with a lantern in his hand.   It was the same dwarf that had once led the boy's mother to King Goldemar's dying Queen.

"Who are you ?" asked the child in astonishment, as he rubbed his sleepy eyes.

"One of your mother's friends," answered the little man kindly ; "dost thou not remember what she told thee about us?   Wilt thou come with me ?"

Kuno rose at once, took the dwarf's hand, and walked away by his side.   They soon reached the clump of ferns that covered the secret entrance, and stepped into the vaulted corridor. The first door opened, and the child found himself suddenly in the enchanted realm of his mother's stories. Yes, this was the crystal hall with the emerald lizards and the sky-blue snakes. The place still glimmered and shone as when the Countess trod its floor; the snakes looked down kindly on the boy with their diamond eyes, and the transparent lizards bowed their crowned heads in friendly greeting.

"I know what the other hall is like," said Kuno in delight to his little guide. "Do not flowers made of precious stones gleam along the silver walls; and in the third hall is there not the Queen's ruby bed swinging from the golden ceiling, and the eagle flapping his golden wings?"

The dwarf smiled. "See for yourself," he said. Then he led him through the halls. Yes, it was all as Kuno's mother had described it; everything was wonderful, and yet he knew it all so well. Last of all, he was led into the throne-room.

The walls and ceiling were of blue crystal, so that it looked like the vault of heaven, and in the high dome shone stars cut out of rubies. There were no lamps in the hall, but from without a hidden artificial light streamed through the crimson stars, and filled the whole room with rosy radiance. At the far end of the room stood a throne made of large and costly pearls, which glowed in the light like rosebuds, and on it sat in her brilliant beauty the Queen of this enchanted palace, with her golden hair flowing to the pearl-built steps of the throne.   Beside her sat King Goldemar in a purple mantle, his noble brow adorned once more with the diamond crown.

With a low obeisance the dwarf introduced the boy to the royal pair.

The lovely Queen was much smaller than Kuno, and yet she looked so dignified that the child knelt and reverently kissed the little hand which she graciously extended to him.

"Thy noble mother was my friend," she said with a gentle voice, "and thou art dear to us as one of our own. Every night, if thou wilt, thou mayest come to us to forget thy little troubles in our hall. Look thou around ; all are ready to love thee and give thee pleasure."

As she spoke she raised her white hand and pointed to the lovely children at the foot of the throne, and to the troops of little dwarfs that were assembled in the hall. Then the royal children came up to greet him, and after them the little dwarfs with their grave wise countenances; they gave him their hands, and met his wondering gaze with friendly looks. And the poor friendless boy, who hitherto had felt himself alone and forsaken, felt happy, now that he found such unexpected kindness and love such as he had never felt since his mother's death. All his troubles vanished from his memory in this enchanted kingdom. Hour after hour flew by, and to the child they seemed but minutes. Then the dwarf who had brought him took his hand and drew him away. Kuno was sorry to go, but he followed his little guide.

"Do not weep," said the latter kindly. "Thou may

come back every night; but take care that thou tell no one of thy visits, or some great calamity may be the consequence."

When they reached the garden the stars had already grown pale, and the first streaks of dawn were showing in the east.

"Let us make haste," said the dwarf anxiously, "for we dwellers below ground can only live under the light of the stars—the sun's rays kill us."

Soon they arrived at the winding staircase at the foot of the tower. The gate was locked, but the dwarf brought out a strangely-formed key, put it into the lock, and immediately the heavy iron-barred door turned noiselessly on its hinges. It was the same with all the other doors as soon as the wonderful key touched them, and softly the wanderers slipped through the rooms and passed the sleeping servants. Kuno reached unseen the room that he shared with Eckbert, and then the dwarf hastened home.

Eckbert had tried to keep awake to receive Kuno with scolding and reproaches, for the child had been missed at supper and sought for, of course in vain. But he had fallen asleep over his generous plan.

Kuno was still slumbering sweetly when Eckbert woke, sprang out of bed, and shook the boy roughly.

"Where were you yesterday? Speak!" he shouted; but Kuno, mindful of the dwarf's warning, kept silence. But when Eckbert raised his arm to strike the child, an invisible hand gave him such a powerful blow on the ear that he staggered half unconscious against the wall. He felt uncomfortable at the thought of the unseen avenger, and he left Kuno in peace, but told the whole story to his mother, wickedly distorting it as he went on. At breakfast she ordered the boy to tell where he had been; but though his heart beat fast with terror, he closed his lips tightly and remained silent.

"I will conquer your obstinacy," said the lady angrily; "you shall sleep in the room in the tower, and go earlier to bed."

In the evening she took him herself to the lonely chamber, from which the winding stair led to the garden; for she thought that fear of the uninhabited and lonely room would force the boy to tell his secret. But when he went without a word, and lay down uncomplainingly on his bed, anger rose high in the proud lady's heart. "Eckbert is right," she thought; "his obstinacy must be conquered."

With a prayer to God, and a fervent wish that his little friends would not forget him, Kuno fell asleep. And they did not forget him. About midnight the little dwarf stood once more at his side, wakened him, and led him into the enchanted palace.

The little folk greeted him joyfully, the royal pair reached him their hands, and amid splendour and pleasure the hours flew by. His friends showed him the rooms that he had not seen the day before—the crystal chambers full of golden ornaments, which every family possessed, and which far outshone the most splendid palaces of earthly kings. They showed him wonderful things which they knew how to make—birds made of precious stones, from whose transparent throats sweet songs poured forth; fruits and flowers, shaped out of jewels, whose beauty and fragrance was like that of the flowers of Eden. Kuno's astonishment and delight knew no bounds; the hours went by too quickly, and when the stars began to pale the dwarf led him back to his room in the tower. And every night at midnight the same dwarf brought him back to the enchanted kingdom. There he forgot all the trials of the day—all Eckbert's spiteful tricks, and Lady Von Allenstein's injustice. But it was not alone to please and amuse him that the little people brought the boy to visit them—they cared also for his mind and heart.

In this magic kingdom lived an aged dwarf with long snow-white hair and beard; a supernatural light shone in his eyes. All the dwarfs, even the King and Queen, treated him with the greatest reverence, for he was the oldest man of their nation, and also the wisest. He could look back through thousands of years; he knew every-thing in the whole earth—all plants and stones; he knew about their origin, and had watched their growth. Often, when the King and Queen were sitting on the throne, the wise man would come into the hall and seat himself on the pearl steps; then the lovely royal children, Kuno in their midst, would gather round and listen as he told with beaming eyes about the wonders of creation, and the mysterious forces of nature. Words of kindness and wisdom flowed from his lips, and it seemed to the boy as if he were sitting in church or at the feet of his dead mother.

But even happier hours than these he spent playing with the children in the crystal hall, letting the beautiful lizards dart down on his outstretched hand, or the sky-blue snakes glide down and wind playfully round

KUNO LISTENS TO THE WISE MAN'S TALK.

his feet.   Once, when he was preparing to go home after one of his visits, King Goldemar held the hand that he had extended in farewell, and spoke to him in a low and confidential tone.   Kuno nodded with a happy smile.

Next morning joy shone from his soft eyes and betrayed itself in his cheerful mood, which made so strange a contrast to the silent gravity of his usual demeanour. The change did not escape the quick eye of the Countess; but she took care not to ask the reason, for she thought she could guess it already.

Earlier than usual Kuno said "Good night," and went to his room, but not to bed. He worked about, fastening wax candles, which he had got beforehand from the steward, on the walls, and trying to give the room a festive appearance; then he put on his best clothes, sat down on his bed, and waited.

At last the castle clock struck twelve, and immediately soft music sounded in the distance; it came nearer and nearer, and soon floated up the winding stair. In a few moments the door opened of itself, and in came Kuno's dwarf friends, marching two and two, and all arrayed in festive garments. They held their invisible caps in their hands, swinging them in measured time, so that the silver bells that ornamented them rang in magic melody. Then followed, escorted by Goldemar and the Queen, a bridal pair, whose wedding feast was to be held in a human dwelling for the blessing and well-being of its occupant. Kuno advanced to meet his guests, and greeted them joyfully; then to the sound of wondrous music the dance began. This was led by the King and his lovely consort, their crowns flashing lightning at every quick graceful movement; then followed the bridal pair in garments gleaming with gold. Kuno had taken the hand of a pretty dwarf-maiden, and now mingled merrily in the splendid throng. All was mirth and gaiety.

Suddenly the music stopped, the dancers stood still, and all eyes turned in indignation towards an opening in the ceiling where the face of Lady Von Allenstein was visible.

Goldemar's eyes flashed angrily.

"Blow out the lights!" he cried to one of his train; and in a twinkling the little fellow had climbed up the wall, and before the lady had time to suspect that this command had anything to do with her, the dwarf reached the opening, and blew into her face.

A fearful scream followed; then the King turned to Kuno and said—

"Accept our thanks, my dear child, for thy hospitality; it is not thy fault that we cannot stay longer. Farewell!"

Then the little people turned quickly towards the door, and soon the boy was alone.

Faint moans were now heard from above, and a sound as of suppressed weeping.

Kuno also had seen the face of the lady, and knew that these doleful sounds were uttered by her. Deep compassion filled his heart; he forgot all the unhappiness that this woman had caused him, and, filled only with the thought of helping her, he took a candle in his hand and hastened to clamber up to her.

He found her crouching on the ground, her hands pressed before her eyes.

"What is wrong, gracious lady?" asked Kuno timidly.

"Oh, I am blind! I am blind!" she groaned piteously. "The dwarf blew into my eyes, and my sight left me."

Kuno, full of pity, seized her hand and led her tenderly step by step down the winding stair, and on to her own apartment.

After calling a maid to her assistance, he returned to say good-night to the poor lady. What he had never done in her days of health he did now—he drew her hand to his lips and kissed it fervently. The lady felt a hot tear drop on her hand ; silently, but with scarce-concealed emotion, she drew it away. This tear burned like unquenchable fire, not only on her hand, but on her soul.

She spent a long and sleepless night ; this unexpected calamity had crushed her hard heart. But though the light was taken from her eyes, a new day dawned within her. Her dislike of Kuno, her hardness and injustice towards the orphan child, all passed through her mind in fiery procession ; and when she thought of Kuno's noble conduct, a flood of penitent tears streamed from her sightless eyes.

Eckbert, on hearing of his mother's misfortune, showed himself as heartless as ever. He railed at the dwarf and at Kuno as the real cause of it. But he had not any idea of sitting through the long tedious hours with his poor blind mother—that was Kuno's business, he thought, for he had been the cause of it all. On the contrary, freed from all restraint, Eckbert amused himself more than ever with the chase and with drinking bouts, and tyrannised worse than before over all around him.

Kuno behaved towards the unhappy lady like a loving son. He sat with her and cared for her wants as if she had been his own beloved mother. When the summer

I

came he led her out every day into the garden or to the rock where his mother lay, and tried to amuse her with his childish talk.

Lady Von Allenstein was often deeply moved when she felt Kuno's tenderness and thought of her own heartlessness. Once her emotion overcame her, and she drew Kuno to her side, and said with tears—" You are so good to me, who was so unkind to you ; can you forgive me for all the wrong I have done you ? Oh ! if I could only get back my sight, I would take every opportunity of making up to you for my injustice."

Kuno was still on the most friendly terms with the dwarf nation, and regarded the enchanted palace as his second home.

Exactly a year had passed since that wedding in the tower-chamber, when King Goldemar again expressed a wish to hold a similar feast in the same room.

Kuno's heart beat high with joy at these words ; perhaps—but he would cherish no presumptuous hopes.

Again the room was festively decorated ; but no one in the castle got the least hint of what was to take place in the isolated room. The little guests appeared, and this time the merriment went on undisturbed.

But dawn, the time of separation, was drawing near, and Goldemar held out his hand to his protégé to say good-bye. Then Kuno held it fast, and looked entreatingly into the good King's face.

" What dost thou want, Kuno ?" asked Goldemar.

" I have one petition, the fulfilment of which will make me happy," answered the boy.

"Name it," said the King graciously ; "it is granted."

Then Kuno led the King to the bed and drew back the curtains. There sat a pale lady in deep mourning, her dark sightless eyes fixed vacantly before her.

"Give her back her sight," begged Kuno, pointing to Lady Von Allenstein.

Goldemar's eyes shone as he looked approvingly on the boy ; then he bent towards the lady and said, "I light the lamps again !" at the same time breathing into her eyes, so that the sight came back immediately.

The newly-opened eyes shone with joy and gratitude, and in a burst of weeping she sank into Kuno's arms, while the royal pair and their train looked on in deep emotion.

"Farewell then, Kuno," said King Goldemar. "Thou hast found what was needed to make thee happy—a mother's heart. We have kept our word. Shouldst thou ever in thy life again need our help, thou wilt find us ready."

With a loving look the King held out his hand, and the Queen and the other dwarfs likewise took an affectionate leave of the boy before returning to their kingdom under ground. Just as they were going through the castle garden towards the entrance in the side of the rock, Eckbert returned from a drinking bout.

"I have come upon these dull fellows unexpectedly," he said, grinding his teeth, when he noticed the procession of dwarfs. "Now they shall suffer for that box on the ear, and for my mother's blindness. I will cut off the last clown's head and throw it in at that stupid Kuno's window."

He slipped softly behind the procession.   When they reached the door in the rock, Eckbert waited till the last had put his foot on the threshold, then he sprang forward and raised his sword.   The same instant the heavy rock door, which so artfully closed the opening, shut to and crushed Eckbert's head to atoms.   Without uttering a sound he fell back, and his blood stained the snow.

The next morning offered a sad spectacle to Lady Von Allenstein's newly-restored sight.   It is true, Eckbert had been an undutiful son, but still it was her child, her own flesh and blood, that now lay before her a mangled corpse.   The place where he had been found with his sword unsheathed made Kuno suspect whose hand had caused his death ; but he was silent on this as on all that concerned his dwarf friends.

Eckbert was buried with great pomp, but no eyes shed tears at the ceremony save those of his mother and of the good forgiving Kuno.   From this time Lady Von Allenstein turned the whole affection of her ennobled heart towards Kuno, who repaid her love with the most heartfelt gratitude ; and no one who did not know their relationship would have thought, to see them together, that they were anything but mother and son.

Winter and spring were past, and the warm summer weather had come.

On a bright summer evening the horn of the watchman on the tower announced a troop of horsemen, and as they drew near with the sound of trumpets Kuno's sharp eye recognised in their floating banner his father's colours.

He had long since recovered, but instead of returning to his castle he had once more offered his strong arm and brave heart in service to his imperial lord. The war was now ended, and the Earl, whom they had long counted dead, had returned, covered with scars and with honours, to clasp his beloved son in his arms.

Lady Von Allenstein still lived in the castle, and presided over it as before, but she was served now from love and not from fear. When she died in a good old age, Kuno knelt at her side; her cold hand rested on his head, and her dying lips spoke words of love and blessing over her adopted son.

HELGA AT HER MOTHER'S FEET.

The Flower of Iceland.

SUBSTANTIAL farm-house stood many, many years ago on the slope of a hill in bleak and frozen Iceland. The owner, who had spent his youth as a sailor in distant climes, had at last obeyed his dying father's summons, and exchanged the palms and orange groves of southern lands for the feeble sunlight and cold lava-fields of his native island. But as a living souvenir of those happy regions he brought home a young and beautiful wife, whose dark and eloquent eyes still shone in the memory of all who had beheld them, long after they had been closed in the last sleep.

"Marietta," her husband had said before the priest had joined their hands in marriage, "have you considered well what you are renouncing when you promise to follow me as my wife? Here in your country an eternal spring reigns, sweet with the fragrance of flowers and musical with the warbling of birds, while the Italian sky shines in never-fading blue. On my island you will find none of these things. A pale sun, a grey sky overhead, and all around barren heaths and ice—ice and snow wherever you look; none but the Icelander can think this island beautiful."

"But you will be there," answered Marietta; "and could I wish for any home but yours?"

So she had gone with him to the far north.

They had one child, a lovely little girl, who bore the name of Helga; she must be a true daughter of Iceland, and to this even her name must witness. But her foreign descent was not to be hid; true, she had the fair skin and beautiful flaxen hair of a northern girl, but her eyes were as dark and mysterious as her mother's.

The Icelanders have no flowers; they know of their beauty only by the tales of their countrymen who have seen them on their travels; but every one who looked into little Helga's beautiful face thought that flowers must look like that, and thus she was called "the Flower of Iceland."

Fair Helga loved her grave father, but she loved still more her beautiful and gentle mother, by whose side she spent most of her time.

Every spring the father set out for the coast with a few servants to get fish for the year's household provisions; for though he dearly loved Marietta and his home, the sea still exercised the old spell on his heart. In summer and autumn he was accustomed to go to the distant trading places along the coast, there to exchange the wool of his large and well-conditioned flocks for the valuable products of foreign lands, with which he loved to please and adorn his dear ones.

At such times Helga would sit at her mother's feet, listening as she told in the soft, sweet sounds of her native tongue about the blue sky and the warm golden sunlight of Italy, of the beautiful flowers and evergreen woods, and of the fine mild nights when the young girls would dance in the moonlight to the sound of the mandoline, and pleasure and melody reigned over land and sea.

Ah! how beautiful that country must be; and here everything was so different. No dance, no song, either from human lips or from the throat of a bird. Helga had never even heard the sheep give a cheerful bleat; everything was stupid and grave; the silence of death was Nature's language here.

Then Helga's dark eye would wander away over Iceland's wide and desert heaths, over the lava-fields that stretched for miles, and which had buried the freshness of nature under their stiff mantle of mourning. She gazed on those giant ice-mountains, untrod by human foot, which rise like monuments of death, with thick mist-veils about their brow. Even when a sunbeam happens to pierce the cloudy covering, the colossal piles of ice shine in the pale light like sarcophagi in a vault· Then Helga would shudder and think with ardent longing on her dear mother's native land.

And she? Ah, her husband had been right. In spite of her love for him, she pined for the sunny valleys of her childhood, all the more as she never told her husband of the grief that gnawed at her heart, for he placed his Iceland before all the paradises of the world. Ten years had scarcely gone by till Marietta's warm heart lay still beneath the sod.

Helga thought her heart would break when they carried her loved mother out towards the hill, whence she had so often looked longingly out over the sea, watching the blue waves as they hastened towards the beautiful but distant south.

"When you bury me," said the dying woman to her husband, "lay me so that my face may look towards Italy." And they did as she wished.

Helga often sat now on the grave, herself the only flower that brightened it; and along with her dear mother's image those distant countries came vividly before her mind, as she had heard them described as long as she could remember.

A distant relation now came to take charge of the housekeeping. She had willingly left her home, bringing with her her only son, in compliance with her rich cousin's request. The stern old woman had no sympathy with Helga's longings, and counted her descriptions of distant lands as fairy tales; nothing, she thought, could be more beautiful than Iceland. But Olaffson, her boy, who was only a few years older than the little orphan, became Helga's eager listener. With equal delight he looked on her beautiful face and listened to her stories; the grave blue eyes, which were usually as cold as the glaciers of his native island, would kindle as she went on, and when Helga stopped he would say, " I will be a sailor, and travel to those countries to see if they are really so beautiful!"

" But you will take me with you ?"

" Oh yes, of course."

Thus the years went by, and the time drew quickly on when the tree, the seed of which had been sown by Helga's hand, bore fruit. Olaffson was no longer a boy, and he decided on going to sea. The head of the house willingly gave his consent, and the time of parting came.

Fair Helga's cheek was pale. Olaffson fancied that it was the separation that troubled her so deeply, and that thought sweetened the bitter hour to him. But ah! it was only her grief at having to stay at home on the cold and barren island, and at not being allowed to see the countries to which, as she thought, she had a much better right than Olaffson.

Another year had gone. Olaffson had come home and given an account of all that he had seen. The hour of parting again drew near. Early next morning he was to set out on a second and longer journey, and in spite of Helga's tears and entreaties to be allowed to go, her father and Olaffson had only shaken their heads and laughed at her childishness.

It was evening. She went with Olaffson to the grave on the hill, there to hear once more about the wonders of foreign lands. Hour after hour flew by; she could not tire of the delightful theme.

"Well, Helga," Olaffson at last concluded, "it is indeed as beautiful in those countries as your mother used to tell you; almost more beautiful—yes, much more beautiful; still, it is not Iceland. There is no place so beautiful as our native land—no place."

Helga looked at him incredulously.

"You may believe me, Helga," he said. "Look; it is now midnight. In those countries there has been night, deep night for hours; the sun has long ago forsaken them, but it loves our island better, for it lingers longer with us. Just look over yonder. It has just sunk into the sea, and on the rosy western sky it paints in silvery outline the beautiful leafy forests which are denied to our soil. Only look how they nod their gleaming heads; does it not seem as if you could hear a mysterious rustling among their branches? And are not the white clouds above like eagles circling over their summits? And now look at the clear light around you! The nights there are as dark as the consciences of criminals; our nights are like the heart of a pious child—light, clear, and still."

"But it is so cold here—so cold that my very heart freezes within me," said Helga complainingly.

"But the cold is bracing," said Olaffson. "There, I

found men weak, cowardly, and effeminate. I could tell you many a sad story to show this. Now look at your own land, Flower of Iceland, for you belong to us; we are honest, brave, and strong as our fathers were, and our sons will be after us, and that we owe to Iceland and its glaciers, its cold but strengthening climate. I tell you, fair Helga, there is but one Iceland, as there is but one flower in it."

Early next morning Olaffson was to set out. Helga's father said he would go down to the coast also with his servants, for it was the time of the yearly fishing, so that they might as well travel together so far.

The farewell was short and silent. Helga struggled to keep back her tears when she saw how merrily they all sprang into the saddle, and when she thought of Olaffson's words about Iceland's brave people; for she must show herself worthy of her race. But her dark eyes rested so longingly on her father's face that he knew what was passing in her heart.

"Come, Helga," said he, stooping down from his horse, "you may go with us as far as the hill where the lava-fields begin." Then he took her up before him on the saddle, and soon the horses were off at a canter. Soon they reached the hill at the foot of which the lava-fields began, whose dark lines stretched for miles along the horizon.

Helga could no longer restrain her tears. She threw her arms sobbing round her father's neck and said, "Don't stay long away, dear father; it is so dreary at home when you are both away."

" I will come back in a few weeks, my Helga," said her father, soothingly ; "meantime be a good girl, and help your cousin with the housekeeping."

He kissed her snow-white brow silently, but tenderly, lifted her down from the horse, and after one more pressure of the hand the little band set out again.

Helga watched them till a sinking of the road hid them from view ; then she went back towards the hill, leant against the side of a rock, and looked into the distance, shading her eyes with her hand. Then they came into sight again, but so far away that Helga's farewell could not reach their ear. A fleeting sunbeam rested on them a moment, making horses and riders shine out clearly from the desert plain over which they were moving. Then a mist, such as only Iceland's mountains could send forth, fell around them, and Helga saw them no more.

She leaned her head sobbing against the rock, closed her eyes, and wept hot tears of grief and loneliness. Then a voice of wondrous sweetness sounded suddenly in her ear, " Why does fair Helga weep ?"

Helga opened her eyes in astonishment. No one was there ; she could see nothing but the mist in the distance and the bare lava-fields at her feet. She closed her eyes again.

" Helga, fair Helga, why are you so sad ?" said the voice again ; it seemed as if it came from the sky.

A slight shudder passed through Helga's frame ; she did not venture to stir, but she timidly opened her eyes and looked up. But what did she see ? Was the azure

Italian sky, of which she had so often dreamt, coming here to meet her? Right before her, on the summit of the hill, stood a form of majestic beauty, which must surely belong to some happier clime. Eyes of deep and mysterious blue shone down on Helga from the kingly countenance, and hair lovelier than her own, golden as the stars of the summer night, flowed down over the robe of purple velvet in which the stranger was clad.

"Why does fair Helga weep?" he asked tenderly.

Helga tried to regain her composure. "How do you know me, O stranger?" she asked shyly.

"Who does not know the Flower of Iceland?" answered he with a smile. "Shall I tell you some things about yourself that will prove to you how long I have known you, and how well I am acquainted with your history? Shall I tell you how often I have seen you sitting on your mother's grave, and what images there passed before your mind? Shall I say what longing a moment ago stirred your soul—how you wished to be permitted to travel with Olaffson, that you might see those rich and wondrously beautiful lands? But no such journey is necessary to the fulfilment of your wish. Your mother's paradise is here—here close beside you."

Helga's eyes shone, half in doubt, half in delight.

"Here, here?" she asked, incredulously. "How can that be?"

"Just come a few steps with me to the other side of the hill, and then you will see that I speak the truth."

Helga took his proffered hand. The stranger who had known her so long and so well was no longer a stranger to her, and he could not be an enemy who was about to fulfil her heart's dearest wish. So she went fearlessly with him to the other side of the hill.

The stranger placed his hand against the rock, which immediately opened, and allowed Helga and her guide to enter. She stood spell-bound with astonishment. Then she passed her hand over her brow, and tried to think if this could be a dream. But no, it was reality. There lay before her a wondrous region, more beautiful than her mother's native land or than all her childish dreams.

Through the crystal dome that stretched above this paradise the sun sent beams bright and warm such as the children of Iceland never see or feel. Their golden light trembled among the green foliage of the majestic trees, played with the flashing fountain jet, and flamed in the cups of the transparent flowers.

In the distance the ocean rolled its deep blue waves round wooded islands, and amid the fragrance of the flowers and the brilliant colours of the lovely scene hovered sweet and magic music, which floated to the shore of the sea, whose waves bore it in soft echo to the happy isles.

Helga looked round with delight such as she had never felt before. Had earth really such beauties, and was she permitted to gaze on them?

She stooped to examine the wonderful flowers, gently stroked the velvet of their leaves with her white hand, and pressed her lips into their fragrant cups. Then her delighted eye watched the fountain, as its waters rose in a line of light almost to the crystal dome, then fell in a graceful curve far beyond its basin, so that the shrubs and flowers bent beneath its shining dew.

Then she turned towards the lofty trees, pressed her face gently against their smooth stems, and looked up at their shining foliage, which rustled softly in the breeze. Snow-white birds hopped from branch to branch, and threw friendly glances at Helga as at an old acquaintance. Was it these feathered songsters that made the sweet music which floated with the sunbeams and the soft spring air all through this lovely place? Or did the tall trees or the distant sea give forth the sweet sounds that soothed with soft caress Helga's heart and mind, bearing away on their melodious waves the past and its memories?

Hours had flown by in this fairy kingdom, and to Helga they seemed but as one moment. At last she turned to the stranger, who had followed her every move-ment with loving eyes, and had noticed her delight.

"Oh, how shall I thank you," she said, grasping his hand, "for bringing me here and satisfying the longing of years? But tell me where I am ; for Iceland's cold hills hide no such paradise."

"You are in my kingdom, fair Helga," answered the stranger in a gentle voice ; "and I am the fairy king of Iceland."

Helga looked at him in astonishment. No lips save her mother's had ever told her of such·things, and *she* knew nothing of Iceland's spirit kingdom. Therefore Helga felt neither terror nor anxiety.

"Ah! if I could only stay here always," she cried earnestly.

"I wish for nothing better," said the king; "and why should you not?"

"Ah! my dear, good father—he has no one but me," said Helga, thinking for a moment of her home.

"But he is now far away," said the fairy king persuasively; "and you can stay at least till he comes back."

"So I can," cried Helga in delight. So she stayed with the fairy king.

One day in this paradise was just like the next, as it will perhaps be in heaven, where there is nothing to remind the blessed of the flight of time, where it is all one gloriously happy present, because they have no past to look back on with sad memory, and the future has nothing more beautiful to excite their longings.

Helga moved with happy heart by the side of the fairy king through this paradise. The white birds flitted around her, now and then settling on her hand or shoulder. The sea with the blue waves gave a sound of pleasant greeting when Helga and the fairy king drew near its shores. Then when he seized her hand and they stepped together on one of the little waves, this fairy boat carried them gently and swiftly over to the happy islands.

At midnight, when Iceland's sun spread its crimson mantle along the horizon, its reflection streamed through the crystal dome, glowed like roses in the fountain and on the birds' white feathers, while the sea rolled to the shore in violet waves.

Then Helga knew that she must close her eyes, in order to strengthen herself for a new day of happiness.

K

She lay down on the soft moss, while the fairy king sat near her and took his harp. From its strings streamed forth magic music which banished memory from Helga's soul. The sweet sounds lulled her to sleep, and carefully guarded the gates of her heart, permitting no dream to knock there which could remind her of the past and its claims. But, once, the chord which nature has placed between the hearts of parent and child, and which never breaks even though seas lie between, sounded with a startling thrill.

Helga's father had come home, and his grief and lamentation at the loss of his beloved child were so violent that Helga's slumbering heart awoke.

"My father!" she said suddenly one day as she stood beside the sea, and drew back the foot which she was just on the point of placing on the wave that stood bowing its blue head before her. "My father! I think I hear you lamenting my loss. Is it not my duty to leave all these beautiful things here and return to him?"

A shadow fell on the fairy king's face. He silently seized his harp and drew from it strains more beautiful, more heart-enthralling than Helga had ever heard before. They floated away over the sea till the waves sank into silence, unwilling to disturb the sweet melodies. And in Helga's heart memory ceased to thrill, and the visions of the past faded from her mind.

Then the fairy king told her how he had chosen her years ago as the queen of this kingdom, and had watched over her since her childhood; that he had prepared all these beautiful things only for her, with the hope that she

HELGA IN THE FAIRY KING'S PALACE.

F. C., p. 154.

would some day be his wife, and thus gain for him that for which his soul had yearned during long centuries— an immortal soul, a boon which is denied to the poor fairies in every land.

"Will you be my wife now, fair Helga?" he asked in conclusion. "I will love you with a faithful love such as you would seek in vain among your degenerate race. You shall never regret having given to the poor fairy king the desire of his heart."

"I will, I will!" said she, seizing his hands with childish frankness. "I will always stay with you."

The king's eyes shone with joy.

"But, fair Helga, the laws of our kingdom are strict; we hold the vows of faithfulness more sacred than you do, although we look for no eternal reward. If you become my wife, and by uniting your soul to mine impart to me your immortality, then you belong henceforth to me, and to me alone. Your father and your home have no longer any claim on you, and if you ever return to them, then I must hold you guilty of robbing me of my soul, and our kingdom will demand your life as the penalty. Canst thou keep such faith as this with me, O Flower of Iceland?"

Fair Helga leaned forward. "Look into my eyes," she said; "do you think me so ungrateful? I will be your wife, and you shall gain through me a never-dying soul. Do you think I could disappoint your hopes of immortality?"

So fair Helga, the Flower of Iceland, was married to the fairy king.

A year had gone by.   The sun shone once more through the crystal dome, and fair Helga's fairy kingdom still bloomed in unfaded beauty ; but the Flower of Iceland was pale and sorrowful, and a tear trembled on her lowered eyelashes.

Was the fairy king's wife not happy ?   Oh yes, she was happy, almost too happy.   Beauty and love surrounded her on every side ; but undisturbed blessedness never lasts long on earth.

Her husband was far away.   The laws of the fairy kingdom compelled him to go every year across the sea to give account of his government to the supreme lord of the fairy race, whose throne stood in the rocky mountains of Norway.   He had promised to return in a week, and now three weeks had gone by, and he had not come home. This thought gnawed at fair Helga's heart, and made her blind to all the beauty around her.   In vain did the white birds flit around her head, stroking her cheeks with their soft wings.   Helga's soul was sunk in sorrow, and the magic music with its soothing power lay asleep in the harp.   At last she rose.

" Ah ! I must be disobedient, my husband ; forgive me, forgive me !   But anxiety will kill me, if I do not go out to look if I can see you in the distance."

She sprang up and went to the door in the rock.   The birds fluttered anxiously around her, but she frightened them away with her hand, and touched the wall through which she had entered a year ago.   The rock, not daring to refuse obedience to its mistress, opened, and fair Helga stepped out on the barren soil of Iceland.   But after being so long accustomed to the warm summer air, she shuddered as she felt the icy breath of her old home, and with hurried steps she went to the point of the rock. Here she stopped, turned her beautiful face, and looked over her left shoulder towards the south-east.

Before the power of this magic glance the veil of the distance vanished. Her look pierced through Iceland's fogs, flew over the eastern mountains, and swam on the Atlantic waves to the steep rock-bound coast of Norway. She saw the mysterious inhabitants of the mountains, and the mighty fairy king seated on his diamond throne, over which thousands of years had passed, leaving it still unshaken. Around him stood his people in their unfading youth and beauty, bowing in lowly reverence. But her husband's noble form was not among them; she could not meet the glance of his deep blue eye, though she anxiously examined every countenance. At last she looked sadly away, and turned to go back to her lonely kingdom.

But when she went round the corner of the rock she saw a tall, manly form standing in the very place whence she had once watched her father and Olaffson as they rode away over the lava-fields. With a cry of joy she ran to the spot. Could it be that her husband had been so near, while she believed him far away? But the man, hearing her light footstep, turned his head, and she looked not on her husband's youthful beauty, but on the care-worn face of her long-forgotten father.

"Helga, Helga!" The words fell on her ear with a strange thrill. "My child, you are still alive, you are still on earth?" and he stretched out his arms towards her, and pressed her to his breast, while the hot tears fell on her brow.

The long-silenced chords now sounded loudly in Helga's heart, memory awoke, and the fairy king's harp was not near to lull it to sleep again.

"My dear, good father," she said, thinking now of none but him, "weep not. Your Helga lives and is happy; but how old you have grown, and how white your hair is!"

"Yes, Helga, I had lost you, my only child; but now that I have found you my youthful vigour will return. Come home quickly, my daughter. How glad Olaffson will be."

At these words Helga's heart trembled. "My dear, dear father," she said, gently stroking the furrowed cheeks, "I cannot go with you; I belong now to another world." Then she told her astonished father all that had happened to her since the hour when she said good-bye to him at the edge of the lava-field.

"I have given my word," she concluded, "and, hard as it seems not to go with you, I dare not, I dare not."

"Alas, my child, my poor unhappy child!" said the father sorrowfully; "into what hands have you fallen?"

"Into the best and tenderest, my father," said Helga, soothingly. "Would that my husband were at home, that you might see him; but I will show you my kingdom, that your mind may be set at rest."

She took her father's hand and led him towards the side of the rock which concealed the entrance into the fairy land. She touched it, but the door remained closed; again and again she passed her hand over the hard stone, but there was no movement.

Helga's heart throbbed as though it would break, and she sank down on the hard ground, begging with bitter tears for admission to her kingdom; but all was still, dead, and motionless.

Poor Helga! Without knowing it, she had transgressed the laws of the fairies by speaking to a mortal of the mysteries of the spirit-world, and now its gates were barred against her. With bitter regret she now remembered her husband's parting command—not to return to the outer world, to which she had no longer any right. Soon, she thought, will the other awful threat be fulfilled, and she sank unconscious into her father's arms.

He was rejoiced to see the fairy kingdom closed against his daughter, and with a lightened heart he bore the precious burden back to her childhood's home.

After long hours and days of darkness, Helga's youthful strength triumphed, and she opened her eyes in full consciousness. Her first glance fell on her father, who sat at her bedside.

"You here, my dear father? Then my meeting with you was not a dream? But now let me get up and go to my husband; he must have come home long before this, and he will believe me when I tell him that I did not intend to leave him."

"My child, look round you," said the father, soothingly. "Let those feverish fancies die. See, you are where you have always been, at home with your old father. All through your long illness you have raved about a fairy king and his paradise, of your marriage and your promises. But these were only fancies, my Helga, such as fever often causes."

Helga looked at him in trembling astonishment.

"That is impossible," she said at last in a faltering voice. "Bring out my clothes, and see whether Iceland has such splendid garments as those."

"Splendid garments?" repeated her father as if in surprise. Then he rose and brought Helga's dress, a garment such as she had always been accustomed to wear.

Helga examined it doubtfully, then she passed her hand over her brow, looked up at her father, and said in a low voice, "I cannot understand it. Can one then dream such things as those?"

"Certainly, my child; it is always so in fever. When I went to the coast a few weeks ago, taking you with me as far as the lava-field, you must have climbed the rock to watch us and fallen asleep there. Then the cold mountain mist crept round you, and almost prevented you from ever awaking. When your cousin thought you were staying too long, she set out with the servants to look for you; there they found you lying on the rock in a state of unconsciousness, and brought you home. A messenger was sent after us, and we returned as quickly as possible. I left my fishing, and Olaffson gave up thoughts of his voyage, that we might be near at hand to watch and care for you."

Helga sighed. Her father had never told her an untruth, so she felt compelled to believe him, though her heart rebelled against his words with bitter grief.

Ah! she little suspected that her father, in the hope of keeping his dear child beside him and hindering her return to fairyland, had invented this story, and carefully taught it to every one about the house.

Helga's bodily strength increased day by day, but over her spirit rested a cloud of melancholy, and she pined in secret for the paradise of her " feverish dreams."

She was at last almost convinced that such they had indeed been, for when she spoke to any of the servants about her lost fairy kingdom, they always smiled and said, " Those were mere fancies ; we were about you all the time and heard you rave about them."

As for the voyage round the world which Olaffson had completed since she went away, of that she heard nothing, nor was she aware that the world's history had advanced a year while she tarried in fairyland. The farm-houses in Iceland are separated from each other by long distances, so that it was but seldom that Helga came in contact with any of the neighbours ; and if a chance stranger came to claim the rights of hospitality, the father or Olaffson took care to warn him beforehand not to disturb Helga's delusion.

But the precaution was almost unnecessary ; for the Flower of Iceland, once so cheerful and talkative, who used to greet the arrival of a stranger as a joyous event, and was never tired of asking questions about the wonders of foreign lands, the same Helga sat silent and listless, and left the room as soon as the conversation turned on beautiful scenery. For the visions of her lost paradise came back to her mind, and it needed a conflict of hours to still her restless heart. "Ah! it was only a dream."

Olaffson had given up his seafaring life, and now busied himself about the farm. Helga's father loved him as a son, and intended making him the heir of his valuable property. But he had hopes of giving him something better still. He was only waiting till Helga should be once more the joyous Helga, till the Flower of Iceland should raise its drooping head. But this time seemed far distant.

"Perhaps she will be better when she is married," said the father to himself, as he looked anxiously at Helga. She was leaning against the grassy ditch that enclosed the farm, and gazing into the glow of the evening sky. He stepped softly up to her.

"What is my Helga thinking of?" he asked tenderly.

"Of the evening rays that are now falling through the crystal dome, of the little waves crowned with the roses of the sunset sky, and of the sweet music of the harp," she answered dreamily.

"Helga," said the old man reproachfully, "will you never shake off these delusions. You have heard from every tongue that they were fever fancies; but you want to vex my heart."

"Oh, no, no, dear father. Do not think so ill of your Helga," she said quickly, as she turned and stroked his cheeks caressingly. "I know very well that they were only dreams, but you cannot believe how deeply they are burnt into my heart. It seems like faithlessness to tear them away."

"That is a remnant of the fever," said the old man. "Ah, Helga, how happy should I be if you were yourself again !"

"And I too, dear father," said Helga, with a gentle sigh.

"I know one way of curing you, and if you love me you will try it."

"That I will, father."

"Do you promise it, my Helga ?"

"Yes, dear father," she answered unhesitatingly.

"Then listen : Olaffson is good and brave, is he not ?" Helga nodded. "He loves you dearly, and my most cherished wish is that you should become his wife, and that you should live under my roof, brightening my old age with the sight of your happiness."

Helga grew deadly pale.

"Ah, father, dear father, I cannot."

"Why not, Helga ? Have you anything against him ? Is he not young, handsome, and strong ? Is he not brave and good ? Could you find me a better son, or yourself a more loving husband ? Tell me, are you influenced in this matter by those foolish dreams, the wild images of your brain ? Tell the truth, Helga."

She looked at him in trembling entreaty.

"Ah, my father, forgive me."

"If you want to make your old father happy, say Yes, and become Olaffson's wife ; if you wish to poison my last days with sorrow, then leave my wish unfulfilled."

With these words the old man turned away in anxious grief, and moved towards the house.

Helga hastened after him.

"Do not be angry, my father," she begged; "I will fulfil your wish, come what will."

"I thank you, my good child; but what do you fear? What could come of it but a father's blessing, with its fruits of happiness and peace?"

So Helga became Olaffson's wife.

Did the Flower of Iceland now regain its freshness and bloom? Alas! no. In spite of her father's tenderness and her husband's love, she still remained sorrowful and pale; deeper, if anything, was the shadow that oppressed her soul. To longing was now added remorse, the bitterest feeling that can disturb a human heart, for it is the only one for which time has no balm.

"How could I ever rob you of your claim to immortality?" she had once said to the poor fairy king; and even though the words had been only spoken in a dream, yet they burned into her soul, and when she consented to be Olaffson's wife, it seemed to her as if she had really shut out that poor spirit from the heavenly paradise.

The short summer passed, and Helga shuddered more than ever under the icy breath of the northern winter; but it too went by, and spring came at last across the ocean to Iceland's snowy plains. The roads were once more passable, and the first sacrament of the year was to be solemnised in the church of the parish to which the farm held by Helga's father belonged. Olaffson asked his wife to partake with him of the sacred symbols, and she gladly consented. Perhaps she thought this feast of reconciliation might bring back her long-lost peace.

She went about her work with more energy than she had shown for many months, so anxious was she to have everything in readiness for the morrow, for they would have to set out early in order to reach the distant church in time for the service. She was just laying the table for supper when she saw her husband passing the window, and by his side a stranger of tall and manly form.

"See, Helga," said Olaffson as they entered, "I bring an honoured guest; set out your best provisions, for he has travelled far, and is in need of refreshment."

Helga looked at the stranger. His face was handsome, but over his youthful features sorrow had passed with heavy hand. But when he raised his deep blue eyes to Helga, and asked in soft and melodious tones—"Will the Flower of Iceland permit a stranger to rest beneath her roof?" a shudder passed through her frame, and the old conflict began in her soul more wildly and perplexingly than ever.

These eyes, this voice, could they have spoken to her only in a feverish dream? And if she had been deceived—what then? The thought threatened to rob her of reason; but Olaffson stepped up to her and said—

"Our guest must be tired and hungry, my Helga; will you not grant him the welcome which the stranger has always met beneath this roof?"

Helga recovered herself by a great effort, and went out to prepare a room for the mysterious guest, while the latter sat down at table with the others. Then she slipped softly back, took a seat in a dark corner, and gazed with mingled anxiety and longing on the stranger's face.

"Look here, sir," said Helga's father, pointing to the sky, "do you ever see anything like that in your native land? Do you not acknowledge Iceland to be the most beautiful country in the world?"

"Yes," said the stranger, "your land is indeed beautiful; but your home and mine are not so very far distant from one another."

He glanced at Helga—of whose presence the others were not aware—then he described the land in which he lived, the same land that Helga was said to have seen only in the delirium of fever.

She listened with breathless attention. It seemed to her as if the splendour of fairyland once more surrounded her. She saw the blue waves rolling at her feet, and felt herself, as in days gone by, rocking on their gleaming crests. She ran merrily to the side of the fountain and caught at the water, that she might sprinkle it in sport on the birds; and she saw the transparent flowers bending their fragrant cups in friendly greeting. Every moment she expected to see the stranger throw aside his disguise, and, standing before her in royal purple, touch the long-disused strings of his golden harp.

Alas! her father had then deceived her that he might keep her at home; her heart had told her the truth, and she, instead of listening to its entreaties, had weakly yielded to persuasion, and broken her sacred promise. And now? Too late, too late—all was over. Full of grief and despair, she hastened out of the house to pour out her heart in bitter weeping amid the stillness of the night.

Next morning, when all was ready for the journey, when the horses were stamping impatiently before the door, the family all assembled to conform to an old Icelandic custom. In that island, before any family partake of the sacrament, each member asks forgiveness of all the rest for wrongs consciously or unconsciously committed. Helga took her father's hand and her husband's. " Forgive me for all the anxiety I have caused you," she begged in a low voice; then she added the mysterious words, "and also for the sorrow that I am about to bring upon you."

" You must also ask forgiveness of our guest, Helga, in case you have offended him," said Olaffson. " You were not to be found yesterday when he wanted to bid you good-night."

She shuddered, cast a farewell glance on her father's face, and moved towards the stranger's room.

Yes, it was as she felt and knew. The dark garment of yesterday had disappeared; before her stood the fairy king in radiant beauty, with his golden hair flowing down over his purple robe.

She clasped her hands in silent entreaty, and her beautiful eyes looked up with love and humility to the face of her beloved but deeply-wronged husband.

" Helga, Helga," said he gravely, " is this how you have been faithful to your love and your promise ?"

" Oh, do not be angry with me," begged Helga; " to

your spirit-eye nothing has been hidden ; you know how it all came about—how my anxiety for you drove me to seek you—how my father found me, and how I was going to show him our kingdom in order to set his mind at rest.   You know that the gates were closed against me, and that I was borne back unconscious to my old home— that they kept me there by cleverly-invented stories, and that at last my father's entreaties forced me to the last and hardest step.   But you know also that I have loved only you, that my heart is yours alone."

"Be judged by thine own words, O Flower of Iceland!" replied the fairy king quietly.   "Why didst thou not listen to the voice of thy heart?   We fairies know nothing of human weakness, therefore we cannot forgive it.   Dost thou know the fate that now awaits thee, Helga ?"

"I know it well," answered Helga firmly, "and if my mouth has been unfaithful, my heart has been true.   I welcome death, for it will reunite me to you !"

Then a happy smile passed over the fairy king's noble countenance ; he stretched out his arms, and pressed Helga dying to his heart.

Finding that his wife did not come back, Olaffson hastened with his father-in-law to the stranger's room. They found fair Helga in the fairy king's arms.   Both were cold and dead ; in the same moment both hearts had broken.   Olaffson tried to take Helga away from the stranger's arms, but in vain.   What life had robbed him of, he held in death with a grasp that could not be loosed.

"Leave them, my son," said the old grief-stricken father ; "she is his by right.   What has all our prudence done for us ? Worse than nothing! The fairy king has reclaimed his own in spite of us."

They laid them in the same coffin, and next morning the soil of Iceland was to receive them into its cold lap. But in the night that followed this eventful day, sleep fell more heavily than usual on the eyes of the mourners. They did not hear the whispering of gentle voices or the hasty tread of many feet. They did not see the multitude of fairies who had assembled from all parts of the island to show the last honour to their beloved king. Noiselessly the spirits lifted the coffin, carried it out of the house, and away to the rock where fair Helga had begged in vain for admission.

To-day it was not denied her. The magic gates sprang open as the coffin approached. With drooping wings the white birds hovered round, and mourned the royal pair in notes of soft lamentation.

At the shore of the beautiful blue sea the faithful spirits lowered their burden. There Helga and her fairy husband rest beneath the flowers of this paradise, and beside the gentle murmur of the waves. On the branches of the cypress that grows on their grave hangs the fairy king's harp. The hand is cold that once touched its chords ; but when the morning breeze sweeps through them, they sound as of old in magic melody. The sweet notes float on the sunbeams through the evergreen paradise, pierce the hard rock, and hover as beautiful and undying legends over Iceland's heaths and snow-clad hills.

L

THE OLD MAN BESIDE THE CORPSE OF
ANTONIO.

THE SEA-FAIRY.

THE evening sun was sinking in a glow of colour on the waters of the North Atlantic and on the rocky coast of Norway as a youth wandered alone by the edge of one of its numerous fiords.

He was alone in the world; father and mother, brothers and sisters, were all dead, and he strove to still the longings of his heart by the wonders of foreign lands.

He had seen the midnight sun from the cliffs of the

North Cape, and his eye now rested in astonished admiration on the firmament and the ocean, which shone in a splendour unknown to other zones. He stepped close up to the edge of the sea, and looked down at the waves, which here broke in gold-sparkling foam. But from yon rock but a few yards distant he would be better able to enjoy the ever-changing play of the waves; so he went up to it, and laid his hand on one of its jagged projections to aid him in climbing. Then he saw something white and golden gleaming at his feet, and when he leant forward to observe it more closely he saw that it was the form of a young woman who was sitting in solitude on this uninhabited strand. Over her garment, white as spring blossoms, down to the purple hem, fell hair golden as the waves at her feet, and her tender hands lay clasped upon her knee, while she, dreamy and motionless, looked out upon the sea.

The young man scarcely ventured to breathe lest he should frighten her; but a stone loosened beneath his hand and rolled rattling to the ground. She looked up and turned her head, and now his glance met a face of unimagined beauty.

"Who art thou?" she asked, in gentle astonishment; "and what seekest thou here on this world-forsaken shore?"

"I wished to see the beauties of Norway," he gathered courage to answer, "and I found them greater than I expected. But who art thou, wondrous being, who venturest to stay alone in this solitude, with none save the ocean and yon stern rocks to bear thee company?"

"I am the sea-fairy," she answered gravely. "The golden evening sunshine, which streamed down into my castle, enticed me to the strand, as it has done many a time before. But thou art the first mortal that I have seen here for thousands of years."

He did not answer, but gazed dreamily on her lovely form. In his soul the fairy tales of childhood shone dimly forth—tales of the crystal castle under the sea, and of the fascinating beauty of the sea-fairy; and now, could these have been no fables, but reality—sweet tangible reality?

For a moment he covered his eyes with his hand, and looked again. No, she had not vanished. The rosy light of the evening sun lay now on her white garment, and her beautiful form seemed still more lovely in this radiance. She rose slowly, and apparently with the intention of going away to the waves, when such burning pain came in the young man's soul that he took his hand from the point of the rock and stepped respectfully, but with firm tread, up to the beautiful lady.

"No, do not go," he begged, raising his hand in earnest entreaty; "do not go, thou vision of my childhood. But if thou canst not tarry longer here, then take me down into thy ocean kingdom. There is no one on earth to miss me; and now that I know that thou really dwellest beneath these waves, I shall feel an unappeasable longing after thee, as in the days of my childhood, when I lay for hours on the shore of my native land hoping to catch a glimpse of the pinnacles of thy castle."

The fairy stood still, and her eye, blue and fathomless

as the ocean at the horizon, looked in the young man's face as if to read his soul.

"Knowest thou what thou askest?" she said earnestly. "If I grant thy petition and take thee with me, it is for no short amusement, which thou canst leave when tired, and wander further at thy will. No; if thou go with me it is to stay in my kingdom, and only with thy life wilt thou be permitted to release thyself from thy vow. Consider it well. In thy veins flows the blood of a faithless race; but we are of a different nature. Ingratitude and faithlessness we punish severely, and our heart knows no weak pity for those who incur our wrath."

"Try me, lady," said the youth, with firm determination. "Take me with thee, and let me serve thee and surround thee with love and obedience; and if thou find me faithless, spare not thine anger."

"Come then," said the sea-fairy, "and forget not that it is thine own choice." And Antonio, for that was the young man's name, walked joyfully beside the wondrous woman towards the waves. She loosed the star-set girdle from her dress, and gave it to the youth. "Put it on," she said, "that those beneath the waves may recognise thee as one of mine;" and he did as she bade him. Then she gave him her hand, and stepped out upon the sea, which grew smooth beneath her foot as a path of crystal. Antonio followed joyfully; the magic girdle prevented him from sinking, and when the shore lay a few steps behind them, the glittering plain opened and disclosed a glassy stair that led down into the depths of the ocean kingdom. Did he step down on them, or did they, rising upwards, offer themselves to his foot? He could not make out how it was, for, now that he was led by the fairy's hand and girt with her girdle, earthly laws had no longer power over him. He only knew that they were descending into the water with marvellous swiftness, and that the waves of the Gulf Stream, which flows with the warmth of spring around these coasts, played softly round his head and shoulders, while he breathed among them as freely as on the air above. And when he looked upwards he saw the crystal steps break and form again into waves as soon as the foot left them, and above his head the sea heaved as was its wont, the great waves following one after the other with a glorious play of ever-changing colours.

Soon he stood at the bottom of the sea; and here there was nothing dark or gloomy, as we are apt to think, but all around the reflection of the evening sky lit the clear depths with golden light.

"Now thou art in my kingdom," said the sea-fairy; "forget not that it is the home of thine own choice."

His eyes shone as he gave a joyful assent. "His home!" And he would never long for another; of that he was quite sure.

They walked together over the soft, shining, golden sand. Not far off purple trees rose on their slender stems, and sent their wide branches out on every side.

"That is my coral park," said the sea-fairy; "it stands in wide circles round the ocean castle, and keeps the wild waves far from this retreat."

Soon they stood at the gate of the magic hedge, and

the fairy laid her hand upon the rock. Suddenly an electric current seemed to stir the whole line of trees. Thousands of little slumbering creatures awoke, and stretched their tiny heads out of the openings between the branches to greet their lady. She, meantime, walked with Antonio through the intricate paths of the coral grove, till they·reached the shining plain where the castle of the sea-fairy stood. Its lofty walls were crowned by a glittering roof, over which the waves glided to and fro with softest music.

Antonio gazed in happy astonishment on the radiant edifice, which excelled in beauty all the childish dreams of which it reminded him.

"And may I stay here? and shall I never be obliged to leave this splendour?" he asked in a gentle whisper; but before the fairy could answer there was a trembling in the waves around. Over the transparent roof, and out of the shadows of the coral grove, came myriads of little star-fishes of violet and rosy hues, and played round the head of Antonio and among the sea-fairy's locks like butterflies on a summer day. Then they fluttered away again, and lost themselves in the trembling dance of the waves.

The beautiful lady, still carefully keeping hold of Antonio's hand, walked now over the watery meadow which surrounded the castle with its gentle waves; and when she reached the high-arched portal the transparent gates opened of themselves, and the empress of the ocean entered her enchanted palace.

Antonio's eye was dazzled by the splendour all around.

Hall after hall followed in brilliant succession, and over all stretched the high arches of the crystal roof, through which the evening sky shed its undiminished splendour. Warm and soft as the breath of spring, the little waves glided through these enchanted rooms and fell back with gentle splashing from the crystal walls—now shining like a flood of crimson, now azure blue, and now like liquid amber; thus they mirrored the changing play of colours in the fleeting clouds overhead.

The sea-fairy looked into Antonio's joyous face. "Thinkest thou that thou canst forget thine earthly home here in my kingdom?" she asked graciously.

" Forget it?" he replied. "If home is the fairest spot on earth, then I have only found mine now. Henceforth all other places lie eternally forgotten. But what is that yonder?" he asked, pointing to tall green pillars whose tops reached nearly to the crystal roof.

" See for thyself," said the sea-fairy, and he moved by her side towards the last hall in which the graceful columns stood. And now he glides between their slender shafts, and utters a joyous cry as he looks up at the transparent dome, beneath which leafy tree-crowns waved, while little star-fishes gleamed brightly as they glided among the leaves.

" Palm trees!" cried Antonio, breathless with astonishment—" palm trees, such as I have heard rustling by the banks of the Ganges! This must be some delusion, some golden dream, out of which I must sooner or later wake. No, no, there are the tender lianas winding round the kingly stems, and there in the shadow lurks my lotos

ANTONIO IN THE CRYSTAL CASTLE.

F. C., p. 178.

flower, the most beautiful of all the gorgeous blossoms of India!"

He dropped the fairy's hand, hastened forward, and looked into the shining cup, whose purple streamers trembled in the waves.

"Yes, indeed, it is the lotos, gleaming in snowy purity like its sisters in the holy stream, in whose cup the goddess slumbers. But oh! how camest thou hither, beloved flower? But what do I ask? The holy river of thy favoured home has caught thy falling seed and borne it onwards to the sea, and there on its protecting wave thou hast been rolled on and on, further and further, towards the south-west, till the warm Gulf Stream received thee. Carried northwards by this current of blessing which careful Nature sends to these icy realms, thou camest with broken palm branches and liana sprays into this northern fairyland, where the hand of the beauteous sea-fairy gave thee a second home—one beautiful enough to make thee forget even the sunny plains of India."

Did the lotos flower think so? Its trembling cup gave no reply, but Antonio thought it did. Henceforth the kingdom of the sea-fairy should be his home, and she herself be dear to him as his father and mother used to be in the old half-forgotten days. His happiness seemed full as he moved by her side through the wide watery realm from one wonder to another, while her grave but beautiful mouth explained to him with easy eloquence the mysteries of the deep, problems in the solution of which curious men spend their lives in vain.

Round them played the gay star-fishes; beside them, on the gleaming sand, thorny ray-fishes rolled like silver balls; behind them followed, in many-coloured throng, the fishes large and small, their fins and scales sparkling in the sunlight like silver and precious stones. They glided fearlessly around Antonio, let him catch and stroke them, and looked up at him with intelligent eyes when he spoke to them in human words. They did not indeed comprehend what he said, but they all understood the star pattern on the girdle, which still surrounded his waist with its radiant circle, and made him known as the friend of their beloved mistress.

Yes, it was pleasant to glide through the waves, with beauty, peace, and harmony all around; but Antonio thought it more delightful still to wander with the majestic fairy through the halls of the crystal castle, to be lifted by gentle waves up to the lofty dome, and to look up through its clear vault to the bright sky far overhead.

But Antonio's happiest moments were spent in the hall of palms, as he rested in the shady corner where the lotos bloomed. The flower would bend its white cup over his dreamy eyes, and the waves moved the purple stamens over his brow as gently as his mother's hand. The water flowed about him soft and warm, high overhead the palm trees waved their leafy tufts, and the sea-fairy glided through the brilliant halls, singing to her golden harp songs sweeter and more enthralling than anything Antonio had ever heard on earth. Is it any wonder then that he forgot his bleak, unmusical home— that he never gave it one longing thought?

The summer sun had often sent its golden light, unbroken by night's darkness, into the sea-fairy's kingdom; the stars of the winter sky had often twinkled through the crystal roof of the ocean palace; but Antonio had taken no heed to the flight of time. The years passed over him in pleasant but monotonous repose; the little waves rippled and sang with unchanging cheerfulness; and Antonio hastened from pleasure to pleasure, without remembrance, without longing, feeling only the present delight.

The sunlight of a new summer was making its way into the ocean realm when Antonio came out of the palace and walked through the gleaming water-meadows. The fairy had been called to a distance by some business in a remote part of her extensive kingdom, and Antonio had thus been left alone in the castle. But the splendid halls seemed to him only half as beautiful without their lovely queen, and he determined to seek the society of the merry fishes without. They came swimming to meet him, slipped through his fingers, splashed the water merrily with their fins and tails, and formed themselves into a wide and brilliant procession behind him as he walked.

Soon the oddly-jagged branches of the coral grove arched above his head. He intended to-day to explore every corner of this lovely park, of which he had hitherto seen but one spot. He went further and further into the maze of trees, and the fishes followed him at every step and glided like silver stars through the deep red branches.

Antonio looked back; the bright sunny plain and the

gleaming palace had disappeared, hidden by the dense grove of coral; but to the side at the outer edge of the forest he heard a sullen, ceaseless roaring, for the ocean billows rolled high and dark beyond the magic circle.

He went further; everything became strange and awful. There was not a glimpse of the bright familiar regions he knew so well. Purple twilight lay around him, and to the side the darkly rolling ocean; but there before him was a faint glimmering of light which became gradually brighter. Could it be the crystal castle which he thought he had left far behind?

At last he reached the light, and looked down on the scene at his feet. Before him lay an open space, over which the sunlight streamed, unhindered, in golden radiance, and under this flood of sunshine rested rows of pale, silent sleepers, heart to heart and arm in arm, as the rage of the ocean or the anger of the sea-fairy had torn them away from their full, warm, joyous life. They had sailed fearlessly in their trusty ships over the sea, perhaps even rejoicing in their nearness to the haven, and in the prospect of happy meetings, when they were suddenly shattered by a hidden reef, or dragged downward by the treacherous whirlpool.

Antonio walked with loudly-beating heart among the sleepers. Here lay an old man with long and silvery hair, and his withered hand rested tenderly on the head of a beautiful boy; beside him lay a man, whose youthful wife, even in the death-struggle, had not loosed her hold on her tender infant; there slept two stalwart youths, their hands clasped as in strong affection—they were brothers, as the likeness of the features showed. And there—and there—and there, wherever Antonio's glance fell, lay forms once beautiful in their youthful strength, now cold and stiff in death. And yet they only seemed to be asleep, for, however long they might have rested there, time had made no ravages among them. Their features were unchanged, save for a deeper peace; and when the coral branches overhead rocked in the waves, sending their purple shadows over the lonely ocean graveyard, there fell on the faces of the dead something like the reflection of their former life.

Antonio bent over them, as if to read the last sad thought of the pale lips—to learn the last unspoken wish, that he might take it with him as a solemn vow, and fulfil it as soon as he could reach the upper world. For the spell of the ocean kingdom was broken at the sight of these white faces, and he longed now for his home, bleak and unmusical though it was. With a deep sigh he took his eyes from this sad scene, and advanced to the outer edge of the coral grove, where the lofty branches bent and formed a low network, which divided the resting-place of the dead from the raging ocean. He leant with folded arms against the fence, and looked out on the billowy sea. The huge waves rose black as thunder-clouds, hurled their white froth toward heaven, and sank with sullen roar back into the deep. It was a scene of fascinating horror, and Antonio could not tear his eyes away.

Then suddenly northwards through the surging waves came something strange, dreadful, horrible. Its long outstretched serpent neck was of changing green, and its wide gaping throat was full of sharp destructive teeth; its gigantic body wound dark through the flood—now drawn together, now stretched out in its immeasurable length, so that even the lifeless waves shrank back, and Antonio's heart almost ceased to beat with dread amazement. Thus the monster of the deep rose in slow but ceaseless movements, and its threatening head was raised above the foaming heaps of water beside the coral fence just as Antonio caught the first glimpse of its poisonous tail.

"It is the sea serpent," he faltered at last, as soon as he recovered his power of speech—" the monster of which the fairy told me that death and destruction follow in its wake. The poor sailors up above on the surface of the water, who have perhaps laughed and mocked at it as an exploded fable, will now see and feel it in the last terror of the death-struggle." And he clasped his hands tightly as he gazed upwards in an agony of fear.

Suddenly a wide shadow darkened the waters, covering with its gloomy wing the purple fence and the golden waves that flowed above the dead. Antonio sought for the cause of this phenomenon, and saw far above in the surging sea a low rock which he had not noticed before. Whether the wild waves had torn it from the coast and driven it hither, or whether the storm had forced it up from the bed of the ocean, he knew not; but there it stood, dark and immovable, with the waves dashing over it, and the sea serpent gliding round it in foaming coils.

Now he knew for what end the ocean was preparing

all its horrors. There, from the south, came a ship with well-filled sails, of firm, substantial build, and guided by a skilful hand; it seemed to mock at the terrors of the deep, for the deadly rock and the lurking serpent were hidden beneath the water; the huge waves surged above both, and covered them with their foam.

The captain of the stately vessel saw the heaving waves, but he knew the powers of his noble ship. With flashing eye he stood on the deck, calming the passengers with cheerful words, and shouting his orders to the nimble sailors. He steered his ship confidently right over the familiar track, in the midst of which the treacherous rock lay waiting his approach.

Antonio watched the ship's advance. His terror-sharpened eye distinguished every mast, every plank. It seemed to him as if he saw smiling, happy, unsuspecting faces bending over the side and nodding friendly greetings to him in his calm, safe depths below. He wrung his hands in despair, and cried in his loudest voice, "Steer to the left; oh! steer to the left, for to the right lurks double death." But the next wave drowned the cry, and granted him not even the faintest echo.

Now, now must the end come—unavoidable and dread. Antonio covered his eyes in trembling anguish. A sudden crash, one single piercing scream, which with awful clearness rose above the roar of the ocean and the hissing of the serpent, trembled through the waves, and thrilled through Antonio's loudly-beating heart. His hands fell from his blanched face, and he looked up through the sea.

The waves still rolled, the rock still stood in dreadful gloom, the serpent still wound its frightful coils, but the scattered planks of the broken vessel were driven round and round by the mad whirlpool, and those who a moment before had smiled in the fulness of life and happiness now wrestled with the waves. Strong men among them, who would not part from life without a struggle, grasped after floating planks, raised themselves above the waves, and looked round for their dear ones. But the sea serpent came darting over the white-crested billows, struck with its tail the floating timbers, and sent their trembling burden down to the hungry depths.

Happy were those who, already choked by the water, had sunk down unconscious to the bed of the ocean, there to slumber undisturbed. The survivors were the prey of the monster. With its tail curled in horrid rage, its green eyes flashing, and its vast jaws gaping wide, it darted on every man whose powerful arm and stout heart would not give up the struggle with the waves, and in a moment his death-cry was lost in the sea serpent's horrid throat. With insatiable rage it glided from one to another till all had perished, and not one was left to carry home the dreadful tale. None would ever know the fate of the goodly vessel and its precious freight.

Antonio had sunk on his knees, and his eyes had followed every motion of the sea serpent till the dreadful work was done.

When all was over, the sea serpent rocked itself in horrid satisfaction on the waves, and let them drive it at their will. But the dark rock retained the power of motion, and sank slowly down into the deep, making the waves foam and toss as they parted right and left to let it pass. Then Antonio perceived that what at a distance he had taken for a rock was a gigantic kraken, one of those sea monsters which often lie quietly for years at the bottom of the ocean, then rise to the surface and lurk with deadly purpose in the path of unsuspecting men. He saw the supple, far-reaching polypus-arms, which, grasping at the masts, had cracked them like reeds, and torn the planks asunder with swifter and more complete destruction than the mere force of the waves could have accomplished. The snaky limbs were feeling aimlessly about the flood, groping down towards the soft sea-bed where the monster would now fasten itself for a long period of repose.

Antonio involuntarily shrank back, although the ocean, with its billows and its still more dreadful monsters, could not break through the coral fence or disturb the sparkling waters of the Gulf Stream. He watched the kraken reach the bottom, settle down in its soft bed, and draw in its long arms as for sleep. Then all became peaceful as before.

The wild waves sank to rest, and the ocean flowed still and clear; a deep blue sky arched overhead, the sun shot golden glances through the billows, piercing to the lowest depths, and dyeing with amber light the waves that flowed above the kraken, which lay like a long dark hill not far from the coral fence, and parted from it by a narrow current.

M

Antonio stepped back hesitatingly to the fence, and looked through. On the sea-monster's back waved a forest of tall grass wrack, which had taken root there during its long years of inaction. Through the waving blades little fishes and sea-urchins glided fearlessly, and lazy turtles crept along in the shade. But in the midst, as in a nest of brown moss, lay something like a swan of dazzling whiteness, with lifeless outstretched wings. Antonio was gazing fixedly on this object, when a gleaming wave swept through the grass wrack, and raised the dead swan's limbs. The next loosed it from its dreadful resting-place, and bore it into the current which flowed towards the place of the dead.

Nearer and nearer floated the bird, till it struck against the coral network, and Antonio stretched out his arms to grasp it. Then he saw that it was no swan, but a lovely maiden in a wide flowing garment, whom the waves had hurled down from the ship to the sea monster's back, and who had thus been borne to her grave. With a sorrowful heart he caught her in his arms, lifted her through the coral fence, and carried her to where the dead lay in their peaceful resting-place. There he laid her by the old man's side, knelt beside the dead maiden, and arranged the long fair hair, tossed by the waves, around the pale but lovely face, and folded her marble hands as if in prayer.

The last duty was fulfilled, and he would now have been free to return to the crystal castle, there to revel in new joy and splendour, but he still knelt beside the maiden's corpse, looking dreamily into the still, white face

as one looks into a dim, far distance. He knew that
from her sleep there was no awaking; for in these deep
waters no living thing could breathe save one that wore,
like him, the sea-fairy's girdle; she was dead, and must

ANTONIO LAYS THE DEAD MAIDEN IN HER LAST RESTING-PLACE.

slumber on till the resurrection morn. The eyes remained closed, and the mouth could never smile again,.
yet Antonio gazed at it as if it were about to tell him
some dear familiar tale—perhaps the story of his own
life. Antonio knew the sweet, innocent, tender face, but

the flood of fear and horror which had raged for hours in his soul had confused his memories, and he only felt that the eyes and mouth now so firmly closed in death had once smiled at him in love and friendship.

At last he rose, cast a last look on the lines of sleepers, stepped back into the coral grove, and made his way through the shadowy paths back to the sea-fairy's castle.

His ocean vision had lost its charm, the paradise of his childish dreams was laid in ruins; the sunny waves, which so short a time before had played around him with the soft warmth of summer breezes, felt now so cold that he shuddered, and his breathing became laboured and painful.

Again he rested in the hall of palms, and the stamens of the lotos-blossom floated caressingly over his temples, in which the blood now flowed more quickly, for the death-cry of the sinking crew still rang in his ears, and before his eyes hovered the pale, beautiful image of the dead maiden.

Where, ah! where had he seen those features? He looked up into the waving summits of the palms. Could it have been on the banks of the Ganges that such a mouth had smiled at him, from the band of Hindu girls who passed him every evening with pitchers on their heads on their way to fetch water from the sacred stream? No, no, it was not there, nor in any of the favoured countries of the new world, that he had seen that face, for there the maidens' hair was of a darker hue. No ; no foreign land had ever shown him those sweet features, and his thoughts turned to his old, half-forgotten home.

The palm-trees beneath the crystal dome changed as he gazed into the old wide-spreading lime-tree in his father's garden, and the song of the waves in the fairy halls sounded in his ear like the tones of the little organ which his father played at evening when the day's work was done.

Antonio closed his eyes. Was it to call up more easily the old long-forgotten scenes, or to hide the hot tears which started to his eyes? It seemed to him as if he lay once more on the round bench below the lime-tree, with his head on his tender mother's lap, and her soft hand upon his brow; above him rustled the lime leaves, and through the open windows floated the soft notes of his father's evening song. Antonio lay there listening in silence. His mother sat with a happy smile on her loved face, and by her side Antonio's old teacher, on whose lips he and his wild companions hung in rapt attention, as he told them of the strange lands which he had visited in his youth.

Oh, what a flood of memories rushed over Antonio's heart!—music and fragrance, his mother's gentle hand, and the old man's wonderful descriptions; and in the midst of all a tender, fairy-like child, in a soft white dress and golden hair, who flitted like a sunbeam through the garden paths! When she had gathered enough flowers, she came softly up, sat down at her father's feet, and wove a garland; Antonio kept his eyes closed, not to sleep, but to listen undisturbed. The little one, thinking him asleep, rose softly and placed the garland on his brow. Then he caught her hands, and playfully held her fast; but she bent over him till her fair locks touched his cheeks and whispered, " Be quiet, Tony; thy father is telling a story, and does not like to be interrupted;" and she looked down at him and smiled.

The riddle was solved at last. It was she. It was the sweet child to whom his wild boyish heart had gone out in tender love, and whose image had gone with him into distant lands till it faded before the brilliant, ever-changing scenes through which he passed. But now it stood before him in its old beauty, and he loved her as though they had parted yesterday—now, when she lay cold and stiff among the dead.

He rose, clasped his hands in anguish, and looked up at the crystal roof, through which the evening sky sent all the bright hues of a northern sunset. But all that he had loved to look on here had no beauty for him now. Within was melody and song and unearthly splendour; without, death, horror, and unutterable grief. He sprang up, ran as if hunted through the glittering halls, and out to the plain before the castle; but the floods which were wont to send fragrance and song and radiance to hail his coming seemed to him now filled with deadly darkness, and the sound of their waves was like suppressed sobbing.

He turned away shuddering, and, for the first time since he came to the fairy's kingdom, he directed his steps to the coral gate which parted the Gulf Stream from the darker billows of the ocean. He passed out, and walked in gloomy silence over the sand, which to-day seemed to have lost its golden glitter. Soon he stood at.

the spot where the crystal steps ended, and he looked up longingly through the heaving flood.

"Oh that I could return just once to the free fresh air," he sighed—"to my old forsaken home!" And his wish was fulfilled, for he still wore the starry girdle which made the elements obedient to his will. The waves parted like the petals of a lily, and formed themselves into glassy steps. With a shout of joy Antonio placed his foot on the lowest one, and he scarcely knew whether he moved himself or whether the water lifted him from step to step. He saw the blue waters become clearer and clearer, until he stood on the last step, his head rose above the waves, and he drew deep breaths of his native air.

With flashing eye and heaving breast Antonio looked westwards, where the sun's radiant ball rested on a bed of purple clouds, while the reflection fell in roseate and amber shadows over the whole heaven, and the distant billows flowed like a mantle of royal purple.

But the waves which bore Antonio to the strand dashed up golden spray just as on that summer evening when he descended to the fairy-land below the sea. There lay also the red rock at which he had first seen the fairy, and with a sigh he bent his steps in that direction. Was there not some one sitting there now? Antonio shaded his eyes with his hand, for he was still dazzled by the unaccustomed light. It was no illusion. There, where the fairy once sat, was to-day a bent and aged figure, and instead of the golden locks flowed silvery hair about the temples.

" A human being !" was Antonio's first ecstatic thought as he ran across the strand.

"Good evening, sir," he cried joyfully.

The old man raised his weary head, and his sad eyes rested with indifference upon the youth. But the last few hours had changed Antonio. The veil had fallen from his eyes and heart, and he saw now with the keen true eye of childhood. The hair on the old man's head had indeed grown whiter since he saw it last, and sorrow had graven its deep lines on the high forehead ; but it was the same clear-cut mouth to whose words Antonio had once listened with burning eagerness, and in the dark eyes still flashed something of the old fire. It was his aged teacher, the father of the pale, beautiful maiden among the dead in the ocean depths.

" Do you not know me, revered sir ?" asked Antonio, with faltering voice, as he bowed in courteous greeting.

The old man looked at him again.

" No," he said slowly, " I did not notice you among the crew ; but though you are a stranger, I am glad that you are saved. I thought I was the only survivor from the shipwreck."

" Look at me once more, sir," said Antonio, trying to steady his faltering voice, "and turn back a few pages in your life's history. Think of a little garden, and of an old lime-tree beneath whose leafy roof you often sat, while the sweet tones of an organ thrilled through the summer air.

The old man's eyes shone more brightly, and his lips trembled.

"Antonio!" he stammered out, "Antonio!" and his white head sank on the shoulder of his favourite pupil, who knelt before him with his arm wound in filial tenderness round the childless man.

"Oh, Antonio! I have lost my child to-day, only to-day. She would not let me go alone to the distant north, to which some luckless impulse drove me in my old age, and so she came with me on my toilsome journey. To-day we struck on a hidden reef, and the same wave which dashed her against the dark rock drove me, despite my struggling, on this barren strand, though I would fain lie with my darling child below the waves."

The old man covered his face with his hands, and Antonio did not venture on any words of consolation.

"If I could even find her corpse," said the poor old man at last, "I could bury her at home; but even the sad consolation of visiting her grave is denied me."

"She has found a better resting-place than you could give her," said Antonio—"she sleeps on a golden bed; a coral grove surrounds the spot; corruption has no power over her fair features, and no worm can touch her. Amid noble companions she slumbers, while the sunbeams kiss her snowy eyelids, and the warm waters of the Gulf Stream flow gently over her."

"How do you know all this, Antonio?" asked the old man in astonishment.

And Antonio told him about that evening when he met the beautiful sea-fairy at this very rock, and descended with her into her ocean kingdom, there to live in forgetfulness of home and friends, until, awakened by what he had seen and felt to-day, the old memories acquired new power over him, and throbbed more strongly than ever in his soul.

"What will you do now, my son ?" asked the old man.

"I will go home with you," Antonio answered promptly. "I will be to you a devoted and obedient son, if you will but let me."

The old man gazed at him with beaming eyes.

"Then let us go," he said, rising, "for I long to leave this place of horror. In a few hours we shall reach the little harbour in which we cast anchor yesterday evening, and there we can embark in a homeward-bound ship."

"Let it be as you will, my father," replied Antonio. "But one duty remains yet unfulfilled. If the sea-fairy had led me by deceit or violence into her kingdom, flight would be but right ; but I went of my own free will, bound myself to obedience and unchanging fidelity, and enjoyed her kindness and hospitality. It seems to me cowardly and ungrateful to go away secretly, without a word of thanks or of farewell, and the thought of this would destroy my happiness at home. To-day she is to return. I will go to meet her, tell her what broke the spell of her kingdom, and beg her to let me go in peace, and with her blessing. Wait for me here. The air of this zone is soft, and its night skies clear. Before the bright night changes to the brighter day, I will come back to leave you no more."

He kissed the old man's hand, and went towards the sea. Meantime the fairy had returned. The open coral gate and the empty halls of her palace told her that

Antonio was gone. Her soul was filled with grief and rage. He was one, indeed, of that faithless race whom she already knew and hated; but his eye and heart had still that divine image which she sought in vain among the cold, dumb creatures of the ocean, and in comparison with which the beauty and harmony of her fairy realm seemed poor and unsatisfying. He had become very dear to her. She had begun to believe in his fidelity. only to find herself once more deceived. But, as she had told him, the weak pity of mortals found no room in her heart. She did not complain, and no word of anger escaped her firm-set lips. She would go up to punish the faithless one, if he was still within her reach, according to her former threatenings.

She passed through the coral gate to the place where the heaving steps led to the world above. She beckoned, and the rocking staircase grew firm beneath her tread. Just as she set her foot on the first step, Antonio began to descend. They met half-way in the midst of the sea. Antonio trembled, as she stood before him in the full splendour of her magic beauty and her overwhelming majesty and might, and his soul shrank from her, and turned with ardent longing to his own loved home.

"Whence comest thou?" she asked sternly, although her keen ear heard the story of the last few hours in the louder beating of his heart. "Whence comest thou?" Then he gathered courage to tell her all, and begged her to let him go in peace.

"Rememberest thou not that summer evening when

thou insistedst on coming with me, notwithstanding my warning?" she asked in the same severe tone.

"Yes," Antonio faltered.

"And dost thou not remember my threat, and thy demand that I should punish thee if thou shouldst break thy faith?"

"I remember it all," Antonio said, with trembling lips.

"And in the face of all this dread and certain future dost thou still dream of leaving me?"

"I cannot do otherwise," he cried passionately; "the ocean kingdom has lost its charm since I have seen the gulf of irreconcilable enmity which divides it from my race—since it has robbed me of what was once my heart's dearest treasure. No, proud lady, let me go; I should be henceforth but a dismal guest."

Her eyes grew dark and fathomless as the deep sea beneath them.

"Go," she said slowly, "but first loose thy girdle."

He drew a deep breath of hope and delight, took the starry girdle from his waist, and gave it to the fairy. She took it, looked once more into his face, and glided down over the breaking steps.

Antonio turned to seek the upper world, but the stair above him had vanished, the step on which his foot rested melted from beneath him, and he found himself floating through the dark, deep waters. But the waves flowed no longer soft and free as spring breezes over his head and breast. With his girdle he had given up his power over them, and now he was but a weak mortal struggling with the raging elements. The waves roared round him, and tossed him hither and thither like a ball, while he strove in vain to breathe. He looked up to measure the distance, then he struggled with all the strength of despair against the waves. His young strong arm bore him upwards; once more he raised his head above the flood and breathed the air of heaven. His eye sought the red rock on which his old teacher sat, with his arms stretched out helplessly towards his adopted son, whose desperate struggles he had no power to help.

"I am coming, I am coming, my father," he cried confidently, but a giant billow swept over the youth and hurled him down into the boiling deep.

The evening hues were fading from the ocean, and the old man still stood beside the rock, his hands clasped, and his eyes gazing fixedly on the now tranquil deep. A dark object came floating from the west, and the waves left it on the beach almost at the old man's feet. He raised his dark eyes and looked at the motionless form, then he rose and walked with tottering footsteps to the spot. There lay Antonio, pale, cold, and dead. He had kept his word; before the bright night had passed into the brighter morning he had come back, but not as he had dreamed and hoped. The old man's trembling hands dug his grave at the foot of the red rock where Antonio had first seen the fairy. Then he turned his footsteps towards his distant, lonely home.

As soon as evening came again to visit earth and ocean, the sea-fairy rose through the waves, went up to the rock, and sat down beside the rock beneath which Antonio lay. There she sat, silent and motionless, her white hands lying idly in her lap, and her dreamy eyes looking out on the heaving billows ; but down her beautiful face ran great tears, that shone in the light of the setting sun, and told the pain that throbbed in her proud and lonely heart.

Not till the hues of evening gave place to the rosy tints of dawn did the sea-fairy go back to her ocean kingdom, never to return to earth.

No mortal eye has since beheld her, and the old saga of the sea-fairy is no longer heard along the coast of Norway.

Antonio's resting-place is desolate, as of old. It is known only to the Norwegian sky, which looks down brightily and sunnily upon it, and the little waves sometimes dash over it, sparkling like the sea-fairy's tears.

The Faithful Goblin.

CASTLE stood long years ago on a lofty hill in the old land of Hesse. Not a stone of its proud walls is now standing, and even its site is well-nigh forgotten by tradition; but in those days its high pinnacles were seen for miles over the country, and a haughty and noble race ruled in its halls.

The beams of the setting sun were falling through the little lead-framed window-panes into a round turret chamber, and rested on the fair hair of a lovely little girl. She was kneeling on an arm-chair beside the window, leaning her head on her little rounded arms, and weeping silent but bitter tears.

"Oh, Margaret, Margaret, why are you so long?" she cried at length, sobbing aloud, as she slipped down from her seat and ran to the door; but the massive door of the castle chamber was too high for the little hand to reach to open it, and the thick oaken panels kept any sound of her crying from reaching friendly ears.

Everybody was far away—everybody, even Margaret her nurse, who, forgetful of her duty, had left the child alone while she was watching what was going on at the splendid banquet which was being given to celebrate the betrothal of the eldest daughter of the noble house.

"Oh, Margaret, dear Margaret, come to your little Maude!" cried the child again, as she rose on tiptoe and tried to open the lofty door. But her efforts were in vain, her entreaties all unheard; and at last she went back to the window, for it was beginning to grow gradually dusk in the high-ceiled turret chamber. She climbed up again to the arm-chair, leaned her arm against the window-sill, and looked with silent weeping into the glowing red of the evening sky, where little white clouds were swimming like swans in a sea of crimson.

"Maude, Maude!" said a clear voice suddenly at the other side of the room.

The child turned her head in astonishment; at the fireplace there stood a little boy, not any bigger than herself, and with just the same lovely golden hair and rosy face. His coat was of red velvet, and his feet were encased in little buckskin boots, richly embroidered with costly pearls.

Maude's tears forgot to flow. Half terrified, half delighted, she kept her eyes fixed on the form of the beautiful little stranger, and at last she asked shyly, "Who are you, little boy, and how did you get in ? The door is still shut!"

The little fellow laughed merrily, and came towards Maude's chair.

"Ah, Maude! you have known me this long time. Just think now; doesn't Margaret always threaten to call me when you won't go to sleep at once at night ?"

"You don't mean to say you are Puck, our castle goblin, who has played so many tricks on people that everybody is afraid of him ?" asked the little girl quite fearlessly; "but they always speak of him as old and wrinkled."

"Yes, I am he," nodded the little boy; "but I only tease wicked people who tease me, and I am old and ugly only in their eyes. But I will not tease you, but serve you whenever I can, and play with you when Margaret leaves you alone, so that you need not be afraid of me. Would you like that, Maude ?"

"Indeed I should," said the child, with beaming eyes, "I am so often alone, now that dear mother is dead. Father is always out hunting. I am too little for my sisters, and Margaret so often goes to gossip with the other servants, and shuts me up here. She has been so long away now that I am hungry, and it is getting dark, and she is not coming with candles and supper."

"You shall have both immediately, Maude; just wait

N

a minute!" cried the little boy eagerly, as he hastened back to the fire, swung himself up by the iron bars, and climbed nimbly and easily up the chimney.

Maude had got down from her chair, and was standing in astonishment looking up after him.

"Oh! you will spoil your lovely coat, dear Puck!" she cried anxiously; but the only answer was a merry laugh from the goblin.   Then all was still, and the little fellow had vanished.

She stood with clasped hands, looking expectantly up the dark, strange road which little Puck had chosen. She felt that it was all so mysterious, and yet so delightful; it was just like waiting on Christmas Eve for the presents.   Then there was a rustling and clattering away high up, and quick as a squirrel the little fellow clambered down the sooty wall, and in a twinkling he laid his burden down before the astonished child.

"Just wait a minute," he cried merrily, "and you will see how light it will be!"

As he spoke he climbed up the wall, and in a moment the silver sconces were radiant with lighted wax candles.

The little girl clapped her hands in delight.

"That is not all," said the goblin with an air of importance; "just look here."

He opened the basket which he had brought with him. With magic quickness, the table was covered and set with the daintiest dishes.

Maude needed no pressing to taste them.

"Oh you good Puck," she said gratefully, "how kind you are to me!   Did Margaret give you all that?"

"Margaret, indeed!" answered the goblin, growling; "she has no time to think of you. She is too busy staring at what's going on, and tasting stolen bits."

"But who gave you all this—this delicious cake and this splendid pie? This must surely be the dish that Margaret says cook is so proud of!"

"Yes, that it is!" said the little fellow, nodding; "and the guests made such faces when it suddenly vanished from before their eyes that I nearly died with laughing at them—ha, ha, ha!"

"Vanished?" asked the child in astonishment.

"Yes, vanished!" laughed Puck; "do you think they would have given it of their own accord; I put on my cap, so that they did not see me, and then I packed up everything that I thought you would like."

Maude dropped the bit that she was just putting to her mouth, and gazed incredulously at her little friend.

"What do you mean?" she asked anxiously.

The little fellow laughed heartily.

"Look," said he, as soon as he was able to control himself; "do you see this little red cap? I have had it under my arm all the time I have been talking to you; now I am going to put it on!"

In a moment he had vanished from the child's sight—though she peered anxiously about the room, she could see nothing. Not a gleam of his red coat nor of his golden hair was to be seen at all, yet his clear laugh close beside her told her that he was there and as near as ever.

"Oh, Puck, dear Puck, don't play such tricks, please," she begged; "I am afraid when you do that."

That instant he stood again before her, handsome and merry, shaking his golden locks and smiling.

"You must not be frightened," he said soothingly; "I will always be visible for you, and my cap will only be used in your service. Now give me something to eat. No, not that cake! Break me some white bread into this dish, and pour some nice white milk over it; that's what I have been accustomed to for generations. In your great-grandfather's time the good maid used to leave me some every evening, and in return I used to help with all sorts of work about the house. Now, men are not so good-natured, and won't give me my dues, and so I don't care to be friendly with them."

"My good Puck," said the little girl, handing him his bowl, "you shall want for nothing now! I get white bread and milk every evening for supper, and I will always go shares with you."

Then the friends ate their supper with keen appetites, chatting all the while like old acquaintances. At last sleep overcame the tired child. Then Puck sat at the foot of her couch, and sang a strange, soft, sweet lullaby. As soon as Maude was asleep, the goblin busied himself in removing all the traces of their feast; and when Margaret returned late at night, with many misgivings about her neglected duty, she found the child in a quiet sleep, instead of being, as she feared, ready to receive her with bitter reproaches.

Margaret breathed more freely, and resolved to be more mindful of her charge in future. For a few days she kept her resolution faithfully, but she soon began to slip out in the twilight to chat with a friend, only for a few minutes, as she assured Maude. It was not long till the minutes became a half-hour, and in a week or two she had forgotten all her repentance and good resolutions, and poor little Maude would have had cause again for bitter tears if it had not been for her little friend.

Scarcely had the door closed after Margaret, when the goblin popped his fair head out of the chimney, and sprang into the room with a merry greeting. Then Maude would clap her hands with delight, for now began the pleasantest hour of the day. There was no end to the stories that Puck could tell for her entertainment. For hours together, while her nurse was away, the child sat motionless, with clasped hands, listening with bated breath to tales about days long gone by. For hundreds of years the little goblin had lived in the castle as an honoured member of the household, and his memory preserved more faithfully than the family chronicle the history of every individual of the long ancestral line. And before the astonished child the grave seemed opened, and the forefathers who had long since mingled with the dust all passed in the bloom of youth before her eyes. Then she would go to the ancestral hall, and standing before the pictures gaze at them, now in love, now in horror, for she knew the story connected with each one of the old portraits.

No one in the whole castle knew of the child's friendship with Puck. She was afraid that the servants might tease him if they knew of his presence, or perhaps drive him away, so she kept her secret carefully.

It was winter. The snow lay deep, the storm howled at night and whistled in the wide chimney, and the windows were covered with thick frost.

"Poor Puck," said Maude one evening, as the goblin came down the chimney, his teeth chattering with cold, "I cannot allow you to stay any longer up there. See, your hair is white with frost and snow, and you are trembling all over."

"Yes, yes," said the little fellow ; "it is very cold."

"Look here, then," said the child, going to her dolls' corner, and drawing aside the curtain ; "I have turned out the dollies. You shall have the big four-post bed, and in the day-time you can stay here too. I have set a little table and chair for you, so that you may have something like a little room till the summer comes."

So all winter long Puck crept at night into the warm, soft little bed, instead of springing back at Margaret's return up the cold dark chimney.

Spring came with its primroses and fleecy clouds, and then followed summer with its splendour of flowers in field and grove.

And now Maude and her nurse used to go out into the woods, to the child's intense delight. But one day Margaret found the sun too warm and the way too long for her lazy mood, and was easily persuaded to sit down and rest while Maude ran to gather wild strawberries.

Scarcely was she out of sight of her nurse when Puck, who had invisibly accompanied her, took off his cap, threw it into the air with a shout, and stood before his little friend laughing his own merry laugh. What delightful hours those were! What rich beds of strawberries Puck knew—what choice flowers he could find! Then, when the child was tired, she threw herself down on the moss, with Puck at her side, and they both gazed up into the green tree-tops.

The goblin understood the language of Nature. He heard what the trees whispered to each other about the trees of Paradise, with the golden stems and the flowers of precious stones; he understood the song of the nightingale as he sang to his mate about the beauty of the bird Phœnix and its undying youth; he saw the beetles gleaming in the grass, and heard even their soft sounds as they talked about their brothers in the distant Indies, whose wings gleam so like emeralds that the dark-eyed Hindoo women use them to deck their raven hair; and even the silent, lifeless stone had an intelligible language for Puck—it told him of the diamonds far away beyond the seas, which the poor slave seeks with eager eyes, trying to find one large enough to purchase his freedom. All this he understood, and told the child about it as she listened in silent rapture, and gazed up into the whispering trees.

Thus, in pleasant alternation, the seasons rolled by, and Maude blossomed into maidenly grace and loveliness. She had become her father's darling. Many an hour that he had formerly spent at the chase or at the wine-cup he now passed with his daughter, amused with her astonishing tales out of the family history. But she never would tell him how she got all her knowledge, for she shrank from bringing trouble on the faithful goblin, who still continued to be her friend, and the companion of her hours of solitude.

Maude's only unmarried sister, Gertrude, was about to be united to a brave young knight, whom she had chosen in preference to a powerful but universally dreaded Earl, whose castle stood at no great distance.

At the marriage, Maude appeared for the first time among the grown-up people, and, as befitted the occasion, she received as attendant page the son of a neighbouring nobleman, who, being an old friend of her father's, had allowed his son to come and learn knightly service in the household of Maude's father, preparatory to his filling an office in the Imperial Court. He was a handsome youth, a little older than his young mistress, with brown hair and dark, dreamy eyes, and Maude took an innocent pleasure in the beauty of her future attendant ; but Puck looked not well pleased when she told him about her new page.

"I will send him away if I don't like him," said he angrily.

"Oh no, dear, dear Puck, you must not do that !" said Maude coaxingly. "If you love me, be kind to him ; he is motherless, as I am."

But the little goblin was offended for the first time since the beginning of their friendship, and when Maude went to rest he refused the soft little doll's bed that had grown so dear to him, and sprang instead up the chimney to the top of the tower. There he sat looking gloomily up at the stars, and many were the sad thoughts that chased each other through his ancient breast.

Next morning, when Gero came to the turret chamber with a bouquet of flowers for his young mistress, he found Puck seated beside her in the window-sill watching her at her spinning. The goblin had put on his invisible cap at Gero's entrance, but it was of no avail, for the page had been born during the ember weeks, and could see the little fellow in spite of the charm.

"Why, Lady Maude," he cried in angry astonishment, "who is this that you have in your company? It cannot surely be one of the goblins who do so much mischief."

"Puck has been my friend and companion from my childhood up," said Maude, a little hotly; "and I have to thank him for many a pleasant hour."

"That may be," answered Gero, "but he must not take my place with my mistress. And now your palfrey is ready, and I will escort you on your ride."

Then the goblin's wrath broke loose. He called Gero a proud fool, and said he would not let him interfere with him. Then he followed Maude, who descended the winding turret stair, her mind full of distress at the discord between her companions. When she sprang to her saddle at the castle gate, Puck jumped up behind her, as was his wont, and went trotting merrily off with her down the mountain. But his pleasure was not to last long, for scarcely had they reached the broad, even road, when Gero rode up to the side of his lady's horse, caught little Puck suddenly, and set him before himself on his saddle.

The goblin would have been able easily to free himself

from the hand of the youth, if it had not been that Gero had wisely taken possession of the invisible cap, and all the little fellow's efforts to release himself only increased his tormentor's mockery. At last, when Gero set him down again at the castle gate, Puck clenched his little fist, and growled, " I will pay you back for this."

"GERO CAUGHT PUCK SUDDENLY AND SET HIM BEFORE HIM ON HIS SADDLE."

From this time on the page had little peace. At night Puck would slip into his room, and disturb his sleep with all sorts of malicious tricks ; and once he even lifted Gero from his bed, and laid him down close to the edge of the great well, hoping that, waking with a start, he might fall into the cold, deep water. Gero escaped the danger, but the adventure taught him to keep on terms of at least outward peace with his little foe.

Maude did her part towards preserving this show of

harmony by allowing Gero alone to accompany her when she went to walk or ride, and by granting the little goblin the old cosy morning and twilight hours.

Puck accepted this arrangement with some grumbling. When the hour came for the ride, he would mount to the top of the tower, and look after the riders, as they trotted along so cheerfully, with a sad look in his eyes.

"But he can't tell her stories like mine," he said exultingly; "no, he can't take my place there."

No indeed; the young page had never listened to the language of Nature, but he had delightful things to tell about tournaments and noble deeds, and the soft voice of the forest trees began to die gradually from the girl's soul, overpowered by the noise and bustle of life.

Very pleasantly the maiden's days went by. The morning hours in the turret chamber grew more and more dear to her; the rides in the green wood and the tales of the unknown world had every day new charms; and in the warm evenings her wise goblin friend used to tell her wonderful things about the stars, as the two stood on the top of the old tower watching the far-off lights peep out one by one.

One night, as she lay dreaming sweet dreams, woven out of memories of the day's delights, she was awakened by Puck's sudden call.

"Quick, quick! do you not hear anything?" cried the little fellow anxiously; "rise and flee for your freedom and your life."

Maude started up in terror.

"What is wrong?" she cried.

"The powerful Earl, whom your sister refused, has heard that your father is absent, and has come to take a mean revenge by robbing your father of his wealth and of his child."

"What am I to do, good Puck?" cried Maude in bitter anguish, clasping her trembling hands.

"Dress quickly, and let us go."

"Through the midst of the enemy?" asked the maiden, trembling, for she heard the oaken stairs creaking with the tramp of many feet.

"Yes, right through the midst of the enemy," said Puck, "but not without my cap. Cover me with your cloak, and put this on your head. Now, no one can see us."

So they passed unseen through the midst of the rough soldiers. Once Maude nearly betrayed herself when she saw Gero fighting single-handed against a multitude of foes. The winding stair that led to his lady's turret chamber was narrow enough to be defended by one, and with the courage of a lion he guarded the way to the place where he believed his precious charge to be.

How hard it was for Maude to keep from telling him that his efforts were needless! But Puck laid his little hand against her lips, and forced her to silence.

"Puck, dear Puck, can you not save him?" cried the maiden, in distress, when they were once outside the castle walls.

"Not till your safety is beyond a doubt," said the little goblin resolutely; "not till you are away in the depth of the forest, where they will never be able to find you."

With trembling haste Maude ran towards the wood, but the way was long, and her eager feet tottered under her. Turning to look towards the castle, she saw flames bursting from door and window. Still more anxiously she pressed on till the tall forest trees hid the castle from her sight. Even then Puck refused to leave her.

"Would Gero, who has, I confess, done his duty by you—would he, since he seems to love you, wish me to go back to save him a little trouble, and leave you unsheltered?"

Further and further they went through the very scenes where Puck had spent so many pleasant hours with his child-friend. But now, the trees that used to whisper so softly looked down like grim giants, and the night-wind in the branches howled "Flee!"

Suddenly a gleam of light broke on their path with a mild silvery radiance. A gentle murmur of water fell on the wanderer's ear, and in a few minutes they stood by the side of a valley, which here, forgotten by the world, lay like a home of peace in the heart of the forest.

There, in the shelter of a mossy rock, stood the cosy cottage of the old forest-warden. The moonbeams flashed back from the single window, and trembled on the stone bench before the door. The cottage was uninhabited, for the good old man whose home it had once been had years since passed away, and his office had never been filled. Yet nothing bore traces of decay. There was even a bright fire on the hearth, and a boiling kettle hung upon the hook above it. For the old forest-warden had been a good friend to Puck, and the little fellow loved to keep the little cottage as neat and home-like as it used to be.

Maude smiled gratefully as she looked around. "Thanks, dear Puck," she said; "now hasten back to Gero. I will lie down on this nice bed of fragrant moss, and I will not be afraid, I promise you."

When Puck returned, he found that the maiden's weariness had overcome her anxiety, but he knew by the tears that trembled on her eyelashes that she was thinking, even in dreams, of her brave page, and he dreaded to tell her when she awoke that he had not been able to find any trace of the faithful Gero. A great portion of the turret stair had fallen in, and among the bodies that lay piled beneath its ruins it was impossible to distinguish any one.

When the maiden woke, she almost for a moment fancied herself in her own turret chamber, for there, at the open window, stood the richly-carved arm-chair, the one carefully-preserved souvenir of her sainted mother, where Maude had so often sat and chatted with her little friend, and there in the corner stood her harp and the silver spindle, with its snowy thread.

But alas! she soon remembered the terrors of the night, and when, in answer to her questioning look, Puck told her, with faltering voice, his fears for Gero, the maiden's grief found vent in bitter weeping.

But Puck would not allow her to dwell on these sad thoughts. Drawing aside a curtain that hung against the wall, he disclosed to her astonished eyes the portraits of her dear parents, which had hung just so in her own room at home. And while she stood gazing on the beloved faces, her hands clasped in silent emotion, the flame was crackling on the hearth beneath the bubbling kettle, and Puck was rummaging in cupboards and chests, rattling with plates and cups, and preparing a meal for himself and his dear charge.

Maude, with the happy buoyancy of youth, half forgot her trouble of the night, while her colour came back with the needed food, and her heart was cheered by Puck's pleasant chatter, so willing was she to believe his prophecies of better days.

"You must stay here, Maude," he said, "until your father returns, and till he has punished the wicked Earl for his malice. For you would not be as safe, even in your father's protection, as here in this forest retreat. So be patient, and I will give you back in time to your friends, even to Gero, if he still lives, though that will be the hardest thing of all. But I know now that he was worthy of you, or he could not have fought as he did last night. It was nobly done!"

And the little fellow rubbed his hands with delight, which he felt, in spite of himself, in thinking of that valiant defence.

"You would have been friends yet if he had lived," said Maude tearfully. "Two such dear, good people could not have been enemies all their lives."

Days and weeks passed by, and still Maude was kept in her place of concealment. From time to time Puck went out to see what was going on between the hostile noblemen. The report brought back was always the same—"The Earl is sending out spies—I see them lurking in all directions—to find out your retreat, for they seem to know that you escaped the fire, or to suspect it from not finding your body among the dead. He wants to take you now as a hostage against your father's vengeance." Then, when Maude's cheek would pale at the words, he would add, "But they cannot find you in the midst of this thicket."

So the maiden still stayed in the forest cottage, and if her grief about Gero and her longing for her beloved father had not gnawed at her heart, she could have been nearly as happy in the lovely valley as she was once in her old home.

Puck was at work every morning by break of day, as if he wanted to make up for a century of idleness, nor would he ever allow Maude to share his household toil. But she sat spinning on the stone bench at the door, while he bustled cheerily about the little cottage. Then, when all the work was done, they would go into the wood, and it seemed as if the old days had come back again. For they still lay on the soft moss gazing into the shady trees while Puck told his marvellous stories.

Autumn and winter came, and the leisure hours were spent now by the cheery fire that burned on the clean-swept hearth. Never was there such a servant or such a merry companion as the little faithful goblin.

At last spring came. And now Puck went away every day to see what was going on at the wicked Earl's castle, for Maude's father had laid siege to his enemy's stronghold, hoping to force him to give up the dear one whom he believed to be imprisoned within those walls. Puck never let the sorrowing father know of his child's safety, for he did not wish her to be removed from his protection till her powerful enemy had been reduced by war, or even slain.

As the wood grew greener, the hopes of the besiegers waxed daily brighter. The fall of the castle was sure, and its defence could last but a few days longer.

This was the news which Puck brought home one day as he came to the noonday meal, and when he again went out to get further information, or, if possible, lend, unseen, a helping hand to the besiegers, Maude sat on the stone bench before the cottage, and tried to busy her trembling fingers with her spinning. But Puck was longer absent than usual, and she asked herself anxiously should she regard it as a good sign or the contrary.

At last she could stand it no longer. She rose and went along the narrow path by which she had come to her place of refuge. She had never before ventured alone through those forest shades; but the birds sang sweetly as she passed along, and she thought their cheerful voices bid her hope.

Soon she came to the scenes familiar to her from her childhood. Here was the place where Margaret used to sit and rest, and there—what memories filled her soul with sad emotion!—there was the old oak-stump on which she had sat by Gero's side, as he told her of the great world of which she knew so little. And now the eloquent mouth was silent, and her faithful page had

o

fallen in her defence, for Puck, in all his journeys to the castle, had never seen Gero among the besiegers.

She leant her head against a tree-stem, and wept long and bitterly. Then she raised her head to take one more look at the sacred spot. But were her tear-filled eyes deceiving her? There sat, as if lost in painful memories, a tall, manly form in gleaming armour, with a well-remembered sash of silver and blue across his breast.

Maude uttered a cry. The knight raised his head, and she looked into a familiar, but now pale and grief-marked face.

"Gero, Gero!" she cried, forgetting every other feeling in her wild delight, and rushing with outstretched arms to where he stood.

The young knight's brain swam. At first he thought the sweet apparition must be his dear one's spirit; but no, he clasped in his arms the trembling form of the lost maiden.

For one moment she lay sobbing on his breast; then, recollecting herself, she tore herself blushing from his arms.

"Forgive me, Gero, my surprise overcame me. So you are alive, and I had mourned for you as dead."

"Did you mourn for me, lady?" asked the young knight. "Thanks for the sweet assurance. I too sorrowed—oh! how deeply—for your loss; and to-day I rose from what I thought would be my death-bed, and came to visit the spot where we had spent so many happy hours together, here to indulge my grief undisturbed. The wicked Earl who caused our trouble fell to-day in the storming of his own castle, but great was our disappointment not to find you anywhere within its walls. And now you are here, and I am not deceived by a blessed dream!"

"No, it is no dream," said Maude joyfully; "but now let us hasten to relieve my father's grief."

As they went together through the wood, Maude told the knight how Puck had saved her, and how he had cared for her in the lonely valley.

"The brave little goblin!" cried Gero, as she finished. "Let bygones be bygones; we will be friends henceforth."

They had now reached the blackened ruins of Maude's former home, but, in the joy of dispelling the grief from the dear face of her father, who stood gazing, in deep sadness, on the scene of desolation, the maiden forgot to mourn at the wreck before her.

Ere the sun set, Gero and Maude were formally betrothed, and the work was at once begun of repairing the ruined castle. Meantime, Maude found a home with her future father-in-law, who was delighted to welcome as a daughter the child of his trusted friend; and Puck found no lack of employment among the busy builders, who wondered sometimes what made the work progress so quickly.

Before another spring the castle stood in more than its old strength and greatness, and no part had received such careful attention as the turret where Puck had made the lonely child his friend.

No guest at Gero's wedding received such marked deference and attention from the bridegroom as his former enemy, and the servants of the new household, catching their tone from their master, treated little Puck with kindness such as he had experienced at the hands of former generations.

The turret chamber was his home henceforth, and all through the long winter Maude's children loved to gather there at twilight, and coax the merry goblin to join them in their games, or tell them tales of the old days of the castle. But perhaps their mother's story was the one that they loved best—the story about the old enmity that changed to such firm friendship between the Lady Maude's page and her faithful goblin.

THE FALLEN BELL.

RE the light of the Gospel had shone on the benighted land of Saxony, there stood on the green banks of the Saale a stately temple, within whose walls a throng of ignorant worshippers presented the offering of praise and of sacrifice to the gods who had been honoured, as they believed, by their remotest ancestors. Then came Charlemagne, who cast out the heathen gods of Saxony, threw down their altars, and introduced Christianity. Among the rest fell the temple on the banks of the Saale. The Christian priest with pious zeal seized the idol which had there been worshipped, and hurled it into the river. From that time on, the rejected god lived as a water-sprite down in the waters of the Saale, cherishing a deadly hatred against the new religion, which had robbed him of his old-established rights. On the site of his former shrine rose now a cloister, and the bell, whose deep rich voice reached even the dwelling of the water-elf, stirring up afresh his bitter wrath and jealousy, called the inhabitants of the surrounding district to the new God and His sanctuary.

But the old honoured faith did not so easily die out from the hearts of the Saxons, and though they were obliged to join in the newly-enforced worship, they clung long to their ancient divinities, and secretly brought them the usual sacrifices.

At last the power of the Gospel triumphed, and the innocent child who had yearly been offered to the water-spirit on St. John's day was now withheld.

Wild was the rage of the mortified elf. All day long he watched among the willows on the bank, whence he could look unseen far over the fields, to see if they had really forgotten him. No sacrifice was brought. He felt that the last vestige of his power was gone. In gloomy anger against the thankless race, he resolved to take by force the victim of which he had been cheated.

A lovely child approached the bank, heedless of danger, holding in its tiny hand a bunch of forget-menots. Close by the water's edge were more of the blue flowers, and he ran forward to pluck the tempting blossoms. Then the waters of the Saale suddenly rose, swept over the place where the child was standing, and carried him down in their cold embrace. From that time people were careful to avoid the river on St. John's day, fearing a similar fate.

As Christianity became more powerful, the cloister, formerly a centre of holy influence, became the seat of arrogance and idle luxury, and the water-elf, who knew that the God whom he hated was a righteous judge, who would punish evil, often sat on moonlight nights among the willows gazing at the cloister, from whose lighted windows came the noise of clinking glasses and wild revelry. Then he murmured between his teeth—

" I shall live to see you brought to shame ! Your God cannot suffer such doings, and I shall have my revenge."

And he did live to see it.

One night, when, instead of pious hymns, drinking-songs were ascending from the cloister cells, a dark storm-cloud spread across the sky. Thunder growled and lightning flashed, making all nature tremble. Men fell on their knees ; the monks alone heeded not the voice of the Almighty. At every peal of thunder they raised their voices in the vain attempt to drown with their wild chorus the tumult without.

Then came an awful flash, which gleamed like a coronet of fire on the summit of the tower, and darted through the roof to the refectory, where in one moment its deadly shaft sent all the profane and godless scoffers before the throne of the eternal. The flame next seized the furniture of the hall, and it was not long till the fire burst from the shattered windows, for every hand was still that might have been raised to check its progress.

The water-sprite sat on a stone at the river's edge, contentedly watching the awful spectacle.

Every moment the flames gained greater force. Their fiery tooth gnawed beam and pillar till they burst asunder with a crash, and at last the devouring element rose from the ruined pile below to the belfry tower. Then the bell, swayed by the heat, began to stir. Faster and faster came the strokes, like a cry of anguish or a mournful knell sounding in wild and awful tones through the uproar of the storm. The beams from which it hung gave way, and with a great swing it fell into the Saale, making the water foam and hiss as it felt the glowing metal. The tower fell in, and the stately building was changed into a mass of smoking ruins.

Gradually the rage of the elements was stilled, and nature sank again to peaceful repose. The clouds were parted, and from the once more azure sky the moon looked down on the heaps of rubbish with the same mild and gentle glance as it used formerly to cast on the proud cloister.

And what of the water-fairy. The downfall of his foes almost reconciled him with his lot. The hated chimes no longer reached his ear, reminding him of what he so wished to forget, his lost dominion. The bell had found a resting-place on a beautiful green meadow which lay at the bottom of the Saale. The sprite planted water-lilies all round it, just as human beings adorn graves with the fairest of flowers. Then he built a crystal castle right in front of it, and brought home as his bride a beautiful water-fairy from the neighbouring river, Elbe.

After a time children played in the shell-adorned halls of the crystal castle, two beautiful boys with bright eyes and little red caps, and their sister, a gentle little water-elf, as sweet and beautiful as her relations of the land, the fairies of mountains and trees.

The sons were like their father ; they hated the human race, of whom the old fairy had told them nothing but evil, and they helped him every St. John's day to entice some heedless mortal down into the stream.

Their lovely little sister was of a very different stamp. A secret longing drew her heart towards the land and its inhabitants, and it was only by the sternest prohibition that her father could induce her to remain at home. But at night, when sleep reigned in the crystal castle, she would rise to the surface of the water, take her stand on the great white water-lilies, which willingly joined to do her service, and thus on this slender raft she would float up and down the stream. Her long fair hair flowed down till it touched the water ; in her white arms she held a golden harp ; and when she touched the strings and sang her sweet songs that told of her longing after the beautiful sunlight, after the blue sky and the unknown human race, the trees bowed their tall heads to the water's edge, the birds hushed their song, and even the night-wind held his breath while he listened to the music of the little water-sprite.

It was once more St. John's day, and the old water-elf was in one of his tempers.

The sun was shining on the river, and its rays flashed back in rainbow hues from the crystal pillars of the water-castle. The meadows in the cool bed of the Saale showed their freshest green, and the long grass waved to and fro among the water, while fishes and water-beetles darted between its stalks like golden stars.

The two boys sharpened their scythes and began to mow the grass, for it was haymaking time. Their sister stood among the lilies beside the great bell, holding one of the white flowers in her hand, and striking the metal with its slender stem, so that it answered her in strange and mellow tones. But she did it softly, very softly, for she knew how hateful the sound of the old bell was to her father, especially on this day. The sound was deep and musical, reminding the little fairy of the chimes which she sometimes heard on quiet nights, as she floated up and down the river on her raft of water-lilies.

Pleased with the dear, familiar tones, she forgot that her father was near, and she struck the bell so loudly that the sound, borne on the waves, thrilled through the castle, where the old fairy was leaning, lost in thought, against a pillar, passing his fingers through his grey-green beard, and dreamily watching his sons at their work.

When the hated sound struck on his ear, he started up with a cry of anger, and looked fiercely at his trembling daughter. But before he had time to give vent to his wrath a shadow fell over the palace and meadow, followed by a crash, as if something had been broken in the castle.

And such was indeed the case.

A boat was passing slowly through the waves above ; the steersman had happened to let the rudder fall, and its iron point struck with such force against one of the crystal panes of the water-sprite's palace that it fell, shattered into a thousand pieces.

This was too much for the enraged fairy. He rose foaming through the water, and stood with flaming eyes before the boatman. " Insolent man," he growled, " what hast thou done ? Repair the injury at once. If the pane is not replaced within half-an-hour, thou shalt pay for it with thy life."

The boatman laughed. " I don't understand glazier's work," said he, " and I shall hardly be able to find any one who could work down there in the water ; so I cannot satisfy your demand. But as for your threats, my good fellow, the time of your authority is long gone by. There is not even a child now who fears you ; and, besides, I have a cargo of steel bars, and you know, my dear waterman, that they would prevent you from coming into my boat to do me any harm."

At the mention of steel, a metal very hurtful to water-elves, the fairy unwillingly retired. He cast one more look of anger on the bold boatman, and on the little girl, who, on seeing the wrathful apparition, had clung terrified to her father's arm ; then he slowly sank into the water. He sat down in his crystal hall, leaned his head on his hand, and tried to devise some plan by which he could entice the little girl from the boat into his kingdom, and, by choosing her as the victim of the day, avenge himself on the boatman.

" I have it !" he cried at length ; " the trick with the green ribbon that I learned the other day from my cousin the water-prince in Bohemia will be of use to me now. To-day there is some great ceremony in the next village, and I am sure the father will send his child there to have her out of my way, and then I may find an opportunity of trying my skill."

So saying, he put on his hat of plaited rushes, drew on his green coat, and rose to the surface to place himself not far from the boat among the willows by the river's brink.

He had guessed rightly. Though the boatman had seemed courageous when speaking to the water-sprite, a secret uneasiness rankled in his heart. It was not for himself he feared, but for his only child ; for he had seen the wicked glance that the waterman had cast on the girl as he disappeared beneath the stream. He consulted his wife about what they ought to do for their child's safety ; for they knew well the dangers of St. John's day, which the mischance with the rudder had unhappily doubled.

In the next village lived a distant relation, and the fair gave an excellent excuse for paying her a visit. The little girl dressed herself in her best, said good-bye to her parents, and received injunctions to stay all night with her friends, and not return to the boat before morning. Joyfully she hastened along the high-road, which lay for some distance by the river-side, till she came to the place where the water-sprite sat so quietly in his summer clothes, that no one would have recognised in him the angry and revengeful spirit of the morning.

" Where are you going so briskly, fair maiden ?" he asked pleasantly.

" To the village, to the dance !" answered the little one merrily ; " don't you hear the music ?"

" My dear child," said the water-sprite artfully, " the girls there are all so finely dressed that you in your plain clothes will look very shabby among them, and perhaps you will not even be able to get a partner. But look at this lovely ribbon, of which I have such a quantity. If you had that twined in among your golden hair, or wound as a sash round your slender waist, you would outshine all the girls at the fair."

The little one, who had thought until the old man spoke to her that she would never get soon enough to the dance, now stopped, and looked with a critical eye, first on herself, and then on the bright green ribbon, which the water-sprite was pulling in endless lengths from the river which flowed on the other side of the willows.

" Look how pretty it is !" said he, and she let him wind it, as if to try the effect, around her slender form.

But immediately she was in the old fairy's power. With a mocking laugh, he said—

" Now, my little one, thou art mine ! We shall see whether thy father will say to-morrow that my authority is overthrown, and that I have no longer power to frighten a child. Come !"

As he spoke he seized the ribbon, and walked towards the river.

The terrified child began to scream, but father and mother were far away. She tried to escape, but the ribbon forced her to follow the water-sprite. Her feet would bear her in no other direction, no matter how she tried. Nearer and nearer to the rushing stream was she drawn by the dreadful ribbon. Soon the water touched her feet.

"Father, mother, farewell!" she cried in a voice of anguish. Then the old water-elf caught her in his arms, and, with a horrid laugh, plunged with her into the stream. The waters did their deadly work on the poor child's body, but the water-sprite kept the soul of the drowned girl prisoner at the bottom of the Saale. She could not mount to heaven; she could not even rejoice in the sunlight which pressed in softened radiance through the water to the meadow on the river's bed, nor might she play like the little water-elf with the silvery fishes. Heedless of her entreaties, the water-man put her under the heavy bell among the lilies, and said, as he went back to his castle, "Here thou shalt stay in punishment for thy father's insolence; and my watchful eye and the weight of the bell will prevent any one from setting thee free."

He went away, and left the soul of the poor little girl alone in her prison. Her sighs and lamentations could not pierce through the thick metal walls, but they were only sent back to her in dismal echo.

Meantime the little water-elf stood outside the bell in

sympathetic grief. She wound a garland of the fairest lilies round the little girl's corpse, carried it gently up through the water, and left it near the boat. The parents would never again see their dear child alive, but she had laid the little body in a soft bed of flowers, to make the sad sight less startling to their loving hearts.

Next morning, when the sun began to gild the waters of the Saale, the boatman left his cabin to make preparations for departure, while the mother, shading her eyes with her hand, stood looking along the high-road, where she expected every moment to see the child appear.

" Look there, wife !" said the boatman, pointing to an object in the water, which slowly approached the boat. " Look there ! What is that ?"

The woman turned to see. The waters of the Saale were gently bringing a great garland of blooming lilies, and in their midst lay, with closed eyes and folded hands, their loved and only child.

The little girl's soul sat beneath the bell. She could not leave her prison. Not a chink was visible, and the heavy bell would not move one hairsbreadth, notwithstanding all her efforts.

"What will my father and mother say if I do not come home ?" sighed the child's soul. " Oh, my poor dear parents ! Never to see the pleasant sunlight or the blue sky ! To stay down here for ever in this narrow, dark coffin—oh, how dreadful !" And if a soul could have died with terror, grief, and longing, that would certainly have been the fate of the little girl's spirit.

The hours passed silently over her and her prison. The hours became days. How many had gone by? The little soul did not know. At last she sank into a kind of stupor, and almost ceased to feel.

But one day something approached her prison, the edge of the bell was raised, and the water-sprite's rough voice said, " Come out."

The opening through which the light was peeping was small, but souls, with their light transparent forms, do not need much space, and in a moment the little spirit slipped out, and now stood trembling before the wicked water-man.

" Thou mayest play here for a little," he said ; " but in an hour thou must return to the bell."

The soul looked up. She had been so long in that dismal tomb, and now she found herself all at once in God's gloriously beautiful creation, though only for a short time, and as a prisoner ! She forgot her past sorrow, and thought not of the future ; she rejoiced in the delightful present, and looked up at the sun, which in noontide splendour stood in the blue canopy of heaven, sending its rays down on the green meadow, their brilliance softened by the crystal flood.

Then she looked around. Before her stood the splendid palace, with its glittering walls and transparent pillars, and round her swam the prettiest little fishes as fearlessly as if the little soul had been an acquaintance for years.

A lovely young girl came out of the shining building, and asked her to play with her.

The old water-sprite frowned in displeasure at his daughter's friendliness, but the little elf did not look at him, and the child's soul thought, "I must go back to prison at any rate, and he cannot do anything worse to me!" So she took the friendly fairy's hand, and rose with her through the silvery flood, chasing the fishes and trying to grasp the sunbeams with her little transparent hand. Then she wound garlands of reeds, and let them rise to the top of the water, after she had pressed sweet kisses on them, and laden them with loving messages for her dear ones up above.

As she stood watching them with tearful longing as they rose nearer and nearer to her home, she heard herself called once more. The water-sprite stood behind her, seized her hand, and led her back to the bell. She turned for a last look at the clear blue sky; the next moment she was back in her dark and narrow prison.

Hours and days passed slowly by. The time seemed endless to the poor little soul. Her only amusement and her only pleasure was to go over again and again that one hour of freedom and happiness.

One day, just as she was doing this, there was a noise outside the bell; the ray of light pierced her prison again, and before the old water-sprite had time to give her permission the little prisoner slipped through, spread out her delicate transparent arms towards the light of heaven, and with a cry of joy greeted the fair, free world. Her playfellow was standing waiting for her, and together they left the bell with joyous haste, slipped

through the waving grass, and danced on the sunbeams
with the dragon-flies and fishes.

"Oh!" said the little soul sadly, "why does this delightful hour come so seldom. Why may I not get out
every day?"

" I do not know," answered the water-fairy ; " but it is
only on Saturday, between twelve and one o'clock, that
the spirits are allowed to leave their prison down here
and play in the sunlight."

" But it is so lonely and dark in the bell," said the
child's soul dolefully.

The little nymph looked at her compassionately.
Both had lost all pleasure in their joyous play, and arm-
in-arm they looked up through the water at the clouds
which were slowly sailing past.

" There comes your father to fetch me," said the little
girl's soul, shuddering. " Oh ! do come once, just once,
every day to my prison ; knock against the bell, and
when the sound pierces through my metal walls I shall
know that I am not quite alone in the world. Will
you ?"

A thought struck the young water-sprite ; she opened
her mouth to tell it to her playmate, but just then her
father came up, and she had to be silent. She could only
nod kindly at the poor little prisoner, whom the old
water-sprite led roughly away to the dismal prison,
whose narrow walls soon shut her out from the cheerful
daylight.

It was night. Souls cannot sleep, but they may have
waking dreams.

Thus the child's spirit was led back in imagination to her home. She saw herself once more in the ship on which she had been born, and fancied herself sitting beside her mother, listening to pleasant stories told by the dear gentle voice, and as she dreamed she forgot the impassable gulf which separated her from the living ones above the stream.

Then the sound of a bell fell gently on her ear. She had been so absorbed in her dreams that she started in alarm at the unexpected sound, and it was a moment or two before she could collect her thoughts to think. Then she remembered her request, of which this was evidently the fulfilment, so she struck softly against the inside of the bell as a sign that she had heard her friend's greeting.

Then the edge of her prison was gently lifted, and with a cry of joy she slipped out into the water. There stood the little water-sprite.

"Will you go up with me to the surface of the stream?" asked she. "Would you like to float up and down on my lily-raft?"

"Indeed I should," answered the little soul. "What do I want but freedom, air, and light? Oh yes, take me with you!"

The lovely nymph took the child's hand, and a little shining wave bore them upwards as on the wings of a swan.

Now they are standing on the surface of the water. The little water-sprite beckoned, and from far and near swam the water-lilies and anemones to make a boat of flowers for their young mistress and her dear little pale companion.

They glided down the stream. Oh, how beautiful it was !

On they moved past lofty mountains crowned by

THE WATER-ELF AND THE LITTLE SOUL ON THE RAFT OF WATER-LILIES.

stately castles—past villages lying in peaceful slumber, whose churches mirrored their graceful spires in the clear flood below—past the willows on the banks, that nodded their drowsy heads as the night-wind played through their branches. And over all these lovely scenes the moon shed her magic light, and the waves sang softly their everlasting song.

Then the little water-elf took her golden harp, and sent her clear voice floating through the stillness of the night. She sang of what was stirring her own heart and filling the child's soul with sorrow—of their longing for happiness on earth or in heaven, which was so far, so far from them both. The sweet sounds floated through the silent night, till the waves checked their song, and the slumbering trees awoke to listen to the enthralling strains.

" Oh !" said the child's soul at length, " why cannot I rise into the kingdom of light ? why must I linger far away from my heavenly home, and pine down below in that dark dungeon ?"

" Because," answered the lovely water-elf kindly, " my father has sentenced you to the bell, and this spell holds you bound, and always forces you to return to darkness and captivity."

" Can this sentence, this spell never be broken ?" asked the little soul.

" Yes, if a human being descends and overthrows the bell the charm will be broken, and you may rise to heaven."

" Ah ! would that that time would come !" said the little one sorrowfully. " The only ones whose love would be strong enough to make them take the risk are far away." And she looked sadly into the distance.

When the moonlight began to pale, and the stars were

dying out one by one, the friends left their lily-raft, plunged into the flood, and the little soul went back reluctantly to her dark prison.

So the days went by. Alone, alone in the dark bell, and once a-week one short hour of freedom and sunlight—that was the lot of the little soul, with now and then a sail on the lily-raft by the side of the water-elf. Unspeakably delightful were these hours, but the longing for their return made the dark days seem all the longer to the poor little prisoner.

And this pleasure was but rare. The little watersprite had to be very prudent, for her cruel father might have made her pay for her nightly journeys with her life, so displeasing to him was her hankering after the human world, and her mild and friendly disposition.

Many a night the old water-fairy rose himself to the surface, many a time did his sons sit among the willows ; and often the water-man could not sleep, and went restlessly through the rooms of his palace to see that everything was right.

It was only on nights when all in the crystal castle were fast asleep, and no discovery was to be feared, that the young nymph hastened to the little soul, opened her prison, by raising the edge of the bell, and rose with her for a sail in the lily-boat.

Years passed by, and with them hope died out from the little girl's soul ; nothing remained to her but memory and longing. In the world above the water, what she had last seen young and fresh had grown gradually old. The playmates of her childhood had been married long ago, and some of them had entered on their eternal rest. Her father had never recovered the shock of that unhappy day, and the secret thought that he had excited the water-fairy's wrath by his defiant words, and had thus caused his dear child's death, gnawed at his life, and brought him to an untimely grave. Her mother alone was left. Her hair had grown white, not so much through age as through sorrow. Once, when in her solitude a deep longing seized her to see once more the place where her child had died, she entrusted the guidance of the boat to her brother's son, who was one day to fall heir to all her little possessions, and told him to take her to her darling's grave.

The boat reached its destination the night before Easter. Here, opposite the clump of willows, which had grown even denser than when she saw them last, and above which the spire of the village church raised its graceful form, the boat had stopped on that unhappy day so many years ago. Here, therefore, was the anchor lowered, and the boatman went to rest. But the mother, when she found herself so near the fatal spot, could not sleep. The most dreadful hour of her life, when she stood watching for the coming of her merry child, and saw instead but her pale, cold corpse, came again before her soul, and she passed the night in bitter weeping.

When the first gleam of daylight played on the stream, she rose and went on deck. All the stars had gone to rest except the morning star, and even its radiance grew gradually fainter; for the young day began to don his golden festive robe. The poor mother leaned over the edge of the boat, and looked down into the water. The sky was one glow of purple, and on the stream lay the roses of the dawn. The Easter sun rose slowly above the horizon, and as its first beam struck the river a sound of solemn melancholy came upwards from its depths.

" What was that ?" said the woman, leaning forward to listen.

A second chime broke the stillness of the morning, and soon the bell began to ring in tones of wondrous richness from the bed of the river. With the chimes, and borne on the sunbeams, which cheerfully plunged into the stream, and rose again radiant from the crystal flood, came a sweet, familiar voice to thrill the heart of the listening mother.

> " Jesus lives, and I in Him :
> Where is thy victory, O grave ?
> Jesus lives to set me free,
> My captive soul His love will save ;
> Jesus will lead me to the light,
> This the sure hope that cheers my night."

So sang her child's clear voice in the words of the hymn which she herself had once taught her, and which the little one used to sing on Easter morning. The child's soul was still imprisoned, but now, on the day of Christ's resurrection, when the bell began to ring as the first sunbeam touched it, she felt a strange, sweet joy, that made her feel inclined to join her voice with its mellow chimes.

On the great Christian festivals all bells that have

sunk in rivers or lakes awake to join in the hymn of all creation, and when, among the rest, the little girl's bell began to sound, her grief and longing generally awoke afresh. But to-day with the first note her sadness suddenly vanished, and a strange joy sprang up in her heart. She folded her delicate hands, and sang the verse of her childhood. But the metal did not send the sound back to her as on other days ; it pierced through the walls, and floated through the waves up to the ear and heart of her sorrowing mother.

Yes, it was her child's voice ; every drop of blood, every pulse-beat of her trembling body told her that. She had indeed found her little daughter's corpse ; but her soul must have remained in the power of the cruel water-sprite, and had been pining all these years down in the stream, shut out from light and liberty and love. All the stories that she had heard of the imprisonment of souls, and which she had always laughed at as childish tales, came into her mind, and filled her with unspeakable anguish. Her captivity must be somehow connected with the bells, or else the chimes would not have mingled as they did with the hymn. She leaned over the edge of the boat, and looked down into the water.

There was a sudden splashing and foaming in the river, and the old water-sprite slowly rose, parted the waves, and stood before the terrified woman. It was the same powerful form, the erect carriage, the long grey-green beard, for the hand of time passes more gently over spirits than over men. The woman recognised him at the first glance, for she had seen him from her cabin window as he vented his wrath on her husband, though she herself was out of sight. She knew that the murderer of her child stood before her, but the water-sprite did not suspect that this was the mother of his little prisoner.

"My wife is ill," he said gloomily. "The chimes in the water always make her ill, but there must have been some special power in them to-day, for she is writhing in agony, and she begged me to bring her a woman of the human race, to lay her warm hand on her aching head, and restore her to health. Come with me," he concluded sullenly ; "it is not for nothing that I ask this."

The woman could have shouted with joy. Her enemy himself was about to lead her to the place where all her affections were centered ; it seemed to her a sign from heaven, and she went fearlessly to the edge of the boat, and prepared to plunge into the stream.

"Not so," growled the water-sprite : "thou couldst not reach the bottom alive—a thing which would have pleased me well enough at any other time, but to-day it would not suit my purpose. Take this ring !"

She placed the glittering circle on her finger, and followed the water-elf into the river. Thus protected, she could walk through the water as on dry land, and breathe in the river as freely as in the air.

They came to the beautiful green meadow, passed the clump of water-lilies, in the midst of which the woman's quick eye had already noted the bell, and entered the crystal castle. There, in a spacious and glittering hall, lay, on a glass bed with shining pillows of fish-scales, the wife of the water-elf. She was tossing in restless pain, and as the woman entered she stretched out her hands entreatingly. The little nymph knelt sobbing by her sick mother's side, and even the rough sons looked on with grave faces.

The boatman's widow went up to the bed, and laid her warm hand on the sick fairy's cold, white forehead. Almost instantaneously the pain vanished, and she fell into a gentle sleep.

The little nymph grasped the woman's hand, and said, while her eyes shone with grateful tears, " Come, I will get you some of our beautiful lilies."

The old water-sprite, in his anxiety about his wife, had quite forgotten the little prisoner below the bell, and, besides, he had no reason to suspect that this strange woman knew anything about the little soul. So, though he did not like to see his daughter so friendly with the human race, he did not try to hinder her from getting the flowers, but sat down quietly to watch his sick wife's slumber.

How the mother's heart beat as she arrived at the lilies, pressed through their intertwining stems, and stood at last close to the bell. With trembling hand she knocked, and the sound thrilled through the child's spirit.

The little water-elf stood in amazement as she watched her visitor making her way so eagerly among the lilies, and great was her alarm when she heard the bell sound, for she thought of her sick mother and her father's wrath. But before she had time to remonstrate, the little soul said, "Who knocks?" She knew it could not be her friend the young nymph, for she came only at night, and this was early in the morning. "Who knocks?" she asked again with trembling voice.

The mother thought her heart would break with joy; her breath left her, and she could not answer just at once; yet the greatest haste was needful, for the old water-sprite might be beside her every moment.

"It is your mother, my dear child," she said at last with trembling lips; "tell me, oh! tell me quickly how I can set you free."

"Mother, mother!" cried the little prisoner; "mother, is it you?"

"It is indeed, my darling," said the mother anxiously; "but we must not lose any time, for the water-sprite may come any moment, and then I shall not be able to help you."

The words brought the little soul back to reality.

"Mother, dear mother, throw the bell down, and your child's soul will thank you for ever in the heavenly world," begged the girlish voice.

The mother put forth all her strength, but the bell, which the spirits moved so easily, would not yield an inch before the woman's efforts.

When the old water-sprite heard it sound, he went to one of the high-arched windows, and saw the widow struggling to overturn her poor child's prison. He beckoned to his sons, and quickly but noiselessly the three left the palace. Once outside, they screamed with furious rage.

The little captive heard the wild cry, and trembled. The mother heard it, and the thought that on one moment hung her own life and her dear child's future happiness gave her gigantic strength ; one desperate effort, and the heavy bell gave way, and lay on its side.

It was almost too late ; for the angry water-sprites had reached the spot, and stretched out their hands to seize the woman.

But the little soul had left her prison, snatched up her mother in her arms, and darted quick as lightning up through the waves. When they reached the land the mother felt her child's arms taken from around her, while a light, cold kiss was pressed upon her cheek. Then the slight, transparent form of her loved one soared like a cloud towards heaven, till it was lost to her sight. With mingled joy and grief she watched the vanishing soul.

"Oh ! leave me not behind, my child ; take me also up to heaven !" she cried, amid streaming tears.

Night came once more, and with his starry mantle covered joy and sorrow, life and death. The poor mother lay on a narrow couch in the cabin of her boat. She was wearied out with the day's lamentations, and a gentle sleep had kindly blotted from her mind her bitter sorrow. It seemed to the sleeping one as if heavenly radiance filled the little room, and an angel with shining wings approached her bed. But when she looked on the face it was that of her dear child, whom she had yesterday freed from the power of the water-sprite.

"Mother, dear mother, come !" said the loved voice ;

" I am sent to fetch thee, that thou mayest keep the Easter feast in heaven with father and me."

And she took her mother in her arms, soared out into the night, high above land and sea, higher and higher, past the glittering stars, till they arrived at last in the glorious heavenly temple, and met the loved father and the beautiful angels.

Next morning, when the nephew found the woman was not rising, he went into the cabin and stepped up to the bed. There she lay, cold and dead, but her hands were folded in prayer, and round her mouth and her closed eyes was a smile of peace and happiness.

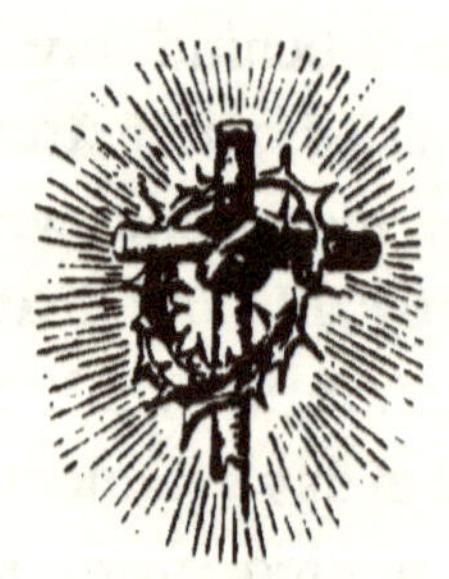

ASLOG RETURNS TO HER FATHER.

The
Last Home of the Giants.

ALE and mountain alter-
nated in beautiful succession beneath the blue sky
of Norway thousands of
years ago just as they do
to-day, and the Gulf Stream
flowed then as now past its rugged coasts ; yet it was a
far different land.   In the thick forests no axe had yet
been heard felling the strong timbers that the Norwegian
rivers would bear down to the sea, to float hereafter as
noble ships upon the breast of the ocean ; in the sheltered

bays no cosy houses nestled with their neatly-kept surroundings of garden and field ; no boat yet flew over the sea with nets and fishing tackle. Man had not yet sought out as a home this beautiful northern land.

A race of giants, of tall and powerful build, dwelt there. Their lifetime was measured by centuries as ours by years. They tore rocks asunder with their hands, and left the great streams a free channel. They bore huge blocks on their shoulders to the shore, and built them into castles whose turrets towered into the clouds. Their voice drowned the roar of the ocean, and scared the eagle from its nest. But this powerful race, beneath whose tread the ground trembled, were of peaceful, harmless disposition. No quarrel divided, nor envy embittered, their hearts. They lived together like the children of one great family.

Their chief was Hrungnir. His companions voluntarily submitted to his control ; for he excelled them all in years, wisdom, and strength, as a father his children.

Hrungnir lived in a splendid castle by the sea. The mountains of Norway had had to yield their most precious metals to adorn the walls of his giant dwelling within and without. The chief's numerous flocks and herds roamed over miles of land, the bears of the thick forests were slain in hundreds by his hands that their skins might cover pillows for his guests, and the tables and drinking-horns gleamed with precious stones. But Hrungnir's most cherished possession was Guru, his only daughter. Her hair shone golden as the stars of the northern night, her eyes were blue as the sky of her native land, and her skin was of dazzling whiteness.

The most powerful giants of the whole country were suitors for Guru's hand, and Hrungnir promised his daughter to him who should excel in swiftness in the race, or whose arm should be strongest to hurl huge boulders. Then the mighty men came down from their castles in the mountains, where the snowstorm sweeps round the hoary peaks, and from sea-side fortresses, till Hrungnir's roof could scarcely give shelter to the host of powerful suitors. The tables smoked with countless dishes, the horns of mead were filled and filled again, and from the windows the songs of the giants sounded forth so loudly that the waves fled back in terror towards the sea.

After the feast, the giants went out to the strand, broke huge masses from the rocks, and hurled them out in the sea as children would throw pebbles. Far out into the ocean flew the masses of stones, but none so far as those thrown by the hand of Andfind, the valiant youth whose castle stood amid the rocks of the storm-swept Doverfjeld, whose wealth almost equalled Hrungnir's, whose beauty bore comparison with that of Guru herself. Then when the suitors arranged themselves on the strand for the race, and the shingle resounded with their golden sandals, Andfind left all his rivals far behind, and his long fair locks floated like golden pennons on the rock that was the goal of the race, while his fellow-suitors were still toiling along the course.

Andfind was victor, and Guru's heart sang for joy, for

she had long loved him in secret, though she was prepared to submit to her father's wish, even if he had
chosen some other for his son-in-law.

Far from grudging envy, the giants loudly applauded
the conqueror, bore him on their shoulders to Hrungnir's
castle, where the chief bade him welcome, and called his
daughter to meet her chosen bridegroom.

The lovely Guru came dressed in a sky-blue robe with
a silver-embroidered hem, which she and her maids had
woven and wrought in the retirement of the women's
room.   Round her white neck and rounded arms lay
gleaming jewels, and her locks were bound with a golden
fillet.   Thus she came to meet the guests.   Hrungnir
took his daughter's hand, laid it in Andfind's right, and
then, as priest of the household, the chief united them in
the indissoluble ties of marriage.

Night fell round the Castle of Hrungnir.   The chief
and his guests lay wrapped in deep slumbers, preparing
for the enjoyment of a new day.   But destruction
approached them, as they slept, with stealthy steps; for
Odin, that crafty king, of whose origin no man could
tell, came with his trusty warriors down from the mountains.   They had heard of the beauty of Norway, and
wished to win it for their home.   They had heard that the
bravest in the land were feasting in Hrungnir's castle,
and they had waited till the hours of slumber that they
might strike unawares the foes with whom they could
not have dared to cope on equal terms.

The moonlight glided through the open windows and
fell on the forms of the defenceless sleepers : the deep

breathing of the warriors and the murmur of the waves were the only sounds that the ear could distinguish. But dark shadows fell in the moonlit hall, tall forms climbed in at the windows, and noiselessly, holding their weapons carefully to prevent them from clashing, they stole into the rooms.   With sure aim they bathed their swords in the heart's blood of the sleepers, so that, with one last groan, each warrior yielded up his brave spirit.   The pavement swam in blood, but Odin's band passed from hall to hall and never slipped on their gory path.

The death-groan, though short, reached Guru's ear.   She rose and listened.   No, it was no dream ; there came that sound again with dreadful distinctness.   She threw on her garments and sprang to the window, and when she drew aside the curtain she saw strange forms in the courtyard, bearing with difficulty a heavy burden.   She looked more closely, and recognised in the clear moonlight the bloody corpse of her noble father.   She stole up to Andfind's couch, and whispered, " Awake, awake, my husband, and let us fly, for treachery and death have entered our house ! "

The bloody work seemed finished in the other rooms, and now the dreaded footsteps were drawing near.

Guru raised a stone from the pavement and disclosed a secret stair.   She bade Andfind descend, and then quickly following him, she carefully closed the opening behind her.

By a narrow passage which led beneath the castle and the rocks to the strand they reached the sea unseen. There a boat lay rocking, which Guru and her maids had often used for pleasant sails. They stepped in. Andfind spread the sail and seized the helm, and the boat flew out into the open sea.

Odin had conquered. The noblest of the land were killed in the inglorious victory of that night, and the weak remnant of the giant race were obliged to leave their old home and seek a refuge in unknown lands. Notwithstanding this ignoble beginning, Odin's reign was one of wisdom, power, and beneficence.

Of Guru and her husband nothing more was ever heard. Whether the sea had swallowed the boat in its hungry depths, or whether the waves had borne them to happier coasts, none had ever brought back the tidings to their old home. But in the winter evenings, when the maidens sat around the blazing pine-log, and talked at their spinning about the days of the Norwegian giants, some aged dame would tell her shuddering listeners of that night of death, and of the mysterious fate of Guru and her noble bridegroom.

Odin's reign was long since ended. His wisdom and his crimes were both alike well-nigh forgotten. Olaf had many years ago brought in the knowledge of the Christian religion, and reared churches on the sites of the old altars ; and to the ancient honesty and strength of the nation was added the mild spirit of the religion of the cross.

On the spot where Hrungnir's castle once stood rose now a fortress as proud, and well-nigh as strong, as that of the giant chief; the flocks that grazed around it were as great as his; and the present possessor, Sämund, like him, counted as his dearest treasure an only daughter.

It seemed almost as if the days of Guru were come back again, for Aslog's golden hair and snowy skin, Aslog's blue eyes and graceful form, attracted the wealthiest and most powerful nobles of the land to woo her.

As each noble suitor was rejected, the father's heart swelled high with pride and hope. "She will only take the best and greatest," he thought. But when the most powerful prince in the land came, and the fair one's lips said "No" to him also, Sämund no longer praised his daughter's prudence. With bitter words he reproached her for her folly, and commanded her to choose before Christmas Eve some one on whom he might bestow her hand.

Days came and went, and Aslog's cheek grew paler and her father's eye more gloomy, for her heart was given to Orm, the poor but beautiful youth whom her father had given her as page. Orm's strong arm had on lovely summer evenings rowed the boat out into the gold-flooded sea; Orm's hand had guided her over the vast snow-fields, as in snow-shoes, with points thin and supple as a beech-leaf, they glided swiftly through the bracing air; and in long winter evenings, while the guests were drinking and singing in her father's halls, Orm used to sit and tell her beautiful stories as she sat by the cheerful fire.

Sämund loved the brave youth, but had any one

spoken of him as his daughter's choice he would have challenged the informant to single combat.

The lovers knew this, and it was with trembling that they awaited the decisive day.

"If she has not chosen before the time I have named," said Sämund to Orm, "I will choose her a bridegroom myself, and you shall have the honour of bearing her bridal train."

Orm gave no answer, but with trembling hand he arranged the table for the guests, and pressed his lips close together to restrain the eager words that his love prompted.

It was the night before Christmas Eve—starry and cold. A secret door opened in the side of the mountain, and two muffled figures slipped out. They were Orm and Aslog. They had brought nothing with them but a little bundle of necessary clothing, a warm skin rug, and a bow and arrows which Orm had slung across his shoulder.

On they hurried over the icy plain, swiftly and terror-stricken, like a pair of hunted doves. They reached the edge of the wide plain. Their snow-shoes were no longer of use, for their road led now towards the defiles and rocky heights of the highlands. It was bitterly cold, the wind whistled through the clefts of the mountain, and its icy breath made Aslog's frail form tremble. Long their path wound among the snow-clad mountains; then they reached a thick fir wood, in the midst of which stood a little hermit's cottage.

"It is I, Father Jerome," said Orm to the old man who came to greet them at the door.

"Welcome, my son!" said the old man, as the youth stooped to press a reverent kiss on his withered hand; "and the maiden at thy side is welcome too to the poor hospitality of the hermit's cell."

The offered rest and refreshment were eagerly accepted by the weary maiden. With pitying eyes the hermit gazed on her grief-marked features, and when Orm begged him to unite them in marriage, the old man, after short consideration, granted their request.

How different was this hour from Aslog's dreams! Not that she gave many thoughts to the splendour and festivity that should have done honour to her bridal, but she felt bitterly the want of her father's blessing.

The ceremony over, there could be no further delay. On the wanderers pressed on their weary way, till Aslog would have sunk exhausted but for Orm's supporting arm. Through the thick fir woods, over rough mountain paths, they hastened on till the first streak of dawn gleamed in the eastern sky. Then Orm pointed to a cluster of dark rocks that lay before them.

"There," said he cheerfully—"there, my Aslog, is rest and safety."

Aslog's courage rose; with renewed energy she pressed over the intervening ground, till they reached a tall jagged rock and entered a cleft in its side. They now found themselves in a cave, which, though narrow at the entrance, became higher and wider as they went on, till it formed a spacious chamber. Out of this gloomy abode Orm's care and thoughtfulness made a home for his loved one that was not wholly lacking in comfort or happiness, and here they lived in secure retirement as long as the winter blocked the mountain roads. But when spring came, and the ways became accessible, Sämund's spies were able to explore more thoroughly, and Orm could no longer go out and in freely among the mountains. But when provisions ran short, he was obliged to tear himself from Aslog's weeping embrace, and sally forth with his bow and arrows. At last, when, after weeks of mild weather, no living soul had been seen near their retreat, their fears subsided, and Orm began to lay aside caution and to venture further from the cave. Perhaps Aslog's father had grown tired of the fruitless search, or perhaps he was even cherishing thoughts of forgiveness. Aslog's heart was quick to believe what she so ardently wished, and Orm began to believe it too. One night, while his wife was sleeping, he took the path towards the valley where the hermit's cell nestled amid the woods. His breast beat high with hope that the old man might be able to give him some good tidings to take back to his loved Aslog, who, although she bore her privations even cheerfully, was yet paler and feebler every day. He drew near a jutting rock, behind which lay the path to the hermit's cottage. In his glad excitement he had forgotten all fear. His bow hung with loose string behind him, and his hand grasped his staff but carelessly. Suddenly he heard a rustling in the thick bushes beside him, and two heavy hands were laid on his shoulder. With a strong effort he shook himself free, stepped back a few paces, and swung his stick menacingly.

" It is he whom we seek," cried his assailants ; " remember the reward."

Then it seemed to Orm as if all the bushes and even the brown rock behind him became alive, so great a rustling was heard on every side.   Quick as thought he brought his stick down on the heads of the two who had first attacked him, and before the others could leave their hiding-places he had turned and fled.

At first there was wild shouting and a sound of eager feet behind, but he never stopped to look back, and he soon passed out of sight of his pursuers.   The way was long and rough, but Orm was strong and fleet of foot, and before him lay his home and Aslog.   At last he was at the cave.

How different was this home-coming from his former hopes !   Aslog lay in sweet sleep, with a happy smile on her lips, as if she dreamt of love and forgiveness; and Orm must soon waken her, and tell her that she must go forth once more a homeless wanderer.

" Awake, awake, beloved one," he whispered, seizing her hand, " and let us flee, for your father's men are on our track, and we must be far from this before to-morrow dawns."

Aslog opened her eyes, and gazed in speechless astonishment at her husband's lips, but when she could no longer doubt, she sprang quickly up and arranged her clothing and the soft skins which had formed her covering in a neat bundle.   Without delay they crept out of the cave by its narrow entrance, and went forth, not, as they had hoped, to Sämund's castle, but to a dark and unknown future.   Westward, where Aslog's home lay, danger and treachery threatened them, so they turned their steps northwards, on untried mountain paths.   The air was mild, the moon shone brightly on their way, and the soft moss kept no trace of their footsteps that might betray them to their watchful enemies.   Thus they wandered northwards for hours.   The cave in the rock lay miles behind them, and they were far from the place where Orm had been seen by his father-in-law's men. Then at last he ventured to turn westwards, towards the sea.   Their way led down towards the lowlands.   The wintry mists were still hanging over the plain.   Orm's keen eye could scarcely pierce their grey veil, and Aslog shuddered as she felt their cold embrace.   They could no longer tell in what direction they were going, but they went on and on, hoping to come ere long to the friendly ocean.   At last Aslog's pale face caught a flush of joy as she heard its distant murmur.   Nearer and nearer sounded the familiar music, and soon the wanderers came to a narrow valley, at the further edge of which rose a cluster of dark rocks.

"It is the coast!" said Aslog joyously, as she almost flew along the ground.

In a little bay at the foot of the rocks lay a fishing-boat.   Orm bore his wife in his arms along the sand, for on this open strand the greatest haste was necessary, lest some hostile eye might see them.   He placed Aslog gently in the boat, sprang in after her, and with trembling hands spread the sail.

The wind seemed to wish the fugitives well.   It swept

down from the mountains and filled the white sail, so that the little boat shot out into the sea like a swan with spreading wings. The sun rose higher and higher, the cliffs of their native coast seemed now but a line of low hills; proud ships glided not far from them, and on the farthest horizon appeared a group of islands gleaming in the golden mist. As the sun sank slowly to the horizon, the great ships passed by without noticing the wanderers, and the little islands were still in the far distance. Aslog's face, that had before glowed with hope, grew pale and wan.

"What is wrong, my darling?" asked Orm anxiously.

"I am hungry," answered Aslog faintly.

Orm sighed deeply. They had had to flee without waiting to get provisions, and now they had been twenty-four hours without food, and the islands lay far, far away. The sun sank into the sea.

"Sleep, my Aslog, sleep!" begged Orm at length; "you will not feel your hunger while you are asleep, and by the time you awake, perhaps we shall have reached one of the little islands before us."

And Aslog smiled submissively, and loosing the skins from the bundle, lay down beneath their protecting warmth at the bottom of the boat. The waves rocked the little vessel gently, the oar splashed in measured monotony, and at last Aslog's eyes closed, and she fell asleep.

Orm now kept watch alone on the wide ocean. Night had come, but a warm breath of spring was still hovering over the sea. The moon rose slowly above the distant mountains of Norway, and flooded the ocean with its silvery light. The waves danced sparkling round the boat, sails and masts shone brightly, and the hair of the slumbering fair one gleamed like waves of gold.

Full of love and grief, Orm's eyes rested on Aslog's pale face. Allowing himself but short rest, and that at long intervals, he rowed on all night, and when morning dawned, a large island with blossoming trees lay before his eyes bathed in the purple light. His cry of joy woke Aslog, who rose and looked at this lovely haven of refuge, which seemed offered to the homeless wanderers. Like a guardian of their future safety a tall grey rock stood upon the shore, in form not unlike a gigantic human figure.

Orm tried to steer between the small islands that lay round this tempting spot; but the waves, which had heretofore played so gently round the shores, now foamed and roared about the boat, and drove it back into the open sea. Nevertheless Orm undauntedly plied helm and oar, only to be driven back irresistibly again and again.

Noon came, and the fruitless struggle still continued; and now the sun was inclining towards the west. Orm's strength and heroic perseverance began at length to fail. His hands bled, his arms trembled, hunger and exhaustion almost overpowered him; while Aslog, who had sunk from a state of the most eager hope into the deepest despondency, clung, well-nigh unconscious, to the mast. Orm thought her dying. Then despair gave him fresh strength. "Almighty God, pity us!" he cried aloud

to heaven. Immediately the waves submitted to the
holy name ; the foaming billows glided gently beneath
the boat; the vessel shot like an arrow through the midst
of the islands, and drew near the haven where the giant
rock with its dark countenance looked down on the little
boat that glided past it to the smooth strand. Orm
sprang out, took the exhausted Aslog in his arms, and
carried her across to the dry, soft sand. He looked
round for something to eat. Fruit-trees waved their
blossoming crowns at no great distance, but the time for
fruit was not come. Orm looked still more anxiously
about the beach. Then he saw a mussel right at his
feet, then another and another. He lifted them, and
offered them to his half-fainting wife ; and so much
refreshed did she feel by the slight nourishment, that she
was able to walk towards the centre of the island, supported by Orm's arm, in search of some place of
shelter.

The blossoming fruit-trees bore evidence of some careful hand, but no path, no footprint told of the cheering
nearness of human beings. They went on further
. through the green island, over which the sun was shed-
ding its last golden beams. There before them they saw
a clear space amid the foliage, and with hearts beating
with hope and fear they approached it. Soon they stood
before a house of very ancient architecture. Its walls
sank deep into the earth, and towered so high into the
air that the firs could scarcely stretch their dark
branches over the hide-covered roof. The windows were
small, and their panes made of fishes' skins. The door

was made of strong planks, and firmly bound with iron
The whole house looked as if it bade defiance to the storms,
and had done so for centuries.

But where were now its builders? Did they lie sleeping in the depths of the ocean? Did the tall grass of the
little islands wave above their last resting-place, or did
they still sit, spell-bound, behind the iron-bound door
and the grey walls of the dreary dwelling? Checking
the slight shudder that shook his frame at these thoughts,
Orm knocked at the door of the mysterious house. No
sound, no footstep told him that he had been heard
within. He knocked again, then a third time, but there
was still no movement. Then he laid his hand on the
heavy latch; the door opened, and they entered a stone-
paved hall. There was no one to bid them welcome or
refuse them entrance. At one side of this hall was
another door. Orm knocked, and when again there was
no answer he opened it, and stepped with Aslog by his
side into a large and lofty apartment. There was no one
to be seen, yet everything bore traces of an orderly hand.
A bright fire burned on the hearth, and above it hung a
cauldron with fish, the smell of which greeted the hungry
fugitives with pleasant invitation.

" Forgive us, noble master of this house !" said Orm in
a loud voice, yet in a respectful tone ; " it is necessity, not
forwardness, which makes us intruders."

They both listened breathlessly; but there was still no
answer. Then Orm poured some of the contents of the
cauldron into two plates, and placed them on the table.
With trembling at first, but afterwards with growing

comfort and courage, the wanderers enjoyed the much-needed food.

When their hunger was satisfied, and their spirits revived, they looked around them. At the farther side of the room stood two beds of gigantic size, and of an ancient, long-forgotten form. The fire below the cauldron was getting low, the evening light had ceased to fall through the windows, and the darkness was only broken by the faint glimmer of the dying embers.

Nature at last claimed her rights. The wanderers' eyes were almost closing, and, laying aside all fear, they took possession of the couches where surely giant forms had once reposed.

When they awoke the sun was shining brightly outside, but its beams could fall but dimly through the rude window-panes. The doors were firmly fastened, and there was no trace of human footsteps, yet the fire burned once more on the hearth, from the bubbling cauldron rose a tempting fragrance, and the table was laid as for a meal.

" See, dear Orm," cried Aslog joyfully, pointing to the fire and the table, " this language is easy to understand, though it be a silent one. The unseen owners of this dwelling know our need, and bid us welcome to their hospitable roof."

When they had again partaken of the contents of the boiling cauldron, Orm and Aslog went into the hall, and found there a stair which led up to a room just below the hide-covered roof. This and the room in which they had passed the night were the only apartments of the house, but they contained all that was necessary for a life of retirement.   There was no sign of any inhabitant, yet it seemed as if some one had lately been there, whose hand had lovingly arranged everything for the poor homeless ones.   They understood the silent language, and they remained henceforth contentedly in the house, enjoying the sweet feeling that they had at last a home.

Orm never cast his net into the sea without drawing out a rich supply of delicious fish; the snares he set in the morning for the birds were never empty at evening. The fruit-trees bore abundantly, and Aslog found plenty of employment in gathering and storing the rich harvest.

Summer passed away, and the short autumn was drawing towards its close, when a lovely baby boy came to cheer the hearts of Orm and Aslog through the dreary winter.   The child was called Sämund, and seemed to his parents a pledge of future reconciliation.

One day Orm was holding his little son in his arms, and watching with delight his baby smiles, and Aslog stood at the fire preparing the midday meal, when a tall shadow passed the window, the heavy house door swung open, and a loud knocking was heard at the door of the room.   Aslog let the spoon fall in terror, and even brave Orm pressed his boy closer to his heart as the visitor entered.

A gigantic woman stepped into the room.   Her stature was greater than Orm and Aslog had ever seen among their own powerful nation.   She wore a sky-blue robe with a silver-embroidered hem; a golden fillet

bound her long snow-white hair, and on her once beautiful features centuries of joy and grief seemed to have
left their traces.

"Do not be afraid," said the majestic visitor, with gentle
gravity; "this is my island and my house, but I gladly
gave them up to you when I knew of your distress.
Only one thing I ask of you. Christmas Eve is drawing
near. For that one night let me have the room for a
few hours, while we hold our yearly festivity. But you
must promise me two things—not to speak a word while
our feast lasts, and not to make any attempt to see what
is going on in the room below. If you grant this request
you may live here undisturbed, and enjoy my protection
until you wish to leave the island."

With lightened hearts Orm and Aslog gave the promise, then the majestic lady bowed her silvery head in
gracious farewell, and passed out through the door.

It was Christmas Eve; Aslog had cleaned and tidied
the room with even more than her ordinary care. The
boards were snow-white, and Orm strewed them with
finely-cloven fir-twigs. The fire burned brightly on the
neatly-swept hearth, and above it hung the shining cauldron. Aslog rolled her baby in the softest of the skins
that served to cover her bed, and went with Orm to the
upper room, where they sat down beside the warm chimney of the apartment below, which passed of necessity
through this second storey.

For a long time all was silent. Suddenly a sweet,
soft sound was heard; others followed, and soon the
music swelled in waves of melody through the night air.

R

Aslog listened entranced, while Orm went to the gable end of the roof, and, since this was not forbidden, opened the shutter which in the daytime served to let in air and light.

There was motion over the whole island. Little shrivelled forms, with grave and aged faces, were bustling about with blazing torches in their hands. They ran dry-shod over the waves, and made their way to the rock that guarded the entrance to the bay. When they reached it they placed themselves in a circle round it, and sat down on the ground in respectful humility. Then a tall form approached from the centre of the island. The dwarfs opened their circle to admit her, and Orm recognised by the flickering light the noble lady who had a few days before paid them so unlooked-for a visit. Her sky-blue robe and the gold in her hair gleamed with even more than their former brilliance. She stepped up to the rock, threw her arms round the cold stone, and remained so for a moment in a silent embrace. Suddenly the stone acquired life and motion. The gigantic limbs were freed from their petrifaction, the hair rolled down over the shoulders, the eyes began to glow once more with life. As if awaking from the sleep of death, the giant rose, seized the hand of the stately lady whose loving embrace had called him back to life, and they both turned towards the house, whither the dwarfs accompanied them with flaming torches and heart-enthralling melody. The ground seemed to tremble beneath the tread of the giants. Soon they reached the house-door. Then Orm shut the shutter,

and groped his way back to where his wife sat beside
the chimney.

GURU AWAKES THE ROCK TO LIFE.

Below there was rattling of dishes and the patter of
many feet; the young couple heard every sound through
the wide chimney. The strong voice of the rock giant
sounded like thunder to human ears, and the voice of
the lady, which Orm and Aslog had heard once before,
was like the powerful notes of some musical instrument.

Tables and chairs were moved, drinking-horns were knocked together; the feast was beginning, and now was heard once more that music which had before so overwhelmed Aslog with delight. Then an irresistible longing seized her to see the wondrous company which Orm had described to her. She rose and groped for a crack in the floor through which it was possible to see into the room below. Orm in silence held out his hand to check her fatal rashness, but the movement woke the sleeping babe, who, terrified by the unwonted sounds below, raised a cry that went to the mother's heart. Forgetting everything now but her child's distress, she began, as was her wont, to soothe him with caressing words. Then suddenly an awful cry and a wild tumult arose below, the music ceased, and through the door rushed the dwarfs in wild commotion. Their torches went out, the noise of their flight sounded but a few moments, then night and silence reigned over the place which a minute before had resounded with festive merriment.

In deadly terror Aslog had sunk back on her seat, tremblingly awaiting the fate that her rashness had called down on her dear ones. They were anxious hours that they spent now in the dark upper room, almost more anxious than those of their flight and of that hard struggle with the waves. At last the morning dawned. A clear sunbeam shot through a hole in the shutter and awoke the boy, who began to cry with cold and hunger. Then her love for her child overcame her fear, and Aslog persuaded her husband to go down with her and learn their fate. They descended the stairs, trembling at every step. Now they stood at the door of the room and listened. There was no sound—all was still as death. At last they lifted the latch ; Aslog pressed her child to her heart and entered the room. A loud cry escaped her lips. At the far end of the room, at the seat of honour at the table, sat the mighty giant whose awakening Orm had witnessed ; but life had again left his veins, and he sat there a cold, grey mass of rock. It seemed to Aslog that the stony hand which still grasped the drinking-horn might yet be raised to hurl destruction at her and her dear ones. She gazed in speechless terror at the rock-giant, her eyes passing slowly from the motionless head to the massive folds of the stone garment. Then she perceived another form, sunk motionless, as in deepest anguish, on the floor. The face was pressed against the cold stone, but the blue robe with the silver-embroidered hem and the flowing white hair told the terrified Aslog who it was.

"Andfind, my Andfind!" moaned the giant lady, raising her face at last, "thou wilt never again smile on thy faithful Guru, and rejoice with her at thy short space of life and freedom."

Aslog uttered a cry, but not, as before, of terror for her own fate, but of anguish and remorse. Her bitter sobbing caused even the grief-stricken giantess to raise her head.

"Do not weep so," she said gently, "and do not be afraid; I could indeed easily kill you, and break this house, which I gave you as your home, like a child's toy.

It is true that your forgetfulness has caused untold anguish to me, but the revenge of the powerful must be— forgiveness!   Then do not weep, for there is nothing to fear."

"Oh, that is not all!" sobbed Aslog.   "The names which you named, noble lady, cut me to the heart. They remind me of a legend which I often heard when a child about Guru, the beautiful giant-maiden, who was obliged to flee from cruel Odin with her beloved And-find.   The story of their fate always touched me deeply, and I thought when I heard these names that you might perhaps be that Guru, and this thought added fresh bitterness to my remorse."

The giantess appeared sunk in dreamy meditation.

"And do they remember us still in the old Father-land?" she said at length; "and are there yet any halls remaining of Hrungnir's castle?"

"No, noble lady," answered Aslog, "they have all long since crumbled to dust, for many centuries have passed over Norway since those days.   It is true a proud castle still looks down on the foaming waves, but it is owned by Sämund, whose only child I am."

"Our fate, O daughter of my former home, is won-drously alike," said Guru ; "but your life will end more joyfully than mine.   We lived here in undisturbed happi-ness for many centuries, for it was to this island that our trusty bark bore us after that night of death.   This house, which my husband's strong arm built for our home, is small and poor compared with my father's halls, but we did not miss the lost splendour.   The days went by in quiet happiness, and we felt no longings after the land which drove out us and our friends. The dwarfs also, who like us had turned their backs on an inhospitable country, settled round about on the little islands, and lived there in the heart of the earth in peace and contentment. Every Christmas Eve we met in this room, and held festival as our forefathers did even before your religion had spread to these northern lands. Centuries passed away, and one evening I was standing with Andfind at the shore of our island looking out over the sea. On the northern horizon appeared a stately ship, and Andfind, whose eye was sharper than the eagle's, and had power to see into the future, recognised in the man at the prow a powerful foe of the freedom of Norway and of our authority. It was Olaf, whom you call a saint, who, not long afterwards, overcame the princes of Norway in one night, and destroyed the last vestiges of the old customs. All this my husband's prudent foresight saw, and with a mighty effort he blew the waves to fury with his breath, so that they threatened to break Olaf's proud ship to pieces. But the invader spoke some prayer such as you uttered when you approached our shores, and the raging sea grew calm. Then Andfind put forth his hand to push back the vessel as it drew near the shore, but Olaf, raising his hands towards heaven, said, in a tone of stern reproof—'Stand thou there a stone henceforth!' Immediately the eyes in which I had been wont to read my husband's every wish were closed, the hand that had grasped mine lovingly grew cold and hard, the form so full of life and beauty turned to unfeeling stone, and my beloved Andfind stood a grey, lifeless rock upon the shore. The invaders sailed on towards the coast of Norway, and I remained in dreary desolation on the now lonely island. Only once a-year, on Christmas Eve, petrified giants are allowed a few hours of life if one of their own race embraces them, and thus sacrifices centuries of his own lifetime. I loved my husband too dearly not to offer this sacrifice willingly, that he and I might enjoy yearly a few hours of inter-course. I never counted how many times he woke to life at my embrace, how many centuries of my life I yielded for his sake; I did not wish to know the day when I, as I embraced him, should likewise turn to stone, and stand henceforth on the shore one for ever with my Andfind. Now all is over," Guru concluded; "I may never more awake my beloved one, for a human eye, a human voice has disturbed the sacred festival of our spirit-race. Stone must my Andfind remain till that day when all the rocks and mountains of old Norway will perish in the ruin of the world."

She threw her arms once more round the cold stone, lifted her golden harp from the floor, and then turned to Orm and Aslog, who had listened in silent grief.

"Farewell!" she said; "I leave you my protection and my blessing. Yours are henceforth the costly vessels that adorned our festive board; I need them no more. Live still in peace and happiness in this house until you return to receive Sämund's forgiveness, and live a life of gladness on the site of my old home."

She passed out, and her sorrowing guests followed her

to the door. Without once looking back, she glided away through the leafless trees; her blue robe gleamed far away over the snow-covered plain. Orm and Aslog watched her crossing the waves to the little islands; then they saw her no more.

Had she descended to the music of her golden harp into the cold billows? or did she go to rule as queen in the kingdom of dwarfs? Orm and Aslog never knew her fate, but her prophecies of good were richly fulfilled.

Sickness and misfortune kept far aloof from their island home. They were happy in their mutual love, strong in body, cheerful in spirit, contented even in their isolation. Their boy grew daily in beauty, strength, and obedience; the trees bore double fruit, the sea yielded its tribute more freely than ever, and the bird-snares were never empty. Sunshine and the fragrance of flowers filled the air, and they drank in life and happiness at every breath. And when winter came, the storm raged round the house, and the thick snowflakes whirled through the cracking fir branches against the window, then the little family sat cosily in their sheltered home; the dry wood blazed brightly on the hearth, and at the cheerful fireside sat Aslog making nets, while Orm carved away at a new oar, and the child listened eagerly to the tales of Old Norway.

Year after year rolled away, and left no traces of care on the faces of the lonely exiles, save that when Aslog thought of her father a shadow crossed her white brow, and the old longing awoke for his love and forgiveness.

It was the beginning of spring. The fruit-trees wore their wreaths of blossoms, and the sunbeams played through the dark fir branches on the roof of the lonely house. The door opened, and Orm, accompanied by Aslog and the boy, stepped out, bearing one of the precious vessels which Guru had left as a parting gift to her guests. The utensils which her motherly hand had provided had become worn out in the course of years, and Orm was going to the coast of Norway to sell the golden goblet, and buy the needed utensils with its price. He had long postponed this step, for he still feared the sharp eye of treachery and revenge ; but their need was pressing, and there could be no longer delay.

The parting was a bitter one. Aslog embraced him again and again, and even Guru's prophetic words had lost their power to comfort. But Orm, although his heart was far from light, soothed her with a promise of a quick return ; then he tore himself away, sprang into a boat, and pushed from the shore.

The boat flew like a sea-mew over the waves, through the circle of little islands, and out into the open sea. A wind as fresh as that which had favoured their flight came now from the north to swell the white sail. Orm drew in the oars and watched how his boat darted over the gleaming waves. He directed his course towards the south-east. As it was drawing towards noon the coasts of his native land appeared above the horizon ; and long before the set of sun the boat sailed up the narrow waters of the Trondheim Fiord, and landed at the quay of the old royal city. Orm passed the streets with hurried steps, and with the precious vessel under his arm he entered the shop of a goldsmith.

The man seemed amazed at the rich metal and the rare and elaborate workmanship, paid without demur the price asked, and Orm hastened gladly to another building to choose his purchases. There was a great crowd of buyers, and fearing lest some old acquaintance should be among them, he turned aside, and examined the wares in silence.

"Welcome, friend! What's the news in your mountains?" said the merchant to a countryman who had just entered.

"Thanks, sir, not much good," replied the newcomer.

"What is wrong?" asked the merchant. "Is your master, rich Sämund, not well? Has he not yet submitted to his fate?"

Orm listened eagerly.

"It will soon be all over with him," replied the countryman; "his grief about his daughter is breaking his heart. He is ill, lonely, and sad. He has had it proclaimed through the whole land that he will forgive the fugitives everything if they will only return; and he has promised a great reward to any one who will bring him the smallest tidings of them. But **they** seem to have vanished from the earth, and it is most likely the old man will die without one of his kin to close his eyes in the last sleep."

Orm thought no more about his purchases; he thought only of Aslog and her dying father. Without being noticed in the crowd he left the shop. Scarcely had he turned the first corner when he ran at full speed to the quay, sprang down the steps, loosed his boat, and by the last rays of the setting sun he steered skilfully along the narrow fiord among all the larger vessels, and rowed towards the ocean. His heart beat with eager longing and delight. Had not a reconciliation with the father of his loved Aslog long been the most cherished wish of his heart as well as of hers, though he had been silent on the subject for Aslog's sake?

It was night when his boat glided out of the fiord and sailed out to sea. The wind, which had blown towards land all day, had turned, and, sweeping now from the Norwegian mountains, drove Orm's boat with the swiftness of an arrow over the waters. The moon rose clear and full above his native land, and the waves dashed their silver spray against the keel. Orm could not but think of that night when Aslog lay hungry and exhausted at his feet—behind him terror and treachery—before, an unknown future. The moon's clear radiance and the sparkling waves were the same then as now, but in all else how blessed was the change!

Thus the night passed, and when the east began to glow with red his boat glided between the little islands, and when the first full beam fell on the fir-tree tops he landed on the shore of his island home.

He scarcely took time to fasten the boat. Then he hastened under the blossoming fruit-trees—with empty hand, indeed, yet with a richer gift than Aslog would have dared to hope for.

And now he stood beside her couch. " Awake, awake,

beloved one!" he whispered as he bent over her; "I bring news of your father, the best news that your heart could wish for—love and forgiveness!"

Then Aslog awoke, and her beaming eyes, the silent tears that fell over her clasped hands, told of even deeper joy than Orm had pictured to himself as he hastened home.

Soon all was bustle in the quiet room. Once more Aslog lit the fire, once more the breakfast bubbled in the cauldron, while she adorned herself and her boy in festive garments, and Orm carried Guru's gifts of gold and precious stones down to the boat. Once more they sat together at the table enjoying the provisions of Guru's hospitable home. They gazed at the lofty walls which had afforded them shelter, and sadly looked on the stony form of Andfind, who had for years been a silent member of the little household. Then Orm seized his wife's hand; and they left the house, carefully closing the door behind them, and followed the boy, who had run on before in his eagerness, towards the strand.

"Farewell, thou lovely island!" cried Orm, as he loosed the rope; "and if ever again hunted fugitives land on thy shore, be to them as sweet a home as thou hast been to us."

The child was already seated in the boat, playing with the beautiful vessels of gold and precious stones, and Aslog sat down beside him to tell him about his new home and his dear grandfather, while Orm dipped the oars, and the boat left the strand of the "Last Home of the Giants."

The sun was just about to sink into the sea ; its rays cast a parting glance on the windows of the lonely castle, on the rock which had once resounded with mirth and revelry.   And now the splendid halls were desolate. The servants, serving not out of love but out of fear, obeyed in sullen silence the commands of their gloomy master.   The daughter, the only one whom his cold heart had ever loved, was lost to him.   His old age was lonely and desolate.   Then his pride yielded.   "What if she has disgraced my house by choosing the servant instead of the prince?—still she is my child, my only one, and dear and loving she has always been to me! Oh, bring back my daughter, my Aslog, that I may look upon her face before I die!"

Rich were the rewards offered by the sorrowing father for the least tidings of his child, but he waited days and weeks in vain.   She seemed lost to him for ever.

"Take me out, that I may see the sun as long as I have sight!" said he to his servants as the evening sun looked in at the castle windows.

The servants supported his tottering steps to the edge of the rock.   Then he beckoned to them to go, and leave him with his sorrow.

The sun sank like a ball of fire into the ocean, and the sea rolled in purple waves from the farthest horizon, and broke them into golden spray at the foot of the castle rock.

"Would that my old age could be calm and clear, like this sweet evening, and would that my life might sink in brightness as the sun into the sea!"

Then he heard in the distance the splashing of oars, and his eye, keen as of old, looked eagerly towards the horizon. A boat, gently urged on by the wind, was sailing from the north-west. Nearer and nearer it came, and seemed to be directing its course to the rock where the old man sat. At the helm sat a manly form, and at the prow stood a graceful woman with a boy pressed closely to her side. Her hair gleamed golden, as his daughter's used to do ; and now she raised her hand, and fluttered a white kerchief as in eager greeting. Sämund's heart beat with glad presentiment, he felt his weakness no longer, but raised himself, unaided, from the stone breastwork, and fixed his gaze on the approaching boat. Now the little vessel came up to the very foot of the rock, he heard the chain rattling round the post, and the sound of familiar voices was borne up to him on the evening air. It was no dream. There were light foot-steps beside him, and when he turned to look, Aslog, his lost Aslog, knelt before him, her eyes full of humble penitence, and by her side knelt a fair-haired boy, who stretched out his hands to the old man, and echoed his mother's words in childish accents—" Oh, grandfather, forgive and love us !"

The old man opened his arms, and pressed the welcome suppliants to his heart, and as he kissed his lovely grand-son, he said in a voice more mild and soft than was his wont—" Thank God, I shall not die in my loneliness after all !"

And he did not die. From day to day he felt more and more of his old vigour, and when he saw how

tenderly Aslog loved her husband, what a faithful husband and father Orm was, and what a dutiful son to
himself, he forgot all his disappointed hopes—even the
royal diadem that Aslog had rejected.   The love of his
children and grandchildren made his last days his
brightest, and thus the wish of that spring evening was
fulfilled, his old age was calm and clear, and his life sank
in brightness as the sun into the sea.

Marcus Ward & Co., Royal Ulster Works, Belfast.

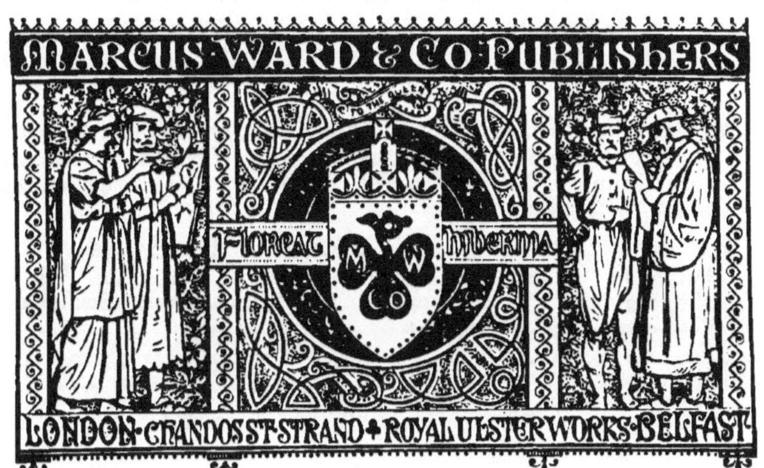

Illustrated & Educational

 Works

PUBLISHED BY

MARCUS WARD AND CO.,

67, 68, Chandos Street, Strand,

LONDON;

ROYAL ULSTER WORKS, BELFAST.

ELEGANT GIFT-BOOKS.

Childhood a Hundred Years Ago. By Sarah Tytler, Author of "Papers for Thoughtful Girls, &c., &c. With Six Chromographs, after Paintings by Sir Joshua Reynolds. Small quarto, cloth elegant, gilt edges, 10/6.

Landseer's Dogs and their Stories. By Sarah Tytler, Author of "Childhood a Hundred Years Ago," &c., &c. With Six Chromographs, after Paintings by Sir Edwin Landseer. Small quarto, cloth elegant, gilt edges, 10/6.

English Echoes of German Song. Translated by Dr. R. E. Wallis, Dr. J. D. Morell, and F. d'Anvers. Edited by N. d'Anvers. With Twelve beautiful Steel Engravings. Small quarto, cloth elegant, gilt edges. 10/6.

Floral Poetry and the Language of Flowers. A collection of choice poems on Flowers, with most complete Indexes to the Language of Flowers, and eight exquisite Chromographs. Small quarto, cloth elegant, gilt edges, 10/6.

The Quiver of Love : a collection of Valentines, Ancient and Modern. With Eight exquisite Full-page Illustrations in Gold and Colours, by Walter Crane and K. Greenaway. Full gilt cover, gilt edges, 7/6.

"Look at it as we may, the book is a marvel, and its cheapness is not its least noticeable feature."—*Morning Advertiser.*

ART VOLUME—NEW EDITION.

Mrs. Mundi at Home. R.S.V.P. Lines and Outlines by Walter Crane. Twenty-four Plates. New Edition, cloth, Decorated by the Artist, gilt extra, gilt edges, large oblong quarto, 15/-.

"A quaint and clever book of drawings."—*Times.*
"Every picture in the twenty-four is a study in itself."—*Standard.*
"An amusing combination of humorous verse and illustrations."—*Daily Telegraph.*
"The humour is so intense, and at the same time so delicate, that the most fastidious hypochondriac must be forced to laughter."—*Morning Post.*
"The binding is very pleasing."—*Saturday Review.*

The House that Jack Built : a New Building on the Old Foundation. Set forth in Twelve Full-page Drawings in Colours, in the Antient Style, by J. R. Harris. Large 4to, cloth extra, 5/-.

"An illustrated children's book, got up in a style which surpasses anything of the kind we have seen."—*Standard.*

The Latin Year: a Collection of Latin Hymns, Ancient and Modern. Edited by the Rev. W. J. LOFTIE, B.A., F.S.A. With numerous Illustrations by R. BATEMAN, after the manner of the best period of early Wood Engraving. Rough edges, quaint binding. 15/-. N.B.—A few copies with special binding may be had. Price 40/-.

Historical Records of the 2nd Royal Surrey Militia. With Introductory Chapters, giving a Sketch of the History of the English Militia, and of events in the Military History of Surrey. By JOHN DAVIS, Captain in the Regiment. Frontispiece and numerous Full-page Illustrations specially prepared for this work. Large octavo. 21/-.

GEMS OF HOME SCENERY.

A series of Topographical Gift-Books. Edited by the Rev. W. J. LOFTIE, B.A., F.S.A. With Six Chromo Facsimiles of Original Drawings by the late T. L. ROWBOTHAM, Member of the Society of Painters in Water-Colours, and numerous Illustrations on Wood. Post 4to, cloth, gold and black, bevelled boards, gilt edges, 6/-.

Views in Wicklow and Killarney.—The Dargle, County Wicklow; Glendalough and Seven Churches, County Wicklow; Glengariff, County Cork; Gap of Dunloe, Killarney; Old Weir Bridge, Killarney; Eagle's Nest, Killarney.

Views in the English Lake District.—Buttermere, Cumberland; Skiddaw, Derwentwater, and Saddleback; Eagle Crag, Borrowdale; Head of Windermere; Rydal Water, Westmoreland; Langdale, Westmoreland.

Views in North Wales.—Caernarvon Castle; Cader Idris, from the Barmouth Road; Moel Siabod, from Bettws-y-Coed; Snowdon; Conway Castle; Beddgelert.

Views in Scotland.—Linlithgow; Ben Nevis, from Bannavie; Loch Leven Castle; Doune Castle; Loch Katrine; Kilchurn Castle.
"Wisely selected and admirably illustrated."—*Daily Telegraph.*
"The most charming gift-books of the season."—*Birmingham Gazette.*

BOOKS AT FIVE SHILLINGS.

𝕮𝖍𝖗𝖔𝖒𝖔𝖌𝖗𝖆𝖕𝖍 𝕾𝖊𝖗𝖎𝖊𝖘.

The Good Old Days ; or, Christmas under Queen Elizabeth.
By ESME STUART. With Five Coloured Illustrations, from Drawings by H. STACY MARKS, A.R.A. Foolscap quarto, cloth extra, bevelled boards.

"Not only will interest be derived from the story, but instruction as to the manners and habits of the people in the days of good Queen Bess."—*City Press.*

Melcomb Manor: a Family Chronicle. By F. SCARLETT
POTTER. Six Illustrations, in Gold and Colours. Foolscap quarto, cloth extra, bevelled boards.

"Altogether a very pretty book, whether as regards the pictures or the story." —*Saturday Review.*

Puck and Blossom: a Fairy Tale. By ROSA MULHOLLAND,
Author of "The Little Flower-Seekers," "Eldergowan," &c. Six Illustrations, in Gold and Colours. Foolscap quarto, cloth extra, bevelled boards.   [*New Edition.*

"Pretty stories, beautifully illustrated in gold and colours."—*Daily News.*

"The fairy pictures are full of life and drollery. . . . The narratives are miracles of wonder and invention."—*Daily Albion.*

The Little Flower-Seekers ; or, the Adventures of Trot and
Daisy in a Wonderful Garden by Moonlight. By ROSA MULHOLLAND, Author of "Puck and Blossom," "Eldergowan," &c. With Twelve Chromographs of Flowers, by various Artists. Foolscap quarto, cloth extra, bevelled boards.

"A charming volume."—*Daily News.*

A Cruise in the Acorn. By ALICE JERROLD. Six Illustrations,
in Gold and Colours. Foolscap quarto, cloth extra, bevelled boards.
                                    [*New Edition.*

"A simple little story, very prettily told, with illustrations in colours and gold." —*Graphic.*

"Told in a charming style, by aid of beautiful print, and illustrated in gold and colours."—*Liverpool Albion.*

BOOKS AT FIVE SHILLINGS.—*Continued.*

Katty Lester: a book for Girls.
By Mrs. GEORGE CUPPLES, Author of "The Children's Voyage," &c. With Twelve Chromographs of Animals, after Harrison Weir. Foolscap quarto, cloth extra, bevelled boards. [*New Edition.*

"A capital book for girls."—*Globe.*

The Children's Voyage; or, a Trip in the Water Fairy.
By Mrs. GEORGE CUPPLES, Author of "Katty Lester," &c. With Twelve Chromographs of Ships, Boats, and Sea Views, after Edward Duncan. Foolscap quarto, cloth extra, bevelled boards.

"Well adapted to the comprehension of children."—*Standard.*

New Series of 5/- Books by Popular Authors.

With Coloured Frontispiece, Illuminated Title-page, and numerous original Illustrations. Post Octavo, Cloth Extra.

Three Years at Wolverton: a Public School Story.
By a Wolvertonian.

Last Cruise of the Ariadne.
By S. WHITCHURCH SADLER, R.N., Author of "The Ship of Ice," "Perilous Seas," &c.

Perilous Seas, and how Oriana sailed them.
By S. W. SADLER, R.N., Author of "The Ship of Ice," &c.

"All through 'Perilous Seas' there is enough stirring incident to arouse, and enough good writing to sustain, the interest of its youthful readers."—*Hour.*

Miss Hitchcock's Wedding Dress.
By the Author of "A Very Young Couple," "Mrs. Jerningham's Journal," &c.

"One of those pleasant stories, in an attractive dress, which are becoming almost a specialty of Marcus Ward & Co."—*Morning Advertiser.*

Ralph Somerville; or, a Midshipman's Adventures in the Pacific Ocean.
By CHARLES H. EDEN, Author of "The Twin Brothers of Elfvedale," "India, Historical and Descriptive," &c.

"There is always an air of reality about Mr. Eden's descriptive passages which makes one feel that they are the result of actual experience."—*Morning Post.*

Myrtle and Cypress: a Tale of Chequered Life.
By ANNETTE CALTHROP.

"The tale is altogether above the average, healthy in tone, and worked out with no little ability."—*John Bull.*

BOOKS AT THREE-AND-SIXPENCE.

TRAVEL AND ADVENTURE.

India, Historical and Descriptive. With an Account of the
Sepoy Mutiny of 1857–58, by C. H. EDEN, Author of "Ralph
Somervil e," &c. Sixty-six Illustrations, Map, and Coloured Frontis-
piece. Crown octavo, cloth extra.

Notes of Travel in Egypt and Nubia. By J. L. STEPHENS.
Revised and enlarged, with an account of the Suez Canal. Seventy-
one Illustrations, Map, and Coloured Frontispiece. Crown octavo,
cloth extra.

Fairyland Tales of Dwarfs, Fairies, Water-Sprites, &c.
From the German of Villamaria. Twenty-five Illustrations and
Coloured Frontispiece. Crown octavo, cloth extra.

Robinson Crusoe. By DANIEL DEFOE. A new and beautiful
edition, with numerous Illustrations, Coloured Frontispiece and Title.
Crown octavo, cloth extra.

The Vicar of Wakefield. By OLIVER GOLDSMITH. Numerous
Illustrations, Coloured Frontispiece and Title. Crown octavo, cloth
extra.

With Full-page Original Illustrations, Coloured Frontispiece, and Illuminated Title-page. Post octavo, cloth, gold and black.

The Ship of Ice : a Strange Story of the Polar Seas. By
S. WHITCHURCH SADLER, R.N., Author of "Perilous Seas,"
"Marshall Vavasour," &c.

"Not only a 'Strange Story,' but one full of exciting interest.   .   .   .
The author writes in a vigorous, manly style, and the book is one which most
English boys, with their love of daring and adventure, are likely heartily to relish."
—*Pall Mall Gazette.*

"A capital book of adventure."—*Manchester Guardian.*

*Chronicles of Cosy Nook : a Book of Stories for Boys and
Girls.* By Mrs. S. C. HALL.

"Mrs. Hall never in her best days wrote a better story for youngsters."—
Morning Advertiser.

"This gifted lady and her husband are known to be among the finest writers of
children's books in this country."—*Edinburgh Courant.*

BOOKS AT THREE-AND-SIXPENCE.—*Continued.*

Country Maidens: a Story of the Present Day. By M. BRAMSTON, Author of "The Panelled House," &c.

"A charming fresh little story, which must give pleasure to both old and young . . . deserves to be heartily commended."—*Morning Post.*

"As charming a tale of home life as we have often met."—*Standard.*

A Very Young Couple. By the Author of "Mrs. Jerningham's Journal," "Miss Hitchcock's Wedding Dress," &c.

"A very lively and pleasant little tale."—*Spectator.*

BOOKS AT TWO-AND-SIXPENCE.

With Coloured Frontispiece, Illuminated Title, and Full-page Original Illustrations.

Mildred's Mistake. A Still-Life Study. By F. LEVIEN, Author of "Little Ada's Jewels," "Maggie's Pictures," &c. Small octavo, cloth extra.

Kaspar and the Seven Wonderful Pigeons of Würzburg. By JULIA GODDARD. Small octavo, cloth extra.

Dobbie and Dobbie's Master: a Peep into the Life of a Very Little Man. By N. D'ANVERS, Author of "Little Minnie's Troubles," &c. Small octavo, cloth extra.

Tom: the History of a very Little Boy. By H. RUTHERFURD RUSSELL. Small octavo, cloth, gold and black. [*New Edition.*

"Almost as good, in its way, as Mr. Carroll's 'Alice in Wonderland.' Parents and lovers of childhood will like it much, as the childish reader is sure to do."—*Illustrated London News.*

"A very good story for boys."—*Globe.*

Tom Seven Years Old: a Sequel to "Tom." By H. RUTHERFURD RUSSELL. Small octavo, cloth, gold and black.

"The truest and purest exhibition of a natural little boy's mind that we have seen in any story of child life."—*Illustrated London News.*

BOOKS AT TWO-AND-SIXPENCE.—*Continued.*

Minna's Holiday, and Other Tales. By M. BETHAM-EDWARDS. Small octavo, cloth, gold and black.

> "Simple, pleasantly-written stories."—*Daily News.*

Doda's Birthday: the Record of all that befell a Little Girl *on a Long, Eventful Day.* By EDWIN J. ELLIS. Small octavo, cloth, gold and black.

> "As pleasant a book as could be given to any little girl."—*Scotsman.*

> "A most suitable book for girls, and one that will delight the little misses immensely."—*Edinburgh Courant.*

> "A charming book."—*Daily News.*

The Markhams of Ollerton: a Tale of the Civil War, *1642–1647.* By E. GLAISTER. Small octavo, cloth, gold and black.
> [*New Edition.*

> "Abounds with thrilling incidents of that eventful period."—*Morning Post.*

> "A well-written story of the civil war, from 1642 to 1647."—*Scotsman.*

> "The story of Charles I. is one that never loses its charm, and when so pleasantly and colloquially told, and embellished by such pretty and characteristic pictures as we have here, it will be sure to find a large and appreciative audience." —*Daily News.*

Eldergowan; or, Twelve Months of my Life, and Other *Tales.* By ROSA MULHOLLAND, Author of "Puck and Blossom," "The Little Flower-Seekers," &c. Small octavo, cloth, gold and black.
> [*New Edition.*

> "One of the pleasantest little books we have met for some time; charmingly illustrated."—*Illustrated Review.*

> "A perfect little gem in its way."—*Civil Service Gazette.*

> "A fine volume for girls."—*Edinburgh Courant.*

Christmas at Annesley; or, how the Grahams spent their *Holidays.* By M. E. SHIPLEY. Small octavo, cloth, gold and black.
> [*New Edition.*

> "A delightful book for children."—*Sunday Times.*

> "Will be read with delight by young folks."—*Lloyd's Weekly London News.*

BOOKS AT TWO-AND-SIXPENCE.—*Continued.*

Turnaside Cottage. By MARY SENIOR CLARK, Author of "Lost Legends of the Nursery Rhymes." Small octavo, cloth, gold and black. [*New Edition.*
"An interesting story, well told."—*Birmingham Morning News.*
"Charmingly written, impressing good and useful lessons."—*Art Journal.*

The Fairy Spinner. By MIRANDA HILL. Small octavo, cloth, gold and black. [*New Edition.*
"Really enchanting, and will enthral the young reader."—*Edinburgh Courant.*
"Well illustrated."—*Daily News.*

Pollie and Jack: a Small Story for Small People. By ALICE HEPBURN, Author of "Two Little Cousins." Small octavo, cloth, gold and black. [*New Edition.*
"Capitally written down to the level of little folks."—*Morning Advertiser.*
"Will be much enjoyed by young folks."—*Figaro.*

New Series of Two-and-Sixpenny Gift-Books.

Nanny's Treasure. From the French of Madame DE STOLZ. Nineteen Full-page Illustrations and Coloured Frontispiece. Small octavo, cloth extra.

The Little Head of the Family. From the French of Mdlle. FLEURIOT. Fourteen Full-page Illustrations and Coloured Frontispiece. Small octavo, cloth extra.

Where the Rail Runs Now: a Story of the Coaching Days. By F. FRANKFORT MOORE. With Illustrations. Small octavo, cloth extra.

Animals of the Farm: their Structure and Physiology. A Handbook for Agricultural Students and Farmers. By JOHN F. HODGES, M.D., F.C.S., &c. Second Edition, revised by the Author. Numerous Illustrations. Small octavo, cloth, 2/6.

B

BOOKS AT TWO SHILLINGS.

Two Little Cousins. By ALICE HEPBURN, Author of " Pollie
and Jack."   Five Coloured Illustrations, Cloth, Illuminated.

"Adorned with bright chromographs, and printed in large, clear type to suit
beginners."—*Standard.*

Percy's First Friends. By M. D.   Five Coloured Illustrations,
Cloth, Illuminated.

"An agreeable account of the early adventures of a motherless boy."—*Lloyd's
Weekly London News.*

Five Little Farmers.   By ROSA MULHOLLAND, Author of
" Puck and Blossom," " The Little Flower-Seekers," " Eldergowan,"
&c.   Five Coloured Illustrations, Cloth, Illuminated.

"Contains a number of cunningly worked-out chromo lithographs, in which
children and their domestic pets are grouped in a most artistic and effective manner."
—*Figaro.*

Maggie's Pictures ; or, the Great Life told to a Child. By
FANNY LEVIEN, Author of " Mildred's Mistake, " Little Ada's
Jewels."   Five Coloured Illustrations, and Illuminated Title-page.
Cloth, Illuminated.

" Will be welcome for the simplicity of its early lessons."—*Lloyd's Newspaper.*

The Twin Brothers of Elfvedale : a Story of Norwegian
Peasant Life.   By CHARLES H. EDEN, Author of " Ralph Somerville,"
" India, Historical and Descriptive," &c.   Coloured Illustrations,
Cloth, Illuminated.   [*New Edition.*

"Full of adventure. . . Schoolboys will welcome the book."—*Guardian.*

"A tale of Norwegian peasant life fifty years ago, cleverly put together, told in
a bright, hearty view, and telling the young reader a great deal about the rough,
simple lives of Northern folk, their customs, superstitions, and amusements."—*Times.*

Our Games : a Story for Children. By MARY HAMILTON.
Five Coloured Illustrations, Cloth, Illuminated.   [*New Edition.*

"A pleasant little book. . . . Attractive illustrations."—*Standard.*

"Adventures of children, drawn in a charmingly natural manner."—*Guardian.*

Ella's Locket, and what it brought her. By G. E. DARTNELL.
Five Coloured Illustrations, Cloth, Illuminated.   [*New Edition.*

"Pleasantly conceived, and prettily told."—*Hour.*

BOOKS AT EIGHTEEN PENCE.

My Dolly. By H. RUTHERFURD RUSSELL, Author of "Tom Seven Years Old." Numerous Illustrations, small 8vo, Cloth extra.

Wildflower Win: the Journal of a Little Girl. By KATHLEEN KNOX. Numerous Illustrations, small 8vo, Cloth extra.

Elsie's Victory. By ELEANOR P. GEARY. Coloured Illustrations, Cloth, Illuminated.

"Sure to delight children."—*Guardian.*

Lily of the Valley: a Story for Little Boys and Girls. By KATHLEEN KNOX. Coloured Illustrations, Cloth, Illuminated.

"A pretty little gift-book, the value of which will be appreciated by the very youngest of readers."—*Leeds Mercury.*

Meadowleigh: a Holiday History. By KATHLEEN KNOX. Coloured Illustrations, Cloth, Illuminated.

"Another of those irresistible little books for children in which Messrs. Marcus Ward & Co. so cunningly combine frolicsome narrative with some of the best executed and most satisfactory coloured illustrations that have ever come under our notice."—*Figaro.*

Katie Summers: a Little Tale for Little Readers. By Mrs. C. HALL. Coloured Illustrations, Cloth, Illuminated.

"We hardly know whether most to praise binding, printing, or literary merit." —*Morning Advertiser.*

"Another tempting story of and for little people."—*Lloyd's Weekly London News.*

Roses With and Without Thorns. By ESTHER FAITHFULL FLEET. Coloured Illustrations, Cloth, Illuminated.

"Suited to children of the tenderest years, interesting and edifying. . . The pictures are a perfect treat."—*Edinburgh Courant.*

"Daintily decorated with delicate coloured illustrations."—*Scotsman.*

Little Ada's Jewels. By FANNY LEVIEN, Author of "Maggie's Pictures," "Mildred's Mistake." Coloured Illustrations, Cloth, Illuminated.

"An exquisite little book for children. . . . No better little book than this could be put into the hands of a good little boy or girl."—*Scotsman.*

"Nicely written, and beautifully illustrated."—*Morning Advertiser.*

Elegant Gift-Books.

***The Garland of the Year; or, the Months, their Poetry
and Flowers.*** Giving an account of each Month, with Poetical
Selections, descriptive of the Seasons and their Flowers; with red
lines, and Floral Designs in Gold and Colours. Small octavo, cloth
elegant, 2/6; gilt edges, 3/-.

" Creditable to the compiler's taste, and comprises many gems."—*Athenæum.*

Language and Poetry of Flowers. A New Edition, carefully
Revised and Amplified. With Six Illuminated Pages in Gold and
Colours. Cloth, black and gold, 2/6; Gilt Edges, 3/-.

LANGUAGE AND POETRY OF FLOWERS. Pocket Edition, Illustrated in
Gold and Colours. Cloth extra, 1/-; gilt edges, 1/3.

The Birthday Register. With Sentiments from Shakspere
(a New Selection of suitable Quotations), printed on writing paper.
With Illuminated Title-page. Cloth extra, 2/-; gilt edges, 2/6; and
in Limp French Morocco, Morocco and Russia, from 3/6 to 10/6.

"The association is a happy one, and in this form is neatly carried out."—
Liverpool Weekly Albion.

CHILDREN'S COLOURED PICTURE VOLUMES.

Struwwelpeter. Funny Picture Stories in the Struwwelpeter
Manner, " In merry mood for children good; with moral sad for
children bad." Twenty-four pages in Colours, enamelled boards.
Price 2/-. *Also, in Two Books, Paper Covers, 1/- each.*

" Much genuine humour, along with healthy, moral lessons."—*Leeds Mercury.*

The Shaksperean Calendar. A Novel Almanac and Daily
Date Calendar, for the Library or Boudoir. Beautifully printed in
Colours. Price 1/-. The Information comprises Sunrise and Sunset,
Moon's Changes, Festivals, Holidays, &c., with an appropriate
Quotation from Shakspere for each Day in the Year.

MARCUS WARD'S CONCISE DIARIES.

For the Pocket—Published Annually—Lightest, Cheapest, Handiest, Best.

THE CONCISE DIARIES meet the universal objection to all other Pocket
Diaries—their cumbrousness and unnecessary weight in the pocket.
They are beautifully printed in Blue and Gold, on a light, hard,
Metallic paper, and combine the following advantages :—

1. Maximum of Writing Space.
2. Minimum of Weight.
3. Useless Matter Omitted.
4. Equal Space for Sundays.
5. Daily Engagement Record.
6. The Writing is Indelible.

THE CONCISE DIARIES are made both in "Upright" and "Oblong" form,
and in Three sizes of each form.

Only one part (Three Months) need be carried in the pocket at once.

All so-called "Useful Information," which few ever read, is excluded.

"By a capital arrangement, the maximum amount of writing space is secured with
the minimum amount of weight."—*Daily Telegraph.*

"The Diary pages are furnished *separately* in quarterly parts, . . . and are
much smaller and handier than they otherwise would be. It is a very good plan."—*Pall
Mall Gazette.*

Season's Calendar for 1877. Size, 4 × 2¾ inches, containing
containing four highly-fiinished pictures, representing "Spring,"
"Summer," "Autumn," "Winter," and four pages consisting of
Calendar and other Useful Information. Price 6d.

Pocket-Book Calendar. A Bijou Almanac, size, 1¾ × 1¼
inches, with gilt edges, suitable for purse, pocket book, or waistcoat
pocket. Price 1d.

POPULAR SERIES OF SUNDAY-SCHOOL CARDS.

SACRED SELECTIONS. A set of Twelve Illuminated Cards,
set in Floral Borders and Gold Grounds, with Sacred Texts and Poetry.
Price 6d.

MEMORABLE WORDS from Scripture. Twelve Mediæval Illuminated
Cards. Price 6d.

PROVERBS AND PROMISES from Holy Scripture. Three packets,
each containing Twelve Floral, Decorated Cards, with Texts. Price
6d. each.

No. 1.—PROVERBS OF SOLOMON. No. 2.—PROMISES (Old Testament).
No. 3.—PROMISES (New Testament).

POPULAR SERIES OF SUNDAY-SCHOOL CARDS.—*Continued.*

FLORAL REWARD CARDS.—Two packets, each containing Twenty-four Cards, with Floral Borders in Gold and Colours. Price 6d. each.
Packet A.—Sacred Verses. | Packet B.—Texts of Scripture.

CHRIST THE FIRST FRUITS. A set of Twelve Floral Cards, with Gold Backgrounds, Texts, and appropriate sacred poetry. Price 1/-.

WORDS OF COUNSEL, from the Sacred Scriptures, Illuminated on Twelve Floral Cards. Price 1/-.

SAYINGS AND BLESSINGS OF OUR LORD. Two Packets, each containing Twelve Floral Cards, printed in Colours on Black Backgrounds, with Verses from Holy Scripture. Price 1/- each.

SACRED TEXTS. Two Packets, each containing a set of Twelve Cards, with Floral Illuminated Borders, printed in Gold and Colours. Price 1/-.
No. 1.—SACRED TEXTS FROM THE OLD TESTAMENT.
No. 2.—SACRED TEXTS FROM THE NEW TESTAMENT.

FLOWERS OF THE MONTHS. A set of Twelve Cards, printed in Gold and Colours, with appropriate Poetry and Descriptive Notes. In Wrapper. Price 1/-.

THE HISTORY OF OUR LORD. Twelve Scenes from the Life of Our Lord, printed in Gold and Colours, with appropriate Selections from Scripture. Price 1/-.

BIBLE PICTURES. Twelve Scenes from Old Testament History, printed in Colours, with appropriate Selections from Scripture. Price 1/-.

SACRED THOUGHTS, in Verse. Twelve Floral Cards, with Black Backgrounds. In handsome Wrapper. Price 1/-.

A PACKET OF POESY. Twelve Floral Cards, printed in Colours on Black Backgrounds. Price 1/-.

HYMNS FOR THE LAMBS OF CHRIST'S FLOCK. Twelve Cards of Birds and Flowers for Children. In handsome Wrapper. Price 1/-.

POPULAR SERIES OF SUNDAY-SCHOOL CARDS.—*Continued.*

THE APOSTLES' CREED. A Packet of Twelve Highly-decorated Cards. In handsome Wrapper. Price 1/-.

THE LORD'S PRAYER. A Packet of Twelve Highly-decorated Cards. In handsome Wrapper. Price 1/-.

POPULAR SERIES OF TEMPERANCE CARDS.

THE WATER PACKET. A set of Twelve Cards, with Borders of Water Plants, &c., and Original Verses by S. C. Hall, F.S.A. Price 1/-.

THE TEXT PACKET. Twelve Selections from Scripture, chosen for their bearing on the subject. Beautifully Illuminated in Gold and Colours. Price 6d.

POPULAR SERIES OF WALL TEXTS,

Suitable for Decorating Schoolrooms, Bedrooms, &c.

GOLDEN PRECEPTS. A Series of Nine Floral Illuminated Texts. Size, $6\frac{1}{4} \times 8$ inches. In Three Packets, price 1/6 each ; or in Mounts, Gilt Bevelled Edges, 3/- each Packet.

ECHOES FROM THE HEAVENLY JERUSALEM. A Series of Floral Illuminated Texts. Size, $8\frac{1}{4} \times 6\frac{1}{2}$ inches. In One Packet, containing Three Texts, price 1/6 ; or in Mounts, Gilt Bevelled Edges, 3/- the set.

CHEERING WORDS FOR PILGRIMS TO THE HEAVENLY JERUSALEM. A Series of Six Floral Illuminated Texts. Size, $6\frac{1}{2} \times 8\frac{1}{4}$ inches. In Two Packets, each containing Three Texts, price 1/6 ; and in Mounts, Gilt Bevelled Edges, 3/-.

LIGHTS FOR LIFE'S JOURNEY. A Series of Texts, Designed in Colours. Size, 19×6 inches. Four in a Packet, price 2/-.

MARCUS WARD & CO.'S

Newspaper Cuttings Scrap-Book.   A Ready Reference Receptacle for Scraps, from our daily sources of knowledge, the Newspapers; with an Alphabetical Index, and Spaces for Marginal Notes.

"When found, make a note of."—Captain Cuttle.

THE NEWSPAPER CUTTINGS SCRAP-BOOK has been introduced by MARCUS WARD & CO. to supply a want equally felt in household, office, or counting-house, as well as in the library of the literary man, or in the chambers of the lawyer.

There are few readers of Newspapers who do not daily meet with paragraphs, notices, or advertisements, which they would gladly cut out and retain, but, not having any convenient means of preserving them, they are passed over and lost; or, even if cut out, are so carefully put away that they cannot be found when wanted for reference.

By the use of the NEWSPAPER CUTTINGS SCRAP-BOOK all such inconveniences are prevented, as the cuttings can be readily fixed in order, and, by means of the Index, may be referred to in a moment; thus forming a volume of permanent interest and usefulness.

LIST OF SIZES, BINDINGS, AND PRICES.

No.	DESCRIPTION.	Pages	Size, in Inches	Price
6020	Fancy Cloth, Lettered on Side	72	7¾ by 9½	1/6
6021	Do. do. do.	100	7¾ by 9½	2/-
6031	Do. do. do.	100	9¾ by 11½	3/-
6043	Do. Extra Gilt, Lettered on Side ...	120	7½ by 9½	2/6
6044	Do. do. do. ...	120	8½ by 10½	3/6
6015	Do. do. do. ...	120	9½ by 11¾	4/-
6017	Do. do. do.			
	and in Colors, Inlaid	150	9½ by 11¾	4/6
6011	Half Roan, Lettered on Back	200	9½ by 11¾	5/-
6008	Half French Morocco, Lettered on Back,			
	Superior Quality Paper	150	9½ by 11¾	7/-
6013	Half Roan, Lettered on Back, Superior			
	Quality Paper	200	10 by 15	9/-

Educational Works.

ATLASES.

Adopted by the Board of National Education in Ireland.

EDITED BY J. HARRIS STONE, B.A.

MARCUS WARD'S SIXPENNY ATLAS.

LIST OF MAPS—Fully Coloured.

Eastern Hemisphere	North America	France
Western Hemisphere	South America	German Empire
Europe	England and Wales	Austrian Empire and
Asia	Scotland	Hungary
Africa and Arabia	Ireland	India or Hindustan
United States & Canada	Australia & Tasmania	New Zealand
Canaan or Palestine		

The largest Sixpenny Atlas ever offered.

MARCUS WARD'S SHILLING ATLAS.

Twenty-four Maps, printed in Colours, in the best style.

WITH GEOGRAPHICAL DEFINITIONS, DIAGRAMS OF THE GLOBES, &c.

This Atlas contains extra Maps and information, suitable
for more advanced pupils, is printed on strong paper, and bound
in durable cloth cover.

LIST OF MAPS.

Eastern Hemisphere	Kingdom of Italy	India or Hindustan
Western Hemisphere	Sweden, Norway, and	Africa and Arabia
Europe	Denmark	North America
England and Wales	Switzerland	South America
Scotland	Spain and Portugal	United States of America
Ireland	Netherlands and Belgium	Dominion of Canada
France	Russia in Europe	Australia and Tasmania
German Empire [Hungary	Turkey in Europe & Greece	New Zealand
Austrian Empire and	Asia	Canaan or Palestine

The largest Shilling Atlas ever offered to the Public.

MARCUS WARD'S HOME ATLAS.

𝕿𝖍𝖎𝖗𝖙𝖞 𝕸𝖆𝖕𝖘, 𝖕𝖗𝖎𝖓𝖙𝖊𝖉 𝖎𝖓 𝕮𝖔𝖑𝖔𝖚𝖗𝖘,

From New Plates, specially engraved, with all the latest information from the best authorities, and Index to upwards of 4000 places.   Crown 4to, Cloth, 2/–; Cloth Extra, 2/6.

LIST OF MAPS.

Explanatory Map	Ireland	Spain and Portugal
Eastern Hemisphere	France	Turkey in Asia, Syria,
Western Hemisphere	German Empire	Persia, Afghanistan, &c.
Europe	Austrian Empire and King-	India or Hindustan
Asia	dom of Hungary	The Dominion of Canada
Africa	Kingdom of Italy	United States of America
North America	The Netherlands & Belgium	Australia and Tasmania
South America	Sweden, Norway, and	Central America and West
Oceania	Denmark	Indies
The British Islands	Turkey in Europe & Greece	New Zealand
England and Wales	Russia in Europe	Canaan or Palestine
Scotland	Switzerland	Bible Maps

MARCUS WARD'S PORTABLE ATLAS.

𝕿𝖍𝖎𝖗𝖙𝖞 𝕸𝖆𝖕𝖘, 𝖕𝖗𝖎𝖓𝖙𝖊𝖉 𝖎𝖓 𝕮𝖔𝖑𝖔𝖚𝖗𝖘, 𝖔𝖓 𝖔𝖓𝖊 𝖘𝖎𝖉𝖊 𝖔𝖓𝖑𝖞 𝖔𝖋 𝕾𝖚𝖕𝖊𝖗𝖋𝖎𝖓𝖊 𝕯𝖗𝖆𝖜𝖎𝖓𝖌 𝕻𝖆𝖕𝖊𝖗, 𝖜𝖎𝖙𝖍 𝖋𝖚𝖑𝖑 𝕴𝖓𝖉𝖊𝖝.

Demy Octavo, handsomely bound in Cloth—India Rubber binding, to open perfectly flat.   3/6.

Advantages of this Atlas over others at similar or higher prices:—

1. Pictorial Illustrations of Geographical Terms.
2. Diagrams to illustrate the use of the Globes.
3. In the Maps of England, Scotland, and Ireland, the Sizes of the Towns by their Populations are distinguished by varied letterings.
4. The Countries where French is spoken are shewn in one Map.
5. The Countries where German or kindred languages are spoken are shewn in one Map.
6. The whole of the Russian Empire depicted on one Plate.
7. The whole of the Turkish Empire depicted on one Plate.
8. Map of Overland Route—Mediterranean to the Indus—Asiatic Russia —Khiva—Kokand—Syria—Euphrates Valley—Koweyt Republic— Persia—Afghanistan—Biluchistan, &c.   Illustrating the advance of the Russian Empire towards India.
9. The British Isles in one Map.
10. Several enlarged Maps of British Colonies.
11. Special Biblical Maps, for Sunday Lessons.

For Opinions of the Press, see next page.

OPINIONS OF THE PRESS (MARCUS WARD'S ATLASES).

"The Sixpenny and Shilling Atlases are *marvels of cheapness*, and the Home and Portable Atlases, each containing thirty maps, with indexes to upwards of 4,000 places, are *very complete for ordinary use.*"—*Guardian, March 15th, 1876.*

"These Maps are cheap, well engraved, and apparently on a level with the most recent and accurate geographical information."—*Standard, March 22nd, 1876.*

"The series of Atlases issued by the Messrs Marcus Ward & Co., of London and Belfast, merit attention. The maps are beautifully printed and neatly colonred; the coast-lines, rivers, and mountains are clearly shown, and the names are not too crowded."—*Public Opinion, April 1st, 1876.*

" . . . Marvels of cheapness, and at the same time of comparative excellence. They are all 'got up' with that artistic taste and neatness which generally characterise the publications of this firm."—*Manchester Courier, March 22nd, 1876.*

"Quite unique. . . . Admirably printed."—*Leeds Mercury.*

Works on Drawing and Design.

Plants: their Natural Growth and Ornamental

Treatment. By F. E. HULME, F.L.S., F.S.A., of Marlborough College, Author of "Plant Form." Containing 44 plates, printed in Colours from Drawings made by the Author, accompanied by a careful Treatise on the subject. Large imperial 4to, cloth extra, bevelled boards. Price 21/–.

" The object of this very excellent work is to show the close relationship that exists between botanical science and ornamental art."—*Morning Post.*

Hulme's Freehand Ornament.

Sixty Examples, for the use of Drawing Classes. By F. E. HULME, F.L.S., F.S.A., Marlborough College. Imperial 8vo. Price 5/–, or mounted millboard, cloth-bound edges, 10/–.

" To the Student of Drawing this book is a mine of well-drawn examples. . . . Cannot fail to be useful to the decorative sculptor, the bookbinder, the manufacturer of textile fabrics of every description. . . ."—*Art Journal.*

☞ *Both these Works have been adopted by H. M. Department of Science and Art, for Copies and Prizes.*

Illuminating: a Practical Treatise on the Art.

By MARCUS WARD, Illuminator to the Queen. With 26 examples of the styles prevailing at different periods, from the sixth century to the present time ; Chromographed in facsimile and in outline. Foolscap 4to, cloth extra, bevelled boards, gilt edges, 5/–, or, in Morocco extra, 10/6.

" A very creditable and remarkably cheap little book."—*Architect.*

Aunt Charlotte's Histories for Young Children.

Profusely Illustrated, Square Octavo, Cloth Extra, Bevelled Boards,
Gilt Edges.   Price 6/- each.

Stories of English History for the Little Ones.

By CHARLOTTE M. YONGE, Author of "The Heir of Redclyffe,"
&c.   In Fifty easy Chapters, with a Frontispiece in Colours by
H. S. Marks, A.R.A.; 50 Illustrations, and an Illuminated Title-
page.   New Edition, with Questions.

"So simple that a child of the tenderest years will be perfectly able to comprehend all that the writer wishes to convey. . . .   adorned with numerous
illustrations . . .   the title-page is a lovely piece of art in illuminated
printing."—*Edinburgh Courant*.

"An excellent and useful little gift-book."—*Scotsman*.

"Any boy or girl who fails to admire Miss Yonge's 'Stories of English
History' must, indeed, be hard to please."—*Bookseller*.

☞ *A Cheap Edition of MISS YONGE'S HISTORY OF ENGLAND,
for Schools, is now ready; with 41 Engravings, and Questions,
neatly bound in cloth.   Price 1/6.*

Stories of French History for the Little Ones.

In Forty-eight easy Chapters, with a Frontispiece in Colours
by H. STACY MARKS, A.R.A.   Twelve Full-page Illustrations,
and an Illuminated Title-page.   New Edition, with Questions.

"The stories are well and clearly written."—*Saturday Review*.

"Charmingly bound, printed, and illustrated."—*Manchester Guardian*.

Stories of Bible History for the Little Ones.

Three Readings and One Picture for each Sunday in the Year,
with an Illuminated Title-page and Frontispiece in Colours.

"Illustrations numerous and well executed."—*Daily Telegraph*.

"Embraces the whole story from the creation to the ascension ; told as
Miss Yonge knows so well how to tell it."—*Guardian*.

"Nicely illustrated, and got up in an attractive style."—*Birmingham
Gazette*.

☞ *A Cheap Edition of STORIES OF BIBLE HISTORY, price 2/-,
just published.*

Stories of Greek History for the Little Ones.

In Forty.five easy Chapters, with Frontispiece in Colours by
WALTER CRANE, Illuminated Title-page, and numerous
Illustrations.

AUNT CHARLOTTE'S HISTORIES—*Continued.*

Stories of Roman History for the Little Ones.

By CHARLOTTE M. YONGE. In Forty-six easy Chapters, with Frontispiece in Colours, Illuminated Title-page, and numerous Illustrations. *[Just Published.*

Stories of German History for the Little Ones.

By C. M. YONGE. With Frontispiece in Colours, Illuminated Title-page, and numerous Illustrations. *[In the Press.*

CLASS-BOOK FOR CLASSICAL AND ART SCHOOLS.

The Mythology of Greece and Rome, with special reference to its use in Art. From the German of O. Seemann. Edited by G. H. BIANCHI, B.A., late Scholar of S. Peter's College, Cambridge. 64 Illustrations, Crown Octavo, Cloth, 3/6.

HANDBOOK FOR AGRICULTURAL STUDENTS AND FARMERS.

Animals of the Farm : their Structure and Physi- ology. By JOHN F. HODGES, M.D., F.C.S., &c. Second Edition, revised by the Author. Numerous Illustrations. Small Octavo, Cloth, 2/6.

Vere Foster's Drawing Copy-Books.

With Instructions and Paper to Draw on.

POPULAR EDITION, 1d. SUPERIOR EDITION, 3d.

In a country where Mechanical, Architectural, and Decorative Skill is in so much demand, a knowledge of Drawing is essential alike to the Artizan, the Employer, and the Connoisseur. The success of Mr. VERE FOSTER'S *Writing* Copy-Books suggested that a knowledge of Drawing might be spread among all classes by a series of *Drawing* Copy-Books by the best masters. It is believed that these books have already called forth much latent talent, and the advantage of a development of Taste and practical Artistic Knowledge cannot be overrated.

A—ELEMENTARY.	K—LANDSCAPE. Four Books.
B—SIMPLE OBJECTS.	M—MARINE. Four Books.
C—FAMILIAR OBJECTS. Two Books.	O—ANIMALS. Ten Books.
D—SIMPLE FLOWERS. Two Books.	Q—HUMAN FIGURE. Four Books.
E, G—FLOWERS. Three Books.	R—GEOMETRY. Three Books.
I—ORNAMENT. Four Books.	T—MECHANICAL. Six Books.
J—TREES. Three Books.	Z—BLANK BOOK.

VERE FOSTER'S
WATER-COLOUR DRAWING BOOKS.
With full Instructions in Painting.

ELEMENTARY BOOKS, 3d.   ADVANCED BOOKS, 6d.

The object of this Publication is to place a knowledge of the higher branches of Drawing, hitherto the accomplishment only of the few, within the reach of all.   It comprises a series of Simple and Practical Examples, in the various departments of Painting, by eminent Artists, together with useful and practical hints for Sketching from Nature.

The prices place them within the reach of every one, and they are adapted either for Self-instruction or for study with the aid of a Master.

SEPIA.—6 Nos., 3d. each.
LANDSCAPE.—6 Nos., 3d. each.
MARINE.—Advanced Lessons—4 Nos., 6d. each.
ANIMALS.—Advanced Lessons—4 Nos., 6d. each.

FLOWERS—1st Series.—6 Nos., 3d. each.
FLOWERS—2nd Series.—4 Nos., 6d. each.
ILLUMINATING.—4 Nos., 6d. each.

VERE FOSTER'S WRITING COPY-BOOKS.
POPULAR EDITION, 1d.   SUPERIOR EDITION. 2d. (No. 10, 3d.)

Quarto Edition (Fine Glazed Paper) of Nos. 4, 5, 6, 7, Sixpence each.

The distinguishing characteristics of this Series are as follows :—
1. Combination in the greatest possible degree of legibility with rapidity.   The formation of the Letters, and notably of *a, d, g, q,* are adapted to this end.   2. The Tailed Letters are of moderate length.   The up and down strokes are of nearly equal thickness, as contradistinguished from the Engraver's style.   3. The writing of each word is continuous from end to end.   4. Exclusion of Large Hand as unfit for small fingers.   5. Systematically progressive arrangement of Head Lines.   6. Two Lines of Copy on a page.   7. Careful selection of Proverbs and Aphorisms.   8. The same clear, simple style of Writing for both sexes, *there being no good reason why girls should be taught a cramped, illegible hand.*

LIST OF VERE FOSTER'S WRITING COPY-BOOKS.

1. STROKES, EASY LETTERS, SHORT WORDS.—Traced Lines under each Copy, to be written over by the Pupil. ROUND HAND.

1½. LONG LETTERS, SHORT WORDS, FIGURES.—Sanctioned by the Committee of Council as satisfying the requirements of the Second Standard, Revised Code, 1875. HALF TEXT.

2. LONG LETTERS, SHORT WORDS, FIGURES,—Guide Lines to regulate the length of Tailed Letters. SMALL ROUND HAND.

2½. WORDS OF FOUR, FIVE, OR SIX LETTERS, for Practice in forming different difficult combinations. SMALL ROUND HAND.

3. CAPITALS, SHORT WORDS, FIGURES.—Analysis of Capitals. Showing how the stiff Printed Capitals become transformed into Running Hand. MEDIUM HAND.

3½. SENTENCES OF SHORT WORDS, spaced by Perpendicular Lines. This is the first book in which Sentences are introduced. SMALL ROUND HAND.

4. SENTENCES, mostly composed of Short Words. The Perpendicular Spacing Lines are omitted in this and all succeeding numbers. MEDIUM HAND.

4½. SELECT QUOTATIONS FROM SHAKSPERE.—Principally Long Sentences. Suitable for preparing Pupils to write from Dictation. MEDIUM HAND.

5, 6. SENTENCES.—Maxims, Morals, and Precepts, in progressively Small Writing ; each Line a complete Sentence. SMALL HAND.

5½. SENTENCES, in Writing of Three Sizes, continuation of preceding Books Nos. 3½, 4½, and 5. SMALL ROUND, MEDIUM, AND SMALL HANDS.

6½. SENTENCES, in Writing of Two Sizes, in continuation of Books Nos. 6 and 7. SMALL HAND.

7. SENTENCES AND CHRISTIAN NAMES. —A collection of over 200 of the Christian Names in most common use, affording scope for a great variety of elegant Capitals. SMALL HAND.

8. SENTENCES.—One Line on each Page. This Book is prepared for those who prefer at this stage to have only one line on each page. SMALL HAND.

9. SENTENCES.—Two Lines on each Page. Smaller Writing than in any of the preceding books. Some prefer this as a Finishing Hand to Nos. 7 and 8. SMALL HAND.

10. PLAIN AND ORNAMENTAL LETTERING.—Single Letters, Words, and Sentences. Alphabets in Thirty-three different Styles. The most perfect Collection yet published.

11. EXERCISE BOOK.—Wide Ruling, with Margin, for Parsing, Dictation, Composition, or other Exercises.

12. EXERCISE BOOK.—Narrow Ruling in Squares, for Arithmetic, Bookkeeping, Geometry, and proportionate enlargements or reductions.

HOME EXERCISE BOOK.—Same Ruling as No. 12 (but Octavo Size). Price One Penny.

COPY-BOOK PROTECTOR AND BLOTTER.—Price One Penny. Keeping the Books fresh, neat, and clean.

Marcus Ward's Royal Ulster Series of
SELECTED STEEL PENS.

These Celebrated Pens have rounded points, are specially manufactured in highest finish from the finest Silver Steel, and are suited for the various requirements of the Public in all Styles of Writing. Sold by all Stationers, at the uniform price of 1s. per box.

42. MARCUS WARD'S "VERE FOSTER COPY-BOOK" PEN.—For Pupils using the earlier numbers of the VERE FOSTER Copy-Books—Nos. 1, 1½, 2, 2½, 3, 3½, 4, 4½, or for ordinary free writing *(Round Hand and Medium Hand)*.   ONE HUNDRED PENS IN A BOX.

41. MARCUS WARD'S "VERE FOSTER COPY-BOOK" PEN.—Adapted for the more advanced numbers of the VERE FOSTER Copy-Books—Nos. 5, 5½, 6, 6½, 7, 8, and 9, and for ordinary neat writing *(Small Hand)*.   ONE HUNDRED PENS IN A BOX. .

51. MARCUS WARD'S "COLLEGE" PEN—*Fine Points.*—A strong, useful Pen for high-class School or College use, suited for the more rapid writing of Advanced Pupils and Students, and for ordinary Correspondence.   SIX DOZEN PENS IN A BOX.

52. MARCUS WARD'S "COLLEGE" PEN—*Medium Points.*—Similar to No. 51, but with broader Points. Suitable also for Professional or Official Correspondence, and for bold, rapid writing. SIX DOZEN PENS IN A BOX.

64. MARCUS WARD'S "BLACK LETTER" PEN—*Extra Broad Points.*—A peculiar pen, specially made for VERE FOSTER'S No. 10 Copy-Book. Adapted for *down strokes* of German Text, Old English, Black Letter, and Engrossing. Will also be found useful by the numerous class of persons who prefer to use a very broad-pointed pen in ordinary writing on rough paper.   THREE DOZEN PENS IN A BOX.

70. MARCUS WARD'S "ITALIAN" PEN—*Extra Fine Points.*—Specially made for the Ornamental Writing in VERE FOSTER'S No. 10 Copy-Book, or for the use of persons who prefer a *very fine-pointed* pen in writing on highly-glazed paper.   THREE DOZEN PENS IN A BOX.

81. MARCUS WARD'S "ROYAL ULSTER" PEN—*Fine Points.*—A splendid pen for Mercantile use, either in Account Books, for Correspondence, or for other purposes. Made of thick but very Elastic Steel, with the highest finish. *Much recommended for Flexibility, Strength, and Durability.*   THREE DOZEN PENS IN A BOX.

91. MARCUS WARD'S "ROYAL PALACE" PEN—*Fine Points.*—Slightly turned-up points. Persons who prefer quill pens will find this the *Softest* Steel Pen made. These pens are suitable for the modern style of large and bold writing, and are peculiarly adapted for writing on the Irish Linen Papers.   THREE DOZEN PENS IN A BOX.

92. MARCUS WARD'S "ROYAL PALACE" PEN—*Medium Points.*—Similar to No. 91, with broader turned-up points, for very bold and rapid writing on the Royal Irish Linen or other rough-surfaced writing papers.   THREE DOZEN PENS IN A BOX.

Samples will be forwarded on receipt of Six Penny Stamps.